Advance Reviews

The hard-boiled detective gets a unique update for our kinder, gentler twenty-first century in the form of Sylvia Jensen, the hard-codependent social worker-turned detective in *Death, Uncharted*, the second in this thoroughly entertaining series. Writer Dorothy Van Soest elevates dysfunction to art as her protagonist—a more realistic and insecure version of Jessica Fletcher—explores crime and murder at the center of America's increasingly corporate approach to education—an investigation that sets her at odds with some very dangerous people.

> — Shawn Otto, award-winning American novelist, nonfiction author,
> filmmaker, political strategist, speaker, science advocate, and
> screenwriter and co-producer of the movie House of Sand and Fog.

In this cold case mystery—a small boy has been murdered in the South Bronx in the late 1960s—we encounter a young teacher torn between her passionate determination to help her disadvantaged students and her increasingly hopeless realization that choosing to side with the children will alienate her from her union colleagues, forcing her out of her profession. As someone who taught in New York City during the epic 1968 teacher's strike, reading *Death Unchartered* sent me back in a time machine, not unlike the heroine, Sylvia Jensen, who returns to the Bronx to solve this crime and connect once again with the angels and demons of her past. In the context of more recent strife over charter schools, this novel invites us to consider a range of destructive forces—whether intractable unions (who are compelled to regard any concession as a "slippery slope") or greedy corporations seeking to "do well by (simulating) doing good"—that block, to this day, equal opportunity for schoolchildren. *Death Unchartered* urges us to translate these conflicts into stark terms, and, like all murder stories, focuses essentially on the question of who people really are: Who are the ones who help? Who are the ones who harm? In mysteries, anyway, if not in life, we enjoy the satisfaction of knowing a passionate detective has set out to prove such harm can be stopped.

— Alan Feldman. Author, *Immortality*, winner of the Mass Book Award for Poetry, Massachusetts Center for the Book

When Sylvia Jensen learns about a child's corpse found in the basement of a Bronx derelict school building that's being razed, she fears it may be the body of a boy who'd suddenly disappeared nearly forty years before. As a third grade teacher in that very school, "Ms. Sylvia," as her students had known her, had championed young Markus LeMeur who'd mysteriously disappeared. Compelled to seek the truth and avenge the boy's death, she returns to the Bronx where she encounters much more than she bargained for. The plot thickens as she revisits her past as a young teacher-activist who'd taken a strong stand against a controversial teachers'strike that threatened to close the school. Embedded in this fast-paced murder mystery are serious themes, including political corruption, the harsh injustices of poverty and racism, and the misappropriation of millions of dollars intended for public education. Surprising twist and turns of plot kept me guessing down to the final page. I couldn't help to compare this to the mysteries of Sue Grafton's whose novels I've enjoyed from "A" through "Y."

— Hal Zina Bennett, bestselling author of *Write From the Heart: Unleashing the Power of Your Creativity*

Death, Uncharted is a captivating read. Every chapter is filled with intrigue and suspense juxtaposing events within a public school that occur in 1968 to ones that converge with the building of a Charter School in 2006. This book shows how ethnic minority children fall victim to unjust and corrupt educational systems. Van Soest brilliantly interweaves the problems that exist in both public and charter schools, with the ethical and moral struggles of teachers who genuinely want to help children. The narrative shows the toll that unjust systems take on both teachers and students and reflexively asks the reader to consider the motives behind charter schools that claim to provide a better education. It is must read for all students and professionals in social work and education.

— Cynthia Franklin, PhD, LCSW Associate Dean for Doctoral Education Stiernberg/Spencer Family Professor in Mental Health Steve Hicks School of Social Work, The University of Texas at Austin

Most murder stories focus on investigative processes. The best provide a side dish of social inspection. But Death, Unchartered takes an additional leap into complexity by providing the subplot of an inner city teacher's efforts to help disadvantaged children at all costs . . . creating a riveting production pairing a murder mystery with ethical and moral conundrums. . . . It's this broader perspective that makes Death, Unchartered more than just another murder 'whodunnit' but an unrelenting probe into the impact of greed and special interests on the educational system . . . a gripping read with a surprising outcome.

— D. Donovan, *Midwest Book Review*

The second novel in . . . the Sylvia Jensen Mystery Series reunites the recently former social worker with Native American investigative reporter J.B. Harrell, setting them on a quest to uncover the truth about the disappearance of a young boy in the Bronx almost four decades ago. . . . Van Soest is a skilled writer, equally adept with dialogue and narrative. . . A solid, engaging mystery with a timely plot.

— Kirkus Review

Death, Unchartered is a haunting read that will cause readers to sit up and take notice. It is a powerful journey wrapped up in an intense mystery/thriller one won't soon forget.

— Paige Lovitt, *Reader Views*

. . . a strong voice exploring a passionate search for justice in a murder mystery . . . involved in social issues, school systems, and the treatment of students while exploring relationships in the past and present, and the fight for justice.

—Five-Star Review, *Readers' Favorite*

ALSO BY DOROTHY VAN SOEST

FICTION

Just Mercy
At the Center

NON-FICTION

Diversity Education for Social Justice
Social Work Practice for Social Justice
The Global Crisis of Violence: Common Problems, Universal Causes, Shared Solutions
Challenges of Violence Worldwide: An Educational Resource
Challenges of Violence Worldwide: Curriculum Module
Incorporating Peace and Social Justice into the Social Work Curriculum
Empowerment of People for Peace

DEATH, UNCHARTERED

A Novel

DEATH, UNCHARTERED

A Novel

Dorothy Van Soest

Apprentice
House Press
Loyola University Maryland

First Edition

Casebound ISBN: 978-1-62720-196-4
Paperback ISBN: 978-1-62720-197-1
Ebook ISBN: 978-1-62720-198-8

Printed in the United States of America

Design: Serena Chenery
Development & Marketing: Kieran O'Shea

Published by Apprentice House

Apprentice
House Press
Loyola University Maryland

Apprentice House
Loyola University Maryland
4501 N. Charles Street
Baltimore, MD 21210
410.617.5265 • 410.617.2198 (fax)
www.ApprenticeHouse.com
info@ApprenticeHouse.com

PROLOGUE
October 1968

I've never been this scared of anyone before in my whole life.

That's why I had to lie to my sister, Mentayer, who's been watching out for me since Grandma had her stroke last summer. I never ever lied to Grandma in my whole life, and I only lied to Mentayer once before. Until now. I can't tell her why I'm so scared because if she knows, they'll come after her. Maybe I can tell Ms. Sylvia. Maybe she can help.

Ms. Sylvia's my normal teacher, but because of the teachers' strike, she has to be the principal for the whole school, which is why I'm in the main office now, waiting for her.

"Markus, what are you doing here?"

I jump and start to stand up. But my head is fuzzy and I fall back down on the bench. Ms. Sylvia lifts up the end of the counter and comes and sits next to me. I look down at the floor.

I try to open my mouth but it's stuck. I lift my shoulders and they stay stuck there.

"Where's your sister?" Ms. Sylvia's voice is higher than usual.

"I told Mentayer to go without me." I look down at my feet, pull them out from under the bench without picking them up, then push them back under the bench again. I pick at the zipper on my jacket, try to pull it up and down. But it's stuck, too.

"You're shaking." She puts her arm around my shoulders and pulls me up from the bench. I let her steer me behind the counter to where the door to the principal's office is hidden behind the filing cabinet. She holds my hand to go in.

It's as big as a gymnasium inside. The ceiling seems almost up to the sky.

"Now sit down and tell me what's going on." Ms. Sylvia points to a chair along the wall. I sit on the edge of it and tap my feet on the floor, first the left one then the right one, over and over, back and forth. She brings a chair next to me and sits down. I don't know where to start, how far back to go, how to explain everything. Mentayer says I don't always think things through. Maybe she's right.

"What is it, Markus? Did something happen?"

I look up at her sideways. If she guesses, then it isn't like I told.

"What has you so frightened?" She puts her arm around me, pulls me close.

I want to tell her. I want her to make everything okay. But I don't know if I should tell her all of it or part of it. I wait for her to make another guess, but all she does is look at me and bite her bottom lip. Then she crouches down and twists her body so she's looking straight at me but I can't look at her.

"You can tell me," she says. "It's okay." She nods and smiles. Her eyebrows are up in her forehead. She blows some air out through her mouth and it makes an impatient sound, but that can't be what it is, because Ms. Sylvia never loses her patience.

She puts her hand on mine and squeezes it. "Maybe it's something we should tell the police?" she says.

I jerk my head up and look at her. I move over to the other side of the chair, farther away. "No. No. Not the cops." I turn away from her and stare at the dark brown wood on the wall. I was wrong. Ms. Sylvia can't help. She doesn't understand. I shouldn't have come.

"Look at me, Markus. Please. Tell me what's going on."

I look at her but only sideways. "It's okay, Ms. Sylvia. I'm fine now."

She doesn't believe me. She keeps asking questions, and I keep saying "It's okay, I'm fine" so she won't call the cops. Maybe if I keep saying it, it won't happen to me, and I won't be scared anymore, and I will be fine.

"We'll talk more about this later," she says. "Frank is out back waiting. We'll drive you to your uncle's."

I have to stay at my uncle's apartment until Grandma gets out of the hospital. I wish I could stay with Ms. Sylvia and her husband, Frank, like Mentayer gets to.

A loud bang on the door makes me jump. Three tall men walk in with a big dog on a leash. They look like some of the men who hang around on the street corner, but I don't recognize any of them. Ms. Sylvia smiles like she's happy to see them.

"Have a good evening, Mrs. Waters," one of them says. "You can go home now."

"Wonderful," she says. "Markus and I are ready to leave."

She holds out her hand and I take it.

"Have a good night," she says to the men, "and thank you."

We walk out the door at the back of the school. Some of the teachers who are striking are waiting in the parking lot. They start shouting at Ms. Sylvia. They say mean things. Lines crinkle up on her forehead, the kind Grandma gets sometimes when she watches the news on TV.

"Hey, buddy," Frank says. "I hear you stayed to help your teacher out today. Mighty nice of you."

Ms. Sylvia's busy getting into the van and doesn't hear him, so I don't have to lie to her again. Next to my sister and Grandma, she is the next best person I love in the whole world.

"You okay, Markus?" She turns around and looks at me in the back seat. The lines are back on her forehead.

I nod and smile to make the lines go away, and they do. She smiles and turns around and looks out the front window until we get to my uncle's apartment building. Frank double-parks in front and I reach for the door handle.

"Thank you for the ride," I say, the way Grandma taught me.

"You sure you're okay?" Ms. Sylvia asks. "Want me to walk you in?"

"I'm fine," I say. "Thank you."

I go to the front door of the building, then turn around and smile and wave. Ms. Sylvia waves and smiles back. I open the outside door, and before going in, I turn and wave one more time. Their van pulls away and moves down the street. I walk up the steps, pass the mailboxes on one side, and then push down on the handle on the inside door. At first I think it's stuck, so I try again. No luck.

Usually it isn't locked, so I don't have a key. None of us do.

I sit down on the top step to wait for someone who lives in the building to either go in or come out, but then I think about Mentayer. She'd never sit and wait like this. If she was here she'd be telling me, *Don't be such a lump on a log, Markus. Get off your butt and go get the super to unlock the door for you.*

I always try to listen to my sister, but especially today to make up for all my lying, so I stand up, walk down the steps, and go outside to the sidewalk.

The super's apartment is around the back of the building. The path between our building and the one next door is almost wide enough for two people to walk next to each other, but not quite. I'm almost to the back of the building when the toe of my shoe hits something. I lean against the side of the building to keep myself from tripping and falling. I hear breathing. It must be me. But then the breathing turns into a raspy, angry voice.

"I've been waiting for you."

I can't see anything, but I know who it is. Inside my head Mentayer starts shouting. *Run, Markus, run! Run for your life, Markus.* I turn, hit my shoulder against the building, and force my feet to move, one after the other.

There's a stomping sound behind me. *Move, Markus! Faster!*

I turn and look over my shoulder and see a shadow, a flash of something, a hand or an arm or something bigger. I try to run but I can't. I can't move. I can't even breathe. I look up and see something coming down on me from behind. I duck but it comes anyway. I'm on my knees and they hurt. The cement's hard. Everything's black and I'm floating. Floating away.

ONE

February 2006

Monrow City Hall Park is abuzz with the clatter of dog walkers and joggers releasing puffs of cold air from their mouths, all sturdy Midwesterners with no qualms about leaving their overheated homes to brave the below-zero temperatures. A ray of sunshine filters through the bare tree branches, the sky clear and blue. A woman with pitted skin sits on a tattered sleeping bag on the ground, her crooked fingers clutching several layers of filthy wool blankets around her shoulders. I drop a ten-dollar bill in her plastic cup.

"God bless you," she says with a toothy smile.

"God bless *you*," I say, pulling my warm wool jacket tighter around me.

At the main entrance to City Hall, a small, makeshift stage has been set up on the steps for our rally this morning. A grade-school class runs past, giggling, as if to remind me why I'm here. Several hundred people are already gathered, a good sign. At the back of the crowd I spot J. B. Harrell's salon hairstyle and black designer topcoat. He looks a bit slimmer than when I last saw him—six months ago, shortly after he and I solved the mystery of how an American Indian boy died in a foster home. From behind he still looks more like a corporate business executive than an investigative reporter. He turns and spots me.

"Sylvia!" He walks toward me with that familiar grin of his that tells me he's as happy to see me as I am to see him. "So you're here to support the mayor," he says, with a glance at the Save Our Public Schools button on my consignment-store wool jacket and the homemade Stop Corporate Greed sign in my hand.

"It's good to see you, too," I say, laughing at his dry joke.

"There's Peter." He points to a man with a gray ponytail standing in a cluster of American Indian, African American, and Latino parents near the stage. They're holding up professionally printed signs in support of the mayor's plan to place our public schools under the management of the CSCH Corporation.

Peter Minter is the Indian Child Welfare Compliance officer with whom I worked when I was a foster care supervisor. We've been friends and allies for years, advocating for improvements in the child welfare system, serving together even now on a statewide reform task force. This is the first time we've been on opposite sides about anything. He heads our way, waving. I wave back with a pained smile.

"Here to cover the mayor's press conference this morning?" Peter says to J. B., shaking hands with him like they're old friends.

"I'm working on a series about charter schools," J. B. says.

Peter nods. "Well, if it's anywhere near as good as the one you did about foster care last year, maybe it'll help." He turns to me with a sadness in his eyes that I've seen many times before. "One Indian kid is graduating high school this year, Sylvia. That's it. One."

"I heard," I say with a shake of my head. "It's awful."

There's a gleam in J. B.'s brown eyes, the one he gets whenever he thinks he's stumbled onto a lead or an angle for a story, a way to articulate the issue through someone's personal experience. "Do you support the mayor's plan?" he asks Peter. "Do you think charter schools are the answer?"

Peter places his hand over his breast, a signal that he's going to tell a story. J. B. reaches in his pocket and pulls out a small notepad and pen.

"A better education is the way out of poverty for us," Peter begins. "We get our inspiration from the stories about the Red School House in Saint Paul, Minnesota. Have you heard of it?" He doesn't wait for J. B.'s answer. "Well, it was founded in 1972 by Indian parents who were concerned about their kids' low achievement and high dropout rates. It was about more than one school, though. It was about the American Indian movement and community organizing, and it was the roots of the first official charter school in the country, in Minnesota in 1992. The long-term effect on Indian people there shows us that change is possible."

J. B. looks at me with his eyebrows raised, but I don't say anything. Peter already knows what I think. I sweat under my arms in spite of the cold weather and unzip my jacket a few inches.

"How can we deny our kids this opportunity, Sylvia? This possible shot at life?"

"I understand," I say. "But desperate people can be vulnerable to exploitation."

Peter pushes his glasses up on his nose, looks over the rims at me. "My people know the difference between hope and trust, Sylvia."

His rebuke is, as always, gentle, but it still stings. I place my hand on my cheek and nod. "Hope is good," I say. "I understand." He smiles, and we part. Still friends, I hope.

J. B. turns to me. "Some charter schools involve people with good intentions who want to address the identified racial inequities," he says.

"And some involve people who are more than willing to exploit the situation," I shoot back at him.

J. B. smiles like he does when he's amused by my passion. "It's complicated," he says. The divisiveness of the gathered crowd reinforces his words. The majority of people protesting are white. They hold homemade signs saying Protect Our Schools from Corporate Greed, Stop the CSCH Scam, and Keep Our Public Schools Public, while the cluster of nonwhite people standing with Peter Minter near the front hold signs saying the opposite: We Support Charter Schools. CSCH: Our Hope for the Future.

Two women—a diminutive white woman wearing a long, quilted coat that makes her look like a square box and an ample-sized, six-foot-tall black woman in a plain brown coat with a red scarf at the neck—approach the microphone. The crowd cheers and whistles.

The white woman welcomes everyone and introduces herself as the coordinator of the Save Our Schools coalition, which she says is made up of twenty-six organizations opposing the charter school takeover. Then the black woman takes the microphone.

"My name is Gillian Sparks. In the city of North Forks, where I live, everyone goes to public school. Except for kids like my son Scott, who are lucky enough to win the lottery and go to a Victory Academy school. You should have seen how big Scott's eyes were the first day of kindergarten. His classroom was fresh, painted in bright colors. There were stacks and stacks of educational supplies, all kinds of shiny electronic equipment, even a mini-library filled with brand-new books."

She pauses, brings a bottle of water to her lips, and takes a drink. The parents gathered with Peter near the front cheer and raise their pro-charter-school signs higher. No wonder they're excited. Our mayor plans to turn over *all* the Monrow City schools to CSCH, so there will be no lottery. All their children will get to go to bright, shiny schools like Victory Academy.

"But, on the first day of kindergarten," Gillian Sparks continues, "my son got detention for not being orderly in the halls." She furrows her brow and runs her tongue over her upper lip. "I thought that was a bit harsh for a five-year-old, but since self-discipline is at the core of the Victory Academy model, I figured they were making that clear from day one. Then Scott kept getting detention again and again, for one reason or another. He started having emotional meltdowns in the mornings. He complained of stomach-aches. He said the teacher made him and three other black boys sit in the back, separate from the rest of the class. He thought they must be conta-gious, because one by one, the other boys stopped coming to school, and he became afraid he would be the next one to get sick."

I scan the crowd, see expressions of growing concern and anger, parental arms tightening around the shoulders of their young children. Some people standing with Peter have lowered their signs.

"I went to see what was going on"—the microphone squeals, and Gillian Sparks moves back a few inches—"and it was like a military camp in the school. Children walked the halls like silent robots. No one laughed or even smiled, not even the teachers."

I glance at J. B., who is busy writing in the little notepad he always carries with him. Fragmented memories from almost forty years ago when I taught third grade in the Bronx flash through my head. The teacher across the hall from my classroom treated his students like army recruits in boot camp.

"The principal said my son was incapable of learning and behaving. She wanted him gone. What could I do? I saw how he was being damaged. When I transferred him to a public school, he said, 'I'm sorry I failed kinder-garten, Mom.'" A collective gasp ripples through the crowd. "Then he asked if they didn't want him at Victory Academy because he had some disease or if it was because he was bad. I'll never forget that." She digs in her pocket for a tissue and blows her nose.

"But." She holds up her hands. "My son's story doesn't end there. He did well in the public school. They understood him. They worked with him. He's still rambunctious, but he's happy and creative."

Gillian Sparks walks off the stage to raucous applause and whistles. "How do we protect our children?" someone in the crowd shouts.

"Just say no," someone responds.

The sign-waving crowd goes wild, with people chanting, "Just Say No! Just Say No! Just Say No!" My adrenaline is pumping and I'm about ready to join in when J. B. taps me on the shoulder.

"Want to go for coffee?" He slips the notepad into his pocket.

I nod, satisfied that the rally has been successful and that I've done my part for the day. I hand my sign to someone else as we jostle our way through the throng of people standing shoulder to shoulder and arm in arm, swaying from side to side.

"So, do you miss it?" J.B says, when we emerge from the park and wait for the red light to turn green before crossing the street. He nods to the Health Services Building across from City Hall, where I worked as a foster care supervisor until six months ago. "Do you like being retired?"

"I'm not retired. I resigned, remember?" I pause, give myself a minute to think about his question. "I miss it when I think about the kids, you know, and the workers. But I'm still trying to reform that system, and to save our public school system, too."

"Why am I not surprised," he says with a grin and a shake of his head.

Inside the coffee shop, we find a small round table for two by the door. J. B. hangs his coat over the back of the chair. He stands and watches me sit down and tuck my short, jean-clad legs and knee-high boots under the chair, then unzip my jacket and adjust the cowl neck of my gray cashmere sweater—another consignment-store find.

"So, you want the usual?" he asks. I nod, and he heads for the counter.

I tuck in a couple loose strands of hair that have escaped from the soft gray bun at the back of my head. Then I start to sort through sections of today's edition of the *New York Times* on the table. I push the business and sports sections off to the side and leaf through the arts and entertainment section, make a mental note of some Broadway shows I'd like to see, even though I haven't been to New York in years. Then I pick up the front section and turn the pages until a headline on page five jumps out at me.

"Dead Body Found in Rubble of Demolished Bronx Elementary School."

I fold the page back and read the first sentence of the article. "Last month P.S. 457 in the Bronx was demolished to make way for a new school."

I blink, read the sentence again. P.S. 457. That's where I taught third grade in the mid-1960s. I hold my breath and keep reading.

The mountain of rubble had been cleared away and the excavation crew was pulverizing the last of the concrete base when they discovered a child's body, likely a boy, estimated to have been of elementary school age.

A wave of nausea comes over me. I grab onto my elbows and squeeze my arms against my chest.

The body may have been buried under the basement floor, and later cemented over, three or four decades ago.

The words blur, move deeper and deeper into the page as if disappearing down a cave. The voices, other sounds in the coffee shop, are a distant hum to the shouting in my head. A dead child. Likely a boy. My school. When I was there. I tighten my hold on the edge of the paper and stare at my hands, my wrinkles and age spots, my misshapen, arthritic fingers.

"Are you all right?"

J. B.'s voice startles me. The bright lights in the coffee shop burn my eyes. A gust of freezing air from the open door leaves me shivering and rubbing my hands together. Cold irritates my arthritis.

"What is it, Sylvia? You look like you've seen a ghost."

I stare down at the squiggles and other illegible marks in the *New York Times*, my hands gripping the newspaper like a vise.

J. B. sits down across from me. He leans forward, reaches for the paper, pries my fingers off one by one.

"What were you reading?"

"The school... in the Bronx," I whisper.

"Hmm, it's written by Daniel Leacham," he says. "Must be important." He tips his head and starts to read—some of the words to himself, some of them out loud. "'Dead body found... P.S. 457... demolished... likely male... between seven and nine years of age... buried... identity has not yet been established. The New York Police Department's Forensic Investigations Division is conducting an investigation.'"

He places the paper on the table and takes a sip of his coffee. He leans back in his chair, stretches his long legs out under the table, and waits, his unasked questions dangling in the air.

"I was there." My voice sounds like it's coming from a distance, like it's not mine. "I... " I swipe at the tears on my cheeks, close my eyes. "Oh my God, oh my God, oh my God." I cover my mouth with my hands. I'm rocking back and forth.

J. B.'s voice is soft, hushed. "Sylvia, you know who the dead boy is, don't you?"

TWO

Summer 1967

"Do you need help, Sylvia?" Frank's offer was less than enthusiastic. "Otherwise, I'll go and finish organizing my office."

I looked up from the boxes scattered around me on the kitchen floor of our new apartment to see him standing with one foot pointed away from me like he was ready to bolt. "Go on," I said with a flick of my hand.

His lips brushed my cheek in passing as he headed for the door. There was a smell of stale beer on his breath. I listened to him turning the three locks on the metal door, lifting up the steel pole that dropped into a hole in the floor, then opening the door and letting it slam shut on its own without being locked.

On the same day Frank and I were married, three civil rights workers—James Chaney, Andrew Goodman, and Michael Schwerner—were murdered in Mississippi. I sometimes wondered if that was why I was angry at Frank so much of the time. As if I held him accountable.

Now it was three years later, the summer of 1967 and hot. I was twenty-four years old, a passionate crusader for equal rights, civil rights, peace, and everything that small-town middle America had taught me, in subtle and not so subtle ways, not to be for, not to even think about. President Johnson's signing of the Voting Rights Act two years ago had encouraged me, Martin Luther King Jr. inspired me, and the Black Power and anti-Vietnam War movements called to me. In such a tumultuous and hope-filled time, I could think of no better place to be than the Bronx.

I was, in fact, the reason we were here. Frank was in the seminary, and when it came time for him to make a decision about where to serve his yearlong internship, I dug in my heels and declared I would not go to any small town or to any church where the minister and his wife were hired as a team or seen as a unit. We decided that an urban church would be our best bet, which left him, in our particular denomination, with one choice: a small church in the Bronx consisting of one-third white old-timers who had remained members even after the neighborhood changed and they moved to the suburbs, and two-thirds black and Latino members who lived nearby.

Our apartment across the street from the church faced its round stained glass window riddled with holes. There was a difference of opinion among the members as to whether these holes came from stray bullets or baseballs or both. I looked out the kitchen window and saw Frank lumbering along the sidewalk by the church, then disappearing through the side door to his office.

I grabbed a wet sponge and wiped off the layer of soot that had accumulated on the windowsill since yesterday, resigned already to the daily ritual. Then I turned to face a stack of still-to-be-unpacked boxes that we'd hauled from Chicago in a rented U-Haul trailer hitched to the back of our beat-up Volkswagen van. I bent my knees and lifted up a box labeled *Dishes*. I was stronger than my whisper-thin ninety-pound body suggested. *A spit of a thing,* some people were insensitive enough to say to my face. *If you stood sideways, you'd disappear,* they'd laugh. I didn't find it funny.

I dropped the box on the kitchen counter and started to open it, but the box cutter slipped from my sweaty fingers. I grabbed a paper towel and wiped my hands, then my forehead, my neck, front and back, and between my breasts. That was when I realized that while I was good at picking up heavy things, I didn't always know what to do with them. I had forgotten that I couldn't put the dishes in the cupboards until I did something about the roaches that had swarmed across the floor when I turned on the light last night. I pushed the box to the side and started to make a shopping list. To keep the roaches at bay, some repellent spray. To sprinkle along the baseboards, some borax. To wash out the cupboards, a strong disinfectant soap. The heat was unbearable. We needed a fan. The hot, steamy air was scrambling my mind.

In the bathroom I added more items to the list. Shower curtain. Toilet bowl cleaner. Clorox. More sponges. There was a miniature mushroom growing between the shower wall tiles, but instead of digging it out, which is what I would normally do, I decided to leave it alone, see how big it would get. I wondered if it might be edible.

In the living room, two tall windows covered by heavy metal security bars opened to a fire escape. An array of dingy underwear, worn jeans, and T-shirts hung on a clothesline operated by a pulley system stretching between two buildings. I added laundry detergent to the list and told myself I would not be hanging our clothes on that line for everyone to see. Little did I know, there would be a lot of things I would do in my time in the Bronx that I couldn't have imagined myself doing.

Playing the role of a good—meaning dutiful—preacher's wife was one thing I knew I couldn't do. I went into the bedroom, where Frank's Bible on the bed stand provided more evidence to me of how impossible it was for me to see things the way he saw them. I didn't pray. I didn't read the Bible. I slept during church services, and I hated the songs in the hymnal because they didn't have a gospel beat. I thought that requiring seminarians to learn the Greek language was the height of absurdity.

I didn't know who or what God was, and I never had. I was too young and had too much of my life ahead of me to worry about whether there was a heaven or a hell, and as far as I was concerned, we should be worrying about the hell on earth that too many people were already being forced to live instead of worrying over an afterlife.

Maybe it was our religious differences that made me irritated with Frank so much of the time. It had been so different when we first met, as freshmen in college. I had been awed by his intelligence and his certainty about his place in the world. I liked the way he noticed things about me—the food I ate, the smell of the lavender soap I used in the bath, even when the split ends on my blond hair needed trimming. He noticed me like no one had before, and it was intoxicating. So when this superior being chose me, I married him, never stopping to think about whether or not I loved him.

I couldn't pinpoint when it happened—I guess it was gradual—but at some point he stopped noticing me, and the things I had admired about him became an irritation. His inquiring mind started to feel like criticism, and in the face of his superior intellect and certainty, my own insecurity was magnified.

My reflections were cut short by the sounds of screaming children out in the street. I walked over to the window. Someone had opened the fire hydrant in front of the church full blast, and scores of kids, of all ages and in all kinds of dress and undress, were having the time of their lives running through the spray.

Frank and I would not be having any children. I'd thought it was my fault. So had Frank. He encouraged me to see a doctor, which resulted in both of us being tested, and it turned out it was his fault, not mine. I had thought I wanted kids, but now that I knew we couldn't, I wasn't sure anymore. Frank, on the other hand, didn't take it well, and we stopped talking about it.

As I watched the kids outside now, I told myself it was all water under the bridge. Then I grabbed my keys, locked all the locks behind me, and went out to join in the fun, pinching my nose against the warring cooking smells in the hall. On the second-floor landing, I bumped against a hunched-over man who, in his heroin-induced nonexistence, didn't notice. The first-floor foyer reeked of pine-scented disinfectant and stale urine. I held my breath and raced out onto a sidewalk layered with grime and broken glass and spray paint.

The building super sat to the right of the door in front of his street-level apartment. He seemed to be a permanent fixture, his stomach bulging under a graying T-shirt, his wrinkled skin exposed between his shirt and pants, and hanging over the edge of his rusted folding chair.

"Good morning," I said. "Quite the scorcher today, isn't it? How long do these heat waves last?" I shifted my weight from one foot to the other, made a few more attempts at conversation, and then said, "Well, nice talking to you."

"Yup, you too," he mumbled as I turned to walk away. I smiled. I would try again tomorrow.

The throng of children running through the water from the hydrant grew larger, their squeals louder as they pushed each other and floated pieces of paper and sticks in the flooded street. For a few seconds I almost forgot that the deck of life was stacked against them, almost believed that their playfulness might be powerful enough to outwit society's best efforts to extinguish it. I ran across the street, plunged into the spray with my mouth open, and swallowed a mouthful of water. The escape from the scorching heat was heavenly.

All of a sudden, the children stopped playing, and I realized they were all staring at me like they knew who I was better than I did: a white do-gooder residing temporarily among people living on the margins. Any idealistic notion I'd had that their squealing was the sound of resilience vanished. There was nothing romantic about children having to play in a flooded piece of street with foul garbage floating around their bare feet and ankles. They should have a real swimming pool, with chlorine in it, and a lifeguard to keep them safe.

I left and went back into the building, having learned my first lesson: that there was nothing romantic about poverty, and nothing honorable about living in its midst when you had a choice.

˜

After passing the New York City teachers' exam and signing a loyalty oath, which I was uncomfortable about but signed anyway, I was assigned to teach third grade at P.S. 457, which was an easy ten- to fifteen-minute walk from our apartment. At the teachers' orientation meeting, I learned that I would teach my class during the morning shift, from seven to noon. Another third-grade class would use the classroom from noon to five. The two classes would have to share books, bulletin boards, supplies... everything. How were we supposed to do that? The principal said it was an unfortunate situation but she knew everyone would make the best of it like they always did. Everyone but me seemed to consider it normal.

Once the orientation session was over, I spent a couple of hours working in my assigned classroom with my teacher-mate, a woman in her midsixties who was more interested in what she was going to do when she retired at the end of the year than she was in children. After leaving the school, I went directly to the parsonage for dinner with Pastor Paul, his wife, Linnea, and their two handsome sons.

Pastor Paul was Frank's internship supervisor, but he preferred to think of himself as Frank's spiritual guide and on occasion treated him like a third son. When I arrived, everyone was sitting at the round picnic table on the patio in the back, a slab of concrete between the church and the house. My neon-pink dress with huge lime-green dots was shockingly short and as out of place here as it had been in the school auditorium. I'd heard someone whisper "Since when did we start letting sixteen-year-olds teach" when I walked in. Everyone but me must have gotten the dress code memo, because all the other teachers wore suits. I spent most of the meeting tugging at the hem of my dress and running my fingers along the edge of my hair where it was trimmed above my ears and trying not to feel like a fish out of water.

"Hur står det till?" Pastor Paul's warm smile and soft voice belied his massive six-foot-three presence. "So how was it today?"

"Worse than I expected," I said.

"God works in mysterious ways," Pastor Paul said. "Maybe P.S. 457 is your calling like this ministry in the Bronx is mine."

I winced at his religious assumption and tried to hide my discomfort by reaching for a slice of watermelon and dropping it on the plate in front of me. I poked it with my fork, cut off a piece, and brought it up to my mouth.

Linnea Winston gave her husband an indulgent smile and an affectionate pat on his arm. "Paul likes to believe we're here because of divine intervention," she said. "He doesn't want to admit that no other church in the denomination was willing to hire a black pastor, much less one with a white wife." She ran her fingers through her wavy blond hair.

"And two black sons who might want to date their daughters." Jake, who was a month shy of turning seventeen, laughed like he thought what he'd said was hilarious.

Fourteen-year-old Ronnie joined in. "What do you mean? We're half Swedish, aren't we?"

"Yeah, and we're probably both gay, too," Jake countered. He shoved his hands in the pockets of his jean shorts and leaned back in his chair, laughing.

Everyone cracked up. Frank and I had been told, before deciding to come to the Bronx, that Pastor Paul had been asked to leave his last church, in Connecticut, after he invited a gay couple to join the congregation. I'd liked this family even before meeting them, and now I liked them even more.

"Hey," Jake said, still laughing. "Be glad the Supreme Court finally declared our parents' marriage legal."

"To us!" Ronnie lifted his glass of lemonade. "Thanks to Loving v. Virginia, we are bastard children no longer." The two brothers toasted each other with a clink of their glasses.

I couldn't help but wonder what it must be like for them to navigate a world of prejudice, and if their joking was a way to disguise hurt and anger. But there was no hint of rancor in their humor. It even seemed pure in a way. I glanced at Frank, who was laughing as hard as anyone, knowing that if I told him what I was thinking, he'd accuse me of being too serious.

"Enough," Linnea said with a giggle. "Time to eat."

The laughter subsided as plates and bowls were passed around the table—hamburgers with pickles and onions on the side, potato chips, coleslaw, potato salad, and brownies.

I took a bite of my hamburger. "Mmmmm, this is delicious. I don't know how you do it." I wiped the juice from my chin with the red and white checked napkin that matched the tablecloth.

"Well, first you fire up the grill," Jake said, laughing again.

"No, I mean, how did you take this drab little patch of cracked concrete and make it into such a beautiful little sanctuary? And the parsonage," I pointed toward the back door, "it's so... so... normal."

"Nobody's ever accused us of being normal before," fourteen-year-old Ronnie cracked.

"*Tack så mycket* to Linnea here." Pastor Paul winked at his wife.

"See what I mean?" Ronnie said. "You know any other black man who speaks Swedish?"

Everyone laughed, me included. "I don't mean *normal*, normal," I said. "More like ordinary. No, I guess what I mean is that your home is such a contrast to everything else around here."

"We want you to think of it as yours while you're here, right, Linnea?" Pastor Paul said.

"A shelter from the storm," she added with a smile.

"So what do you think of P.S. 457," Ronnie said. "I went there when we first moved here. I thought the building was falling apart around me."

I put my silverware down and held my head in my hands. "It was built for a thousand students," I said, "and they're expecting over twenty-five hundred. That's more than twice the population of the town where I grew up. The playground is filled with mobile classrooms, and that still doesn't solve the overcrowding."

"So how are they going to manage?" Pastor Paul said.

"By running the school in two shifts," I said. Everyone shook their heads and made *tsk tsk* sounds.

"A way to make two schools out of one," Linnea said.

"Is Miss Huskings still the principal?" Ronnie asked. "She was one scary lady. And creepy?" He lifted his hands up in mock horror. "She used to roam the halls to check on what was going on. We were all afraid of her."

"I'm a bit intimidated by her, too," I said. "I get the impression she's supportive of the teachers but that you'd better not cross her."

"You can always quit," Frank said.

I stared at him. Quit? I picked up my hamburger, licked away the mustard oozing from the side of the bun, and bit into it. Three years of marriage and four years of dating before that, and my husband still didn't have a clue who I was.

~

The first day of school finally arrived, delayed for two weeks by a teachers' strike that I didn't understand. At five minutes before seven, the gymnasium was packed, teeming with brown-faced children and pale-faced teachers. I stood with my back against the concrete under a sign in thick black marker posted on the wall that said *Mrs. Waters, Third Grade, Section 8*. My heart skipped a beat at the sight of the thirty-five students gathered around me, a surging swarm of curiosity and anticipation in a rainbow range of Bronx skin tones. I smiled at them. Some of them smiled back. Others stared, wide-eyed, like deer caught in the headlights.

"Welcome to the zoo," I heard someone to my right say. I turned to see a short, squat man with a handlebar mustache, about ten years my senior, wearing a wrinkled off-white short-sleeve shirt. A blue and tan striped tie dangled at his neck. With a sinister smile, he waved his palm in mock blessing over his students, who, unlike mine, stood at attention in a straight line. The sign on the wall behind him said *Mr. Frascatore, Fourth Grade, Section 1*.

"It's pretty noisy and crowded in here, all right," I said, trying to be pleasant.

"An extension of the neighborhood." With a look of scorn on his face, he tipped his head toward the heavy-duty wire mesh covering the towering gymnasium windows along one wall. "Better be careful out there. You could get punched in the face at any time for no reason at all, or worse yet, stabbed in the gut. My name's Anthony, by the way."

"I'm Sylvia." I paused, then added, "I live within walking distance of here. We moved here this summer."

He snorted and dipped his head toward my students. "They are trainable. But don't expect them to learn anything." Then he smiled, exposing square, yellow teeth.

An ice cube settled in the pit of my stomach. I crossed my arms and looked down, kicked at an invisible piece of dirt on the floor. I wanted to say something, but didn't. I was new, and it was my first day of school. And, having grown up in a family that was averse to arguing, I'd never developed a knack or an appetite for overt disagreement. I turned away from his negative energy, tried not to engage with him or make it seem in any way that I agreed with his reprehensible views.

"Don't listen to him." It was the teacher to my left, a sturdy, bosomy middle-aged woman. The reddish-blond hair tied up in a loose bun on the top of her head contributed to the confident look she had of someone who belonged here and knew her way around. She rolled her eyes in Anthony Frascatore's direction and reached out to shake my hand. "My name's Bonnie. Bonnie Goldmann. I teach third grade, too. Welcome to P.S. 457. Looks like we made it. We lost a couple of weeks because of the strike, but it could have been worse."

"What was the strike about?" I asked.

"Depends on who you ask. I support my union." She gave Anthony a look that I didn't understand and spoke to him more than to me. "But, in my opinion, walking out now was a mistake. Unnecessary... *and* counterproductive."

"The UFT has to take a stand," Frascatore said. "We have show that OHB board and those ATA folks we won't compromise." He swiveled the upper part of his body toward me, saw the confused look on my face, and scoffed. "See that, she doesn't even have a clue what I'm talking about."

He was right. All those acronyms—OHB? ATA?—sent a blush up my neck and onto my cheeks. Bonnie gave Frascatore a swat on his arm. "So how much did you know, big shot, when you were new?" She turned toward me. "Forget about him. He's always like that."

"I signed up as a UFT member," I said, "so of course I know the United Federation of Teachers is our union." I made a face with my lips, an apologetic shrug. "But otherwise he's right. I don't know what he's talking about."

She slipped her hand through my arm, pulled me close and spoke in a low, confidential voice. "OHB is the Ocean Hill—Brownsville school district, where the mayor is conducting a community control experiment in an attempt to improve the quality of education in the black community. A school board made up of folks from that community is in charge of the Ocean Hill—Brownsville schools. It's a good thing, in my opinion, for the community to have power over how its own schools are run. The ATA is the African-American Teachers Association, which supports community control. The UFT, our union, opposes it." She pulled away from me then and turned toward Frascatore, raised her voice. "And you know, Anthony, that there would be no need for the ATA if the UFT had lived up to its mission and commitment to integration and civil rights."

Frascatore stuck his thumbs between the waistband of his black slacks and his belt and leaned back on his heels. "Look, when you're in a battle, Bonnie, you rise or fall as one unit, you look out for each other. You can't have a bunch of Muhammad Alis in the ATA marching off to the beat of another drummer to fight a different war." He marched in place and his shoes squeaked on the gymnasium floor. Then he winked, squeezing together the lids of his left eye and holding it like that for too long to be joking or teasing. Long enough to ridicule but not long enough to be a threat.

The seven o'clock bell rang with a deafening blast that shook the windows and reverberated through my insides. On cue, all the students in the gymnasium silenced themselves and formed lines in front of their assigned teachers.

I smiled at my students and pointed to the sign on the wall. "Good morning! My name is Mrs. Waters, as you can see, but I would like you to call me Ms. Sylvia, okay? May I hear you say it, please?"

"Good morning, Ms. Sylvia."

One voice rang out over all the others, a voice strong, sure, curious, and ready, a voice deep for a girl, for any child her age, with a resonance that welcomed me in like an open door to a mystery, offering a gift of discovery, an adventure.

"Ms. Sylvia! Ms. Sylvia! My name is Mentayer LeMeur and I have a question about your name." The girl's smile was contagious.

"Yes?"

"Why? I mean, why does the sign say your name is Mrs. Waters, but you want us to call you Ms. Sylvia?"

"Good question," I say, stumped. "It's what I prefer." I could see the "why" expression on her face, the questions written all over it: *Why do you prefer your first name? Why say Ms. instead of Mrs.?* I cleared my throat and smiled at her. "And now, class," I said, "if you would please follow me."

As I turned toward the exit, I saw, from the corner of my eye, a smirk on Anthony Frascatore's face.

THREE

April 2006

It's been two months since I read the article in the *New York Times* about the boy's body found in the rubble of P.S. 457. Since then I've spent untold hours searching for more information from every source I can think of—the computer, the public library, every New York City publication sold by our local newsstands. All the major TV channels. The news is dominated by the war in Iraq, beheadings, suicide bombings, protests against anti-immigration legislation, broken promises post—Hurricane Katrina, recent political scandals—but nothing about the dead body. The story has evaporated into thin air, disappeared without a trace, a boy forgotten.

But not forgotten, never forgotten, by me is a boy named Markus LeMeur, and I won't rest, I can't, not until the body is identified and I know whether or not it's his. There's one source I haven't yet tried: Markus's sister. Mentayer would know, if anyone does.

So often over the years, I've wondered why I never heard from her. So many times, too many to count, I've considered contacting her. Each time I lost my nerve and talked myself out of it. And as more and more time went by, it seemed best to leave it alone, let sleeping dogs lie, let the past be the past. But now I can't do that. It's time to call her.

I hold the receiver in one hand and the phone number I got from operator information in the other. I almost put the phone down, but I don't. I can't let this go. Not until I know. My finger trembles as I push the numbers. The phone rings several times, and with each ring, my body quivers. I hold my breath. Will she answer? What will she say? What should I say?

"Hello." The woman's voice on the other end of the line is clear, strong, confident... and unfamiliar.

"Hello, I'm trying to reach Mentayer LeMeur." My voice echoes in the receiver, high-pitched, almost shrill, not sounding like me at all.

"This is Dr. LeMeur speaking. May I ask who's calling?"

"Mentayer?" I ask, "Dr. Mentayer LeMeur?"

"Yes?"

"This is Sylvia Jensen. I mean, Waters. Frank and I are divorced. I took back my maiden name. Ms. Sylvia. I'm sorry. It's been a long time, and hearing a voice from the past like this must seem strange." I slap my forehead with the palm of my hand. I sound like an idiot.

"Oh my."

A stone settles in the pit of my stomach. What do those two words mean? Is that an off-putting edge in her voice I hear, or is it the tone I feared hearing all those times I didn't call? What if she doesn't want to talk to me? What if she doesn't even know who I am?

"It's Ms. Sylvia. Do you remember me?" I hold my breath and wait for her answer.

"Yes, of course."

"I guess it must be a shock to hear from me out of the blue like this."

"As a matter of fact, it is."

"I thought of calling you so many times over the years." The words escape through my lips like a sob. There's silence on the other end, an impenetrable, awkward silence that reduces me to babbling, trying too hard.

"So you're a doctor," I say. "That's wonderful. What is your field, if I may ask? Oh my, it's been so long, it's been a lifetime."

There's a pause, then she says, "I have a doctorate in education."

"That's fantastic, Mentayer. Congratulations. From where?" I wait for her answer with my fingers crossed. In the summer of 1968, when I took her on a tour of the Columbia University campus, she had announced, "This is where I'm going to school. I am, Ms. Sylvia. I swear I am." How amazing it would be, I think now, if that turned out to be true.

She pauses, this time for what seems like minutes, not seconds, and I hold my breath.

"Columbia," she says at last. I jump up, put my hand over my mouth. There's another pause, and then she adds, "I got my undergraduate degree in childhood education from Hunter College, then my master's and doctorate at Columbia University Teachers College."

"Good for you," I say. "So are you a professor now? A teacher? A principal? Superintendent?"

The prolonged silence that follows squelches my enthusiasm and lets me know she is not interested in talking to me about this, or anything else. But I can't let her go.

"I heard that P.S. 457 was torn down," I say.

"They should have done that years ago," she says with a finality that makes clear her desire to end our conversation.

"I'm calling about... well." I pause, dig my fingers into my neck. "It's about Markus. I'm calling about your brother."

More silence. A silence that says, *No, we are not going to talk about this.* A silence that lasts for so long I wonder if the phone has gone dead or if Mentayer has hung up. I feel like I'm going to crawl out of my skin any minute.

At last she sighs, a long, heavy sigh that lets me know she's still there. And then she says, "Markus is fine."

The decisiveness in her voice declares it to be true. Markus is fine. He's alive.

My relief is too huge for words. I have to work to keep myself from hyperventilating.

"I'm so glad," I blurt out between jagged breaths. I have so many questions. Where is Markus? What is he doing? Whatever happened to him? And what about her? Where does she work? Is she married? Does she have children? Is she happy? I open my mouth to ask more about Markus, but she cuts me off.

"My brother is fine," she says, "and the school will be fine, too. The CSCH Corporation is building a new one in its place." She pauses. I wait for her to say more. She doesn't. I open my mouth and try again, not wanting to let her go.

"So, what's Markus—"

She interrupts, her voice sharp, explosive. "Look, Ms. Sylvia. I don't know what you're up to. You disappear into thin air and I don't hear from you all these years, and now you call and start asking all kinds of questions? I appreciate your concern, but it's a bit late." She pauses. "Decades late." Then, with a voice so resolute it leaves no doubt in my mind that this conversation is over, she says, "Thank you for calling."

The sound of the phone clicking sends a bullet straight into me. I sit back on the couch with the receiver pressed tight against my abdomen and absorb the sting. Then the tears come. They wash down my cheeks and splash onto the cushions, tears of relief mixed with tears of grief, tears of loss, years of tears, too many tears. When at last they dry, I sit up and push the couch pillows to the side. I go into the bathroom and splash cold water on my face. Then I go to the kitchen and pour myself a cup of the coffee left over from my breakfast. It smells like sludge, but I'll drink it anyway.

I take it into the living room and sit back down on the couch. Outside the patio window, dark clouds block the morning sun. I sip the bitter coffee and think about how the shock of Mentayer's anger eclipsed the good news that Markus is alive, plunging me into an abyss of regret. But Markus *is* okay. He's fine. Isn't that what Mentayer said?

And then there were the things Mentayer didn't say. Like why didn't she ask me what caused me to be concerned about Markus now? And why did she blow up at me? Why did she say she'd never heard from me? It's true that after a few years of not hearing from her, I stopped writing. It hadn't been a conscious decision; my drinking had gotten out of control, and my relationship with Frank was pretty much over even though we hadn't yet divorced. I do remember thinking that Mentayer must have moved on. I didn't think she cared if she heard from me or not.

Something's not right. Something doesn't make sense. What is it?

Mentayer said Markus was going to be okay, and then, in the same breath, she said the school was going to be okay, too.

Then it hits me. I'd been so upset by her anger that what she said next hadn't registered with me. The reason P.S. 457 was going to be okay was because the CSCH Corporation was building a charter school in its place. Really?

I punch in J. B.'s number on my phone.

"Harrell here."

"It's me, Sylvia. I have to see you. It's about the dead body they found in the Bronx."

"Has it been identified? Was it who you thought it was? Markus, was that his name?"

"I talked to Mentayer LeMeur. She's Markus's sister. She says her brother is fine." I rub my forehead, squeeze the skin together with my fingers.

"But?"

"I don't know. Something's not right." I stop, careful not to betray Mentayer by questioning her veracity. "She told me the CSCH Corporation is building a school to replace P.S. 457. What are the odds?"

"There are no—"

"Coincidences. I know."

We meet for lunch an hour later at the Higher Ground and Spirits Café, a favorite haunt of mine from when I was in graduate school. I've always liked its funkiness, but today its idiosyncratic décor is of no interest to me.

"You must be relieved about Markus," J. B. says.

I close my eyes, and images of the impoverished world of the Bronx appear, as vivid as ever: what I left behind, who I left behind, Markus walking into his uncle's apartment building, waving good-bye for the last time, my not walking in with him to make sure he was safe, never finding out what happened to him. Still not knowing where he's been all these years, what he's been doing. I open my eyes. "The past isn't the past," I say to J. B. "It's right here, right now, whether I like it or not."

He looks at me askance. "What do you mean? Where is Markus now?"

"That's the thing. I don't know." I grip the edge of the Formica tabletop with my hands. "And why hasn't there been any news about the body?"

"They probably haven't identified it yet," J. B. says.

"Mentayer said Markus was fine, but I'd feel better if... " I pause, take a breath. "Why wouldn't they have identified that body yet? It shouldn't be that difficult."

"After so many years," J. B. says in his matter-of-fact journalistic manner, "it actually is. It's hard for forensic pathologists to identify remains when there's not enough skin intact to get fingerprints. They can x-ray the teeth, of course, and compare them with previous dental records. DNA testing of the bone fragments is possible, too, but the DNA would have to then be compared with the DNA of family members."

"So why don't they do that," I say.

"At this point, unless they can narrow the suspect pool, looking for family members would be like looking for a needle in a haystack, or more like many haystacks. It's still possible, but more likely to be done if the police had some idea about the boy's identity first. Then they could use forensic testing to either confirm or deny their suspicions."

I think about what he's saying. The dead boy could be any one of thousands of boys in the Bronx. I suppose if there was a list of every boy who went missing in the Bronx thirty or forty years ago, that could narrow it down, but unless the police had a way to at least make some educated guess about who the boy was, it's unrealistic to think they would consider it worth trying.

"Why would the police care about a boy who died decades ago anyway," I say. "Why invest the time and money on some poor little black kid from the Bronx?"

"Why are you so invested in this, Sylvia, now that you know Markus is fine?" He pauses and gives me a meaningful look that stops short of a scold. "Sylvia," he then goes on, "if for some reason you still think the body might be Markus, you should let the police know. Do you know something?"

"I don't. I don't know anything. His sister says he's fine."

He raises both eyebrows.

"And how would I contact the police anyway," I say. "Make a cold call to 911? No one will listen to me. Besides, I don't know anything." My foot starts tapping, and I press down on my knee to stop it.

"You know you don't believe Mentayer."

My stomach goes into spasm from the betrayal I'm about to commit. "I still don't know what happened to Markus," I say. "Mentayer was angry at me for calling, and I can't shake this feeling that she doesn't know what happened to Markus either. I think it's strange that neither of us even mentioned the dead body on the phone."

J. B. leans toward me, an intent look on his face. "It's also strange that the article in the *New York Times* never mentioned the fact that the dead body was discovered on the CSCH building site. That might not seem unusual on the surface, might not even be considered to be a relevant fact. *Except* that Daniel Leacham, who's an award-winning journalist with a reputation for being thorough, wrote the article. And I know he's written several articles about CSCH in the past. So why didn't he mention CSCH in the article? It isn't plausible that he didn't know."

"What are you implying?"

"It's curious, that's all."

"Call him," I say. "Ask him."

"I already did," he says. "He was pretty evasive, but he piqued my interest when he said something about CSCH being an exposé waiting to happen. This is getting interesting, don't you think?" He falls silent, and there's an air of concentration about him, a tension in the air that I recognize as his suppressed excitement at the potential discovery of a new lead. "That's why I'm going to New York," he says at last.

"I'm going with you," I say without skipping a beat. "I have to know if that dead boy was Markus, because if it was, then his death is my fault."

FOUR

Winter 1967

Even though P.S. 457 was bleak and overcrowded, a physically and emotionally violent place, the energy of my thirty-five eight-year-old students lightened the building's dull gray walls. It even freshened the air, despite the strange mildew smell that made my nostrils itch. From day one I set out to create for them a safe learning space from seven to noon five days a week. We followed the same routine every day so they always knew what to expect. I was quick to praise and encourage, and they, in turn, were eager to please. I kept the door closed to keep the sounds of other teachers' voices, at the end of their nerves and at the top of their lungs, from filtering into our classroom. I never raised my own voice. I never had to.

During the first few months, I visited the neighborhood projects and crowded tenements and met with my students' parents and other caregivers. I wanted to understand the circumstances in which they lived so I could better meet their individual needs in the classroom. I experimented with new ways of teaching and sometimes ran them by Frank.

"I have a brilliant idea," I exclaimed one night when he was sitting in our faux-leather thrift store chair reading, as usual. He turned his book facedown on his lap and puffed on his pipe, which was a status symbol among seminarians. In many ways, we were a typical couple: me the annoyed and annoying wife, he the clueless and distant husband, who preferred reading to listening to me, who in spite of wearing tweed jackets with patches on the sleeves, watched sports and left the toilet seat up.

"Do you know the song *Apples, Peaches, Pumpkin Pie*," I asked.

He nodded and took a sip from his glass of bourbon.

"Kids love it," I said. "I have the record here. I could bring our little record player to school, maybe let my students dance to the song at first, get them loosened up a bit, you know? So this is what I'm thinking. I write the words on a big piece of newsprint with the key words I want them to learn to read underlined in red. While they sing along to the music, I point to the words. After a while, I turn off the music and point to the words again, see if they can repeat them after me. On another piece of newsprint, I post the words in a list, separate from the lyrics and in a different order, and have them read them by sight. You know what I mean? What do you think?"

"How much time will it take?"

I sucked in my breath and counted to ten while his question morphed from curiosity to criticism inside. "I don't know how long it will take, Frank."

"How do you know it will work?"

"I don't," I said with a drawn-out sigh. "But what I do know is that most of my students don't know how to read. At least a third of them barely speak English. The rest of them are bored to death during reading time. 'See Dick run. See Jane skip. Go, Spot, go.' I have to do something different. I have to at least try."

Frank grunted, took another sip of his drink, and went back to reading. When I started playing the record, he disappeared into the bedroom and closed the door. Late into the night I listened to Jay and the Techniques over and over again, stopping to write the lyrics in big black letters on newsprint, making sure I got them exactly right.

Early the next morning, I woke Frank and told him that because I had to carry the record player and the rolls of newsprint, I would be driving to school instead of walking. He groaned, rolled out of bed, and pulled on his jeans. It was his job to put the car battery in the van; after two of them were stolen, we kept it inside at night. He stumbled out of the apartment carrying the battery and leaving behind a trail of air sticky with residual irritation. He came back in, gave me a perfunctory peck on the cheek, and went back to bed.

My students' faces lit up like never before as they danced and sang and shouted out the words, with and without the music. Every day they called out the titles of other songs and asked if they could learn to read with those, too. How could I refuse? Class preparation became the kudzu of my evenings. I was soon familiar with the late-night silence of the neighborhood and came to appreciate the absence of the sounds of screeching cars and of the human bustle of everyday life.

"You have an uncanny ability to focus," Frank said almost every night around midnight when he headed off to bed.

That was, of course, his way of saying I was obsessed. Maybe he was right. I'd always been intense about mastering whatever I decided to do, and maybe I did work too hard. But I had high expectations of my students, too, and their growing confidence was obvious when their little chests filled with pride at the daily display of their accomplishments on the bulletin board. I always placed them right next to the achievements of their new cultural heroes—Harriet Tubman, Sojourner Truth, Matthew Henson, Charles Drew, Cesar Chavez, Langston Hughes, Martin Luther King Jr., Malcolm X, Muhammad Ali. My students and I were happy... until something happened that changed everything.

My class was working in their math groups. I heard a commotion, a banging noise out in the hall, and went out to investigate. I saw Anthony Frascatore, whose classroom was across the hall, slam a student against the wall, then pin him there by the collar of his shirt. He screamed at the student, his mouth mere inches from the boy's ebony face: "What did I tell you to do?"

I swept toward him. "What the hell are you doing?" I said.

Frascatore looked surprised. He released his hold on the boy's shirt, grabbed his wrist, and thrust him through the open classroom door. "Get back in there, and from now on you do what I tell you to do."

"What are you doing?" I asked again. I was gritting my teeth so hard the roots hurt.

"Taming the animals in this zoo. What do you think I'm doing?"

"Assaulting a child."

He sneered. "It's called discipline, Mrs. Waters. You won't find my students singing and dancing."

I glared at him. He glared back. I crossed my arms, tucked in my chin, and stared.

"You do know that I've been teaching here for a long time, don't you?" Frascatore glowered like he was about to slam *me* into the wall next.

"What I know," I said, "is that you better never, ever let me see you lay a hand on any student again."

He snorted. "Or what?"

"Or I will tell Miss Huskings what I saw."

Frascatore clenched his fists, his face flushed. Then he turned on his heels, stormed into his classroom, and slammed the door.

I went back to my classroom, sat down at my desk, and tried to calm myself. You could have heard a pin drop, my students were so quiet. An hour later, when I hugged them and dismissed them for the day, they still looked anxious.

I went to meet Bonnie Goldmann for lunch in the teachers' lounge. The room made my already gloomy mood worse. Its grayish-brown walls were dull and its furniture—metal chairs, a scratched Formica table, and an ancient brown refrigerator—was depressing. There wasn't a single picture or plant. Most teachers avoided the room, which was why Bonnie and I started having lunch here, so we could share ideas about teaching third grade.

It wasn't long before she had become a friend. She was a refreshing New Yorker—frank, pushy, talkative, well-meaning—who never judged me or made fun of my naive Midwestern earnestness. Her reddish glasses, propped halfway down her nose, complemented the color of her hair and gave her the air of a disheveled intellectual. A female Einstein, if Einstein had been attractive. She grew up in the Bronx with parents who were Romanian holocaust survivors. She seemed to know everything about the Grand Concourse and P.S. 457, where she'd taught for many years. I was sure she knew all about Anthony Frascatore, too. And today, that's what I wanted to talk to her about.

"Mr. Frascatore and I got into it this morning." I bit into my peanut butter and raspberry jelly sandwich and talked while chewing in an attempt to hide the angry tremor in my voice.

"He's got a short fuse sometimes." Bonnie waved her hand like she was swatting at a fly. "He hasn't talked to me at all this year."

I was about to ask her why when Frascatore appeared in the doorway. The last person I wanted to see. He sauntered over to the refrigerator and held the door open, turning and glaring at me as if the putrid stench of someone's long-forgotten tuna fish inside was my fault.

"Geez," Bonnie said, holding her nose. "Shut that."

Frascatore grabbed a brown paper bag from inside and slammed the door. "Damned people leave their rotten food in the refrigerator," he grumbled.

"So, Anthony," Bonnie said, her voice a tease. "You still not talking to me?" She looked sideways at me and winked. I looked down at my sandwich.

"Why should I?" He put his lunch down on the table like maybe he was going to stay a while. I reached into my lunch bag for a potato chip. A strange smell emanated from Frascatore, some combination of aftershave, bologna, and sweat.

"Because maybe it wouldn't hurt to listen to somebody other than Al Shanker and his cronies once in a while," Bonnie joshed.

"You think I should listen to someone like *her* instead of our union president?" He jabbed his finger in my direction.

I opened my can of Diet Coke and it hissed.

"Admit it, Anthony," Bonnie said in a now half-serious tone. "Going out on strike at the beginning of this year made things worse. We're more divided than ever."

He grunted. "Yeah, well, we gotta watch out for ourselves," he said with a shrug. "We're in the minority here. You know the stats same as I do, ninety-seven percent of our students are black and Hispanic."

"Being taught by white teachers," Bonnie said. "It's our kids who are the ones getting the short end of the stick, not us."

Frascatore's face turned red, his mouth twisted in fury. "Don't you start with that crap. We have to stand up for ourselves as teachers. If we let communities control our schools, it will be the end of our rights."

"Not that simple," Bonnie said with a shrug.

Frascatore grabbed his lunch from the table. "Mark my words," he said. "Mark my words."

I breathed a sigh of relief as he walked out the door in a huff.

"At least he didn't go on and on about our right to discipline students," Bonnie said with a roll of her eyes. "I swear, that's all that man seems to care about."

The tension was building inside me, waiting to be released. Did she know that Frascatore, in the name of discipline, thought teachers had the right to slam students against the wall? I would bet that if she'd seen what Frascatore did today, she'd be down at the principal's office right now reporting it to Miss Huskings. I wanted to tell her what happened, but she had already started talking a mile a minute, and I couldn't get a word in.

"Did I ever tell you about my dad? He scored at the top on the city teachers' exam, and they still wouldn't give him a job until he took a speech course to correct his Yiddish accent. Thanks to the union, they can't deny someone a job because of accent or race anymore. Frascatore's right that we need to be united, but he doesn't understand what's at risk here."

"What do you mean?" I asked.

Bonnie glanced down at her hands for a second. Then she sat back with a sad sigh. "Look, Sylvia, my family is Jewish. I know what it's like to be persecuted. For generations. It's painful. It hurts me to see it happen to others. My friends feel the same way. What Anthony doesn't get is that if the union keeps fighting the community control experiment in the black Ocean Hill—Brownsville district, the bond between us Jewish teachers and the black teachers is going to be broken."

She paused and looked off into space before continuing. "My dad always said that one of the most precious and fragile links of our democracy is the solidarity of black and white working people through the unions. What scares me most, Sylvia, is that this conflict about who gets to control our schools is going to destroy that."

She took in a quick breath like she wasn't finished, but then she glanced up at the clock on the wall and started packing up her leftover food. "I'm sorry, hon, but I have to run. I've been going on and on without paying any attention to the time. I have to leave for a teachers' conference this afternoon and I'm already late. It'll be so nice to have a break for the next couple of days." With that, she gave me a peck on the cheek and rushed out the door, leaving me alone with the last bite of my peanut butter and jelly sandwich sitting on the table and not knowing what to do about Frascatore.

So I did nothing for the next few days while I waited for Bonnie to come back. I avoided any conversation, even a greeting, with Frascatore, while at the same time keeping my senses on full alert and tuned in to his every movement. I listened for the sound of his voice. I kept my classroom door open so I could keep an eye on him across the hall. And the whole time, my conscience nagged at me. I hadn't told the principal right away, but if he ever laid hands on another student again, I would not hesitate to do so.

Three days later, a sixth-grade student brought me a note from Miss Huskings. When I read *Come to my office at twelve-thirty*, all the muscles in my body tensed. I felt like a student being called into the principal's office for doing something wrong. But what had I done? Maybe someone else had told the principal what I'd seen Frascatore do, and she wanted to know why I hadn't come to her. Maybe someone had complained about my students singing and dancing during reading time, and Miss Huskings was going to question my unorthodox teaching methods. Maybe it was about something else. But what could it be?

By the time I hugged my students good-bye for the day and headed for the main office, I was pretty much a basket case. I leaned on the counter that ran from one wall to the opposite one. Behind me, a cluttered bulletin board was crammed with colorful pictures and announcements, cartoons, happy children's faces, most of them white. In front of me, three desks on the other side of the counter were filled with uneven stacks of papers. To the left of them, a tall gray filing cabinet was piled high with haphazard stacks of ragged reading books. And behind the cabinet, hidden from view, was the door to the principal's office, that narrow, secret opening in the wall known to suck in students who misbehaved. And teachers.

"You can go ahead and knock on Miss Huskings's door," one of the secretaries said as she lifted up the end of the counter and let me in.

I pulled my shoulders back, remembering when I was in elementary school, everyone said the principal had a stick in his office that he beat kids with. I never saw it myself. I'd never talked to Miss Huskings alone before, either, except to say hello and how are you in passing. Her mere presence on the auditorium stage during school assemblies and monthly teachers' meetings was daunting enough. As I stood at the door working up my courage to go in, I heard ripples of laughter and animated voices on the other side.

I knocked. No response. I knocked harder.

"Come," the principal ordered in her raspy smoker's voice.

I turned the knob and pushed in the door. Miss Huskings, slouched down in a leather chair behind her mammoth desk, looked like a wrinkled lump of clay. Creases of skin puckered toward her lips, from one corner of which a cigarette dangled. She plucked the cigarette out with yellowed fingertips and balanced it on the edge of an ashtray overflowing with what looked like a week's deposit of ashes and butts.

"Mrs. Waters," she said.

"I guess I'm early," I said.

Miss Huskings picked up the cigarette and brought it to her lips. She took a puff and blew out a perfect smoke ring. "Anthony and I were reminiscing a bit."

I followed her gaze and saw Frascatore sitting off to the side with one leg crossed over the other. He was smiling and nodding like a bobblehead doll, the embodiment of superiority and clueless self-importance. I grimaced. What was he doing here? Was he the person who had complained about me?

"Sit." Miss Huskings flicked her hand toward the chair next to his.

I pulled the chair a few inches away from him before sitting down. I wished I were invisible, like when, as a child, no one noticed what I said or did. I longed for the advantage that comes with the ability to pass unnoticed through whatever was to come. But it was not to be.

Miss Huskings's pointy green eyes were stuck on me in a way that made it clear I was not at all invisible to her. "I'll get right to the point," she said. She heaved her thick body up and took another drag from her cigarette. "Some parents complained that their son was assaulted by a teacher. Now I know that if *any* of my teachers saw something like that, they would have reported it to me right away." I froze, prepared myself for the attack to come. "So that's not what this is about," she continued. "Anthony here mentioned that the two of you had a conversation about discipline, and I thought it would help if we talked."

This was my chance to set the record straight. But what could I say? How could I tell her that Frascatore had assaulted a boy, but I hadn't reported it to her? She'd want to know why I didn't speak up before, maybe accuse me of collusion and reproach me for putting her in a bad position with the student's parents by not coming forward earlier. For a split second, it crossed my mind that she might already know it was Frascatore, but then why was he here? Wouldn't Miss Huskings want to talk to me alone? Now that he *was* here, that made speaking up impossible. If I told her what I saw, he would deny everything. And why would she believe me over him?

I folded the note she'd sent in half, then in half again, kept folding until it was the size of a piece of hard candy. Then another thought occurred to me, one even more terrifying than the others. Maybe Miss Huskings already knew what happened. Maybe the student had told his parents I was a witness. What if this was all a test? What if my principal was playing games? I shifted my position in the chair, and it scraped on the floor with a high-pitched sound.

"No need to be nervous, Mrs. Waters." The principal coughed into her hand.

I let out my breath. *Then why am I here?* I bit my bottom lip. There was a lead weight in my stomach.

"I told Ada here that you have an unusual philosophy about discipline," Frascatore said in a casual, matter-of-fact tone of voice.

Ada? What was his relationship with Miss Huskings, anyway?

The principal blew out another puff of smoke. She leaned toward me and waited, eyebrows raised.

"I don't think like he does," I muttered. I was confused, thrown off-balance. "That's all."

"She doesn't realize that sometimes it's our job to knock some sense into our students." Frascatore wrapped his arms around the back of his chair, expanded his chest. A button came undone on his dingy shirt.

I clenched my fists. "There are alternatives to violence." I knew I was mumbling and kicked myself for it. I sat up straighter, ready to explain, and be more assertive, until I saw Frascatore shoot Miss Huskings a "didn't I tell you" look.

"Are you saying that Anthony believes in physical discipline of his students?" the principal asked. Was it an accusation? Did she really want to know?

Frascatore cleared his throat and looked me straight in the eye. It was a dare if I ever saw one. I looked away. I didn't know how to respond, didn't know whether Miss Huskings was after him or me or something else. She was watching me, waiting. I had to say something.

"I guess you could say," I said at last, "that Mr. Frascatore believes in controlling students and I believe in motivating them."

He twisted his body toward me, a look of disdain on his face. "Here's the *deal.*" The reminder was delivered with a smile. "I'm not sure Mrs. Waters here believes in any form of discipline at all."

I tightened my jaw. So this was how Frascatore was setting me up. If I told Miss Huskings what I'd witnessed, he would argue that I had skewed ideas about discipline, that what I thought I saw was not what happened. I opened my mouth, angry enough now to tell the principal everything, get it over with, let the chips fall where they may. But then I saw the two of them smile at each other, and I squeezed my lips together. I was the one at risk, not him. The two of them had a cozy relationship. They'd known each other for many years. He was the union representative for the school. He had tenure.

"We can't teach if we're not in control," Frascatore said.

A sharp pain shot through my temple. I spoke up, but my voice was weak. "I don't believe teachers have a right to punish students with impunity," I said. "Students can't learn if they're afraid." I leaned back in my chair feeling nauseous.

"Ah, the self-righteousness of the young and inexperienced," he said.

"Nothing wrong with idealism, Anthony," Miss Huskings scolded. "It's in short supply around here, I'm afraid."

I sat up, feeling a bit emboldened by what seemed to be support. "We need to find ways to encourage our students," I said in a stronger voice. "We need to motivate them."

"Uh-huh, like having them dance in class."

I whirled toward him. "Are you saying my classroom is out of control? Are you accusing me of letting my students do whatever they want? Is that what this is about?"

Frascatore crossed his short legs, one foot resting on the knee of the other, and smiled in a triumphant, bare-your-teeth way.

"Is this meeting about me, Miss Huskings?" I asked. "Have I done anything wrong?"

"No, no." The principal's response was quick and firm. "I know this is your first year with us, Mrs. Waters, but I've been at this long enough to spot a gifted teacher when I see one. I would like you to consider supervising a student teacher next year."

I blushed and looked down at my lap.

"And you've been a big help to me," she added.

"How," I asked, looking askance at her.

"This discussion has helped me clear a few things up in my head. It seems like everything these days comes down to a difference of opinion about discipline." She stood up, glanced at her watch, and grabbed a pack of cigarettes and a folder from her desk. "And now I've got a meeting to get to downtown." She rushed toward the door with a side-to-side gait and a wave of her purse.

"Thanks, Ada," Frascatore called out as he swaggered from the room behind her.

I sat there, stunned, and didn't move until a secretary popped into the office with a stack of mail. Then I left in a daze. I'd been duped. Anthony Frascatore had set it all up. Had set me up. He'd protected himself by making sure I didn't tell the principal what I'd seen.

I didn't tell Frank about the meeting in Miss Huskings's office. I couldn't bear to listen to any of his critical questions or have him tell me I should pray about it or maybe suggest we get a puppy. After dinner we both did what we always did. He sat in his chair with a book and a drink. I did the dishes and cleaned up the kitchen before preparing lesson plans for the next day, ruminating the whole time about what happened in the meeting.

By the time I went to bed I was so tied up in knots that sleep was impossible. I had double-binded myself. My original sin had been not reporting what I'd witnessed to the principal right away. I'd done the easy thing, not the right thing. Yes, Frascatore had suckered me, but I had walked right into it.

I stared up at the sinister shadows slithering across the ceiling. The burden of my transgression was heavy, and much as I wanted to, I couldn't put it down. I castigated myself for being so passive. I'd had another chance to tell the truth during the meeting, and had still remained silent, even as every fiber of my being was calling out to me to do the right thing.

It wasn't the first time. My actions often were miles behind my passion. After years of careful training while I was growing up, it had become second nature for me to remain silent. I learned to not express my opinions, to not make waves. But I hadn't been born passive. My passivity had come in small steps. Like colluding with evil came in small steps.

Enough already, I scolded myself. *You might as well wear a sign saying you're sorry for the Vietnam War, the bombing of Laos, and everything else that's wrong in the world. Better yet, while you're at it, why not apologize for your existence. Cut yourself a break!*

I pulled off the covers and slipped out of bed, careful not to wake Frank. I went to the kitchen for a glass of water. No roaches scattered across the floor when I turned on the light. At least that was something. Then the water, cool on my throat, calmed me into a new thought. If my passivity had come in small steps, then why couldn't it be undone in small steps? Why not, indeed?

I went back to bed, lay down with my hands on the back of my neck, and stretched my legs out. I closed my eyes, and images of my students and their apartments zoomed by as if I were a photographer snapping pictures of travels to new places. One scene in particular came into such sharp focus that it was almost as if I were there again.

~

I'm standing in the foyer of a four-story apartment building, waiting to be buzzed in. I push the apartment bell for the third time, and still no response. I walk outside, ready to give up and leave, when Mentayer's brother comes running up to me. He's out of breath.

"Ms. Sylvia," he says. "I was s'posed to be watching out for you and tell you they was out back. I'll show you the way."

"Thank you, Markus," I say. "So, is second grade still going well for you?" Every day at noon, Markus came to my classroom to meet his sister so they could walk home together. He was a cute kid, small for his age and full of energy, eager to chat and clean the blackboard for me and help me put things away. When Mentayer pulled him away with a reprimand, he'd tag along behind her with a skip in his step and without complaint.

"Yes, ma'am." He nods, and his mouth falls open the same way his sister's does. His resemblance to her is remarkable in other ways as well: a small gap between his two front teeth, a lopsided smile, and curious brown eyes.

His little hand grips mine as he leads me along a narrow, cracked strip of concrete to the back of the building. There, in a postage-stamp yard, sits his sixty-six-year-old grandmother, square of body yet wiry in the face and arms and dressed in a rumpled muumuu with magenta flowers and chartreuse leaves. She's perched on a wooden crate scooping pigeon poop with a rusty metal spatula onto pieces of newspaper, which she then folds and tucks under the crate. Mentayer stands next to her.

"Grandma," she says, "why don't you put it in the garbage can? You come back later, there's gonna be little pieces of poop scattered around for you to pick up all over again."

"Rats gotta eat, too, girl. Everyone and everything's gotta eat something."

Mentayer spots me, and her eyes light up. "Look, Grandma, it's Ms. Sylvia. My teacher. She's here, like I told you." Her gap-toothed smile widens as she takes my hand from Markus and pulls me forward. "Grandma, this is Ms. Sylvia," she says.

"It's nice to meet you, Mrs. LeMeur," I say.

"Everyone calls me Grandma. Don't expect you to be no different."

I smile. This might take some getting used to. "Is this an okay time?" I ask.

Mentayer's grandmother nods. She wipes her hands on her dress and stands up with effort. "You two go on in the house," she says with a shooing motion of her hands and a flick of her wide hips. "Be sure to watch your feet now. Don't you be dragging any dog shit or other garbage into the house again, you hear?" Mentayer scrapes the bottom of her shoes on the concrete and Markus scrambles behind her around the corner to the front of the building.

"Now, tell me, Ms. Sylvia," Mrs. LeMeur says. "What trouble did my granddaughter get herself into this time to make her teacher come to here? I swear, Markus has more sense than she does even though he's the younger. I tell that child every morning to try and act more like her brother, but it don't seem to make no difference."

"I'm delighted to have Mentayer in my class," I say. "I wanted to meet you. I'm visiting all my students' homes. You're the first."

She squints at me. "Huh! You sure she's not giving you trouble? She was a handful for all her other teachers, don't know why third grade would be any different."

"She's smart, as I'm sure you know. She's a fluent reader, way above her grade level. School can be boring for a child as bright and quick as she is."

"Her momma was smart, too." A deep sadness gathers around Mrs. LeMeur's mouth. "But that didn't make no difference. Drugs took hold of her after Markus was born. Killed her in the end. I don't want Mentayer going that road."

~

Frank rolled over, and when his arm brushed against my cheek, I scooted away from him and faced the wall, not wanting the images in my head to go away. I kept thinking about Mentayer. She bored easily, the work much too elementary for her, and then would act out in ways that were challenging in their ability to disrupt, yet thrilling in their creativity. She'd grunt, pant, tap her fingers on her desk, her feet on the floor, sometimes burst into dramatic energy, her crowning achievement a swoon and a roll of her eyes. I designed challenging projects for her to tackle when I sensed she was restless, and more often than not the advanced work absorbed her interest.

I went to see her grandmother two more times after our visit in September. The first time I went to show her a story Mentayer had written and to praise her granddaughter for how well she was learning to manage her impatience in class. The second time I went to confer with her about an incident involving Mentayer in the gym. An older boy had sneaked up behind her when she was jumping rope and pulled out one of the ribbons braided in her hair. She gave chase with the rope and, in her words, "slapped that boy silly." The boy took off crying, "like a baby," and Mentayer ended up getting in trouble with the boy's teacher. Who, thankfully, wasn't Frascatore.

We met in the living room that time, Mrs. LeMeur sitting in an overstuffed brown chair, and Mentayer and me across from her on a ragged couch that was scratchy and had wooden legs. Markus was there, too, sitting in the corner on a chair he'd brought in from the kitchen. His eyes were wide with curiosity and his mouth open as he watched the scene unfold.

The apartment was immaculate and smelled of fresh paint. According to Mentayer, her grandmother made the landlord strip off all the paint down to the wood because there was lead in it, and then he repainted the whole apartment, which was why they all had to stay with an uncle for a week.

"What do you think about what happened in the gym?" I asked Mentayer.

"I think that boy won't ever mess with me again."

"That ain't no excuse for doing what you done," Mrs. LeMeur said. She wagged her finger to make her point.

"You know he won't, Grandma." Mentayer crossed her arms over her chest.

I had to agree with Mentayer about that. "But you came close to cutting his eye," I said. "You could have blinded him."

"I didn't mean to do that." Mentayer looked contrite.

"We know you didn't," I said.

"No matter. It could have been downright awful," her grandmother scolded. "You woulda been suspended for sure."

"He started it." Mentayer poked out her bottom lip. "I didn't go asking for trouble."

"Both of those things may be true," I said.

Mentayer stuck her chin out. "They are."

"You're not responsible for what that boy did," I went on. "But you are responsible for what you did after he messed with you. Maybe there was some other way you could have handled things? Some way that wouldn't have gotten you in trouble."

Mentayer didn't say anything. Her grandmother gave her what Mentayer had described to me as her evil eye. In the corner behind his grandmother's chair, Markus sat up straight, without moving, his hands folded on his lap.

I stifled an urge to smile. I liked Mentayer's stubbornness. "If you could do it over," I said, "what do you think you could do different? Or if it happened again, how could it end better? You know what I'm asking, right? The usual questions."

"But, Ms. Sylvia," Mentayer whined, "that boy isn't in our class, so he hasn't learned how to work things out like we have. He doesn't understand the process."

I felt myself melting away and folded my hands over my chest. The girl was a challenge and I had to improvise, even be cunning at times, to stay a step ahead of her. But I had grown fond of her. Her brother, too. Markus was as bright as his sister but without her impatience. And I liked their grandmother. She hovered over both of them, Mentayer more than Markus. She was like a one-woman PTA whose singular charge was to raise her granddaughter to flourish in a world that was certain to ignore and even try to destroy her unstoppable curiosity and free spirit.

I closed my eyes and, thinking about the LeMeurs with a smile on my lips, fell asleep at last.

I woke in the light of dawn to the sounds of the city coming alive. A garbage truck screeched to a halt outside; sanitation workers shouted to each other as they threw rubbish onto the back. Smells of human refuse wafted through the bedroom window. Soon people would go into the bodega around the side of the building and come out with their morning cups of coffee. The super would bring out his chair to sit guard in front of his door; maybe he'd talk today, maybe he wouldn't. Thirty-five third-graders would expect me to show up again today. Their eyes would be bright and their young voices hungry for approval as they shouted "Good morning, Ms. Sylvia."

Another day. Another chance. If Frascatore ever hurt another child, I would act right away. Next time, God forbid there be a next time, things would be different.

Little did I know how different they would be.

FIVE

Spring 1968

Several months passed without another incident. Until not long before the school year ended. It was almost noon and I was wrapping up my class for the day, thinking about how much I was going to miss my students, when I heard a sound that sent a chill through me. The sound I'd been listening for.

"No! No! No!" I flew out the door and down the hall in the direction of the sound, flailing my arms, running past three classrooms, a distance that felt longer to me than a football field.

Frank had told me it would never happen again. Whenever something triggered my fear that it would, he contended that I'd squashed Frascatore. In the wake of the tumult and unrest spreading across the country after Martin Luther King Jr. was assassinated, whenever a new undertow of despair threatened to pull me under, he insisted that Frascatore would never dare hurt another child again. I tried to believe him. Tried hard. I squeezed every ounce of hope for the future of humanity onto my students. My belief that at least I could provide for them a safe haven from the violence and degradation of the outside world kept me going. And every day that passed, I found solace in the absence of the sound I'd hoped to never hear again. But Frank had been wrong. Frascatore had done it again. He was doing it now.

I was close enough to see the fear-filled eyes of the boy being pinned against the wall. Frascatore's white knuckles pressed down on the small shoulders, his bared teeth close enough to touch the boy's face.

"Stop!" I screamed. *"STOP!"*

Frascatore turned, his eyes drilling into me. He dropped his arms to his sides, opened and closed his fists.

I recognized the boy. His name was Dion Brown. He lived in the building next to the one where Mentayer and Markus lived. I put my arm around his bony shoulders. He was trembling.

"Are you all right?" I asked.

Dion nodded. He stared down at his feet.

"You sure?"

He nodded again but didn't look up.

"What grade are you in?" I asked.

"Sixth."

"Who's your teacher?"

"Mr. Bernstein. Can I go to the bathroom, please?"

"Of course. Then go on back to your class, okay?"

"Yes, ma'am."

I watched Dion walk to the end of the hall and go into the boys' restroom. Then I turned my attention to Frascatore, ready to unleash on him the full force of my anger. But he was gone. The bastard had slipped away.

My breath started coming in short spurts, making my chest shake. I pressed my back against the wall and imagined barging into his classroom, imagined throwing him up against the blackboard, his students cheering me on with their eyes. Then I pulled myself together and went back to my classroom. My students were sitting with their hands folded on their desks. There was fear in their eyes. Mentayer, in her self-appointed role as class spokesperson, shot her hand up in the air.

"Ms. Sylvia, we would like to know if everything is okay."

Something caught in my throat. I coughed. I had never lied to my students before, and I wasn't about to start now. "No, I'm afraid everything is not okay, but I promise you that it will be."

The bell rang, but my students didn't jump up from their desks like they usually did. "Form a line," I said. Then I gave each of them a hug with an extra special squeeze.

"When Markus comes," I said to Mentayer when it was her turn, "would you help him wipe the blackboard and straighten the desks before you leave, and give him a hug from me?"

She nodded and stood to the side to wait for her brother. I gathered up my books and papers and headed for the principal's office to keep my promise.

I walked down the steps slowly in an attempt to control the heat of my fury and my skyrocketing blood pressure. I strode into the main office filled with determination, to the surprised looks of the office staff. I yanked up the end of the counter and bolted around the filing cabinet without asking permission. I pushed in the door to the principal's office without knocking.

"Mrs. Waters," Miss Huskings said from behind her desk. "I've been expecting you."

I blinked. So Frascatore had already got to her. I stiffened my back and stepped into the room. *He isn't going to get away with it again. Not this time.* "Then I guess you already know why I'm here."

The office smelled of tobacco fumes and ash; a smoky haze floated up to its towering ceiling. Gray clouds outside the soaring windows added to the gloom of the room's dark mahogany walls.

"Have a seat, Mrs. Waters." Miss Huskings's tone contained no inflection, no hint of impatience or anger.

"Anthony Frascatore assaulted a student," I said.

She peered into a plastic bag filled with what looked like homemade chocolate chip cookies, then held it out to me. "Have you had lunch?"

I took two steps toward her desk, then paused to take a breath. "He slammed a boy's head against the wall." I took another step forward. "But I'm sure that's not what he told you."

Miss Huskings poked a fork into a Tupperware container on her desk and lifted a forkful of pasta up to her mouth. A mantra played over and over in my head: *Will she believe me? If she does, what will she do? If she doesn't believe me, what will I do? Will she believe me? What if she doesn't?*

She stopped chewing, placed her fork down, and moved the container off to the side. "Are you saying you saw Anthony hit a boy?"

I hesitated, confused by her neutral tone of voice.

"I heard it."

Miss Huskings scrunched her eyebrows together. Not a good sign. She motioned for me to sit down with a tip of her head. But I didn't sit. Instead, I leaned forward and pressed the palms of my hands onto the edge of her desk.

"I know what happened. I heard the boy's head hit the wall. When I got there, Mr. Frascatore had him pinned against it. The boy wasn't even in his class. I saw him holding him there by his shoulders. He was right in his face.

I yelled and he let go. He knew what he was doing was wrong. He knew I caught him. That's why he made sure he got to you first. I'm sure he told you a different story."

"Slow down, Mrs. Waters. Can I get you some water? Or coffee?"

I shook my head, sharp, shook it again. I lifted one foot, then the other, then back to the first foot, back and forth. I kept shifting my feet until I was almost stomping, but my insides felt like they were being tied into knots. I tried to speak, but all that came out was a squeak. I gave up and dropped down onto a chair.

Miss Huskings scrutinized me but said nothing. I crossed my legs, and my dress crawled up my thighs. I uncrossed my legs and pressed them together. My chair creaked. I yanked the hem of my dress down to cover my knees. I tugged at my oversized silver hoop earrings, first the left one, then the right. I rubbed the back of my neck.

The room was silent. A heavy white mug appeared on the desk in front of me. I saw the principal's hand withdrawing. I reached for the mug, took a sip of coffee, my hand shaky. It was thick and bitter. I almost spit it out.

Miss Huskings scrunched her upper body forward and encircled her container of pasta with her flabby upper arms. "I had hoped, Mrs. Waters, that you and Anthony might have resolved your differences about discipline by now."

I slammed the mug down on her desk. Coffee sloshed over the rim. "What he did to that boy was *not* discipline."

"Maybe not what *you* think of as discipline," Miss Huskings said. She picked up a pack of Camels, tapped it on the desk, and pulled out a cigarette. She brought it up to her lips and lit it with a gold-plated lighter. "You know"—she inhaled, blew out the smoke—"I've always prided myself on how well my teachers get along. I want the two of you to work this out."

I stared at her, my mouth open. Was she kidding? Was this for real? "What did Mr. Frascatore tell you?" I managed to ask. "I'm sure it's not what happened."

"He had to run to a special union meeting," Miss Huskings said. "There's a lot of tension right now. Hundreds of cops had to go into Ocean Hill—Brownsville to break up a parents' blockade this morning. The community board is acting like a bunch of vigilantes. And as if that weren't enough, some union members have walked out in protest. Anthony's under a lot of stress right now."

"That's no excuse for assaulting a child."

Miss Huskings took another drag from her cigarette. "Mrs. Waters," she said. "I know you don't rely on discipline to control your students, and I applaud you for that." She flicked the ash from her cigarette into the ashtray. "Anthony could learn something from you."

I blew out my breath. Drops of rain were now hitting the windows, a clap of thunder in the distance.

"Some appreciation of his years of experience and his union position would go a long way," Miss Huskings said. "All he wants is for his students to respect his authority."

"Like a drill sergeant," I mumbled.

"Let's face it, Mrs. Waters, our students could do a lot worse with their lives than enlist in the army."

I bit my tongue. It was useless to argue. Everyone knew Miss Huskings made sure all P.S. 457 students were trained, starting in kindergarten, to respect authority. I'd cringed the first time she visited my class. Without any prompting, my students jumped up from their desks, stood at attention, and shouted "Good morning, Miss Huskings" like they were in a military brigade.

"Miss Huskings," I said with a quick intake of breath, "do you remember last November, when you told me that you expect your teachers to let you know right away if they ever see a teacher assault a student?" I pause and wait for her confirmation. She takes another puff of her cigarette. "Well, I am here to tell you that Anthony Frascatore assaulted a student. Only. A. Few. Minutes. Ago."

The principal put her cigarette down, left it burning in the ashtray. I stood up. Shoved my chair back. She didn't believe me; she didn't want to. So what did I do now? Frank would tell me I'd done all I could do and that I should let it go. But he was wrong. I wouldn't let it go. I couldn't. No. Not this time.

"The boy's name is Dion Brown," I said. "If his parents complain, I will back them up. If they don't, I will file a complaint myself."

Miss Huskings picked up her cigarette and took a puff, studying me as she inhaled. I stood still as a statue in front of her desk and studied her. We both jumped when someone pounded on the door. A secretary burst into the office, out of breath.

"I hate to interrupt, Miss Huskings, but someone found a student unconscious on the floor in one of the bathrooms. His teacher called 911. The ambulance is here."

Every nerve in my body shot out in an electrical current. *Please, oh please, oh please, don't let it be Dion.*

The secretary's thick fingers shook as she held out a piece of paper. "Here's the phone number for the boy's parents. His name is Dion Brown."

Beads of sweat sprang up on my forehead. "Where is he? Is he okay? What are they saying? Are they still upstairs?" I turned and took a step toward the door, ready to run out.

"Hold on, you're not going anywhere, Mrs. Waters." The unusual harshness in Miss Huskings's voice stopped me in my tracks. "I'm sure the boy will be okay." She put out her cigarette and pulled herself up in the chair.

"I think they're going to take him to the hospital," the secretary said.

"Find out which one," Miss Huskings said. "I'm sure his parents will want to know more about his condition, too. Who's his teacher?"

"Mr. Bernstein. He's with them now."

"Good. Tell him to come see me after he's talked to the medics."

The secretary rushed from the room. Miss Huskings brought the piece of paper close to her face and squinted at the number. Then she picked up the receiver and dialed.

I fell back onto the chair and covered my face with my hands. I felt tears stinging my eyes. "This is my fault. I should have walked back to his class with him. I should have stayed to make sure he was okay."

The principal covered the receiver with her hand and shot me a warning look. "Please, Mrs. Waters, your anxious self-regard is wearing a bit thin."

"I should have told you before. I should have told you the first time."

Miss Huskings shook her head and placed the receiver back on the hook. "Their phone's been disconnected," she said. "*Please,* Mrs. Waters. You told me. Now pull yourself together. First we'll go and attend to the boy, then we'll figure out how to contact his parents."

I gripped the edge of the chair and pushed myself up. "I saw him walk to the bathroom, and he seemed fine," I said as we walked together toward the door. "I know a way to get a message to his parents." I knew I could call Mentayer's grandmother. She would know how to find them.

We stopped in the hall outside the main office. Two medics were carrying Dion on a stretcher, headed toward the front entrance. Mr. Bernstein walked behind them with his head down, his hands clasped behind him.

I brushed past Miss Huskings and called out to them. "Is he all right? Is he still unconscious? What hospital are you taking him to?"

The medics glanced at each other with questioning eyes. They nodded and put the stretcher down. It was a good sign that they didn't seem to be in a hurry. I ran toward them. I hoped I might talk to Dion before they took him to the hospital. But then I saw the looks on the medics' faces. I followed their eyes down to the stretcher. Dion was covered with a sheet, even his face.

I cried out and took a step back. Mr. Bernstein wiped his eyes with the sleeve of his white shirt and stared up at the ceiling. Miss Huskings reached for my hand.

"This is our principal." Mr. Bernstein said. Outside, a long low roll of thunder cut through the crack in his voice.

The veins on Miss Huskings's hand throbbed against mine.

"I'm sorry, ma'am," one of the medics said. "There was nothing we could do. He was already gone when we got here."

Within minutes, the school was crawling with police. Students and teachers were sequestered in their classrooms, questioned one at a time in the halls. I waited in Miss Huskings's office. She suggested I go home and take care of myself. But I refused to leave. Not until I'd talked to the police myself.

The detective in charge came in to report to the principal some of what they'd learned, said he wanted to double-check with her. Someone said Dion had been playing football in the gymnasium before school, maybe that was how he got hurt. Someone else said that wasn't true, that no one was allowed to play football in the gym. Someone saw Dion fall down the steps, but that was a few days ago. I fumed as I listened to the police officer repeat what they'd heard in the interview process. Dion was a clumsy boy, always tripping over his feet. It was an accident. His father beat him. There were troubles at home. A suspicious man had been seen outside the school. Dion asked to go to the bathroom and got into a fight while he was gone. The police officer said they'd know more after the medical examiner had a look at the boy's body. An investigation might be in order.

"I already know what happened," I said. "I told you, Anthony Frascatore, a fourth-grade teacher, shoved Dion's head against the wall. I was there. I saw. I know. Everything else is rumor."

"Mrs. Waters heard a noise in the hall," Miss Huskings said, "and when she went out to investigate, Mr. Frascatore was there with the student. Dion was fine then."

I glared at her. "I know what happened. Why won't you believe me?" I turned to the detective. "Anthony Frascatore has assaulted boys before. This isn't the first time."

The detective wrote something in his notebook, adding what I said to what was already there as if what I saw and knew had no more significance than the nonsense others had provided.

"Why aren't you questioning Anthony Frascatore?" I said with accusing eyes. "You need to talk to him."

The policeman looked at me askance and closed his notebook.

"You need to go home now, Mrs. Waters," Miss Huskings said. "Leave it to the police."

SIX

April 2006

"Ladies and gentlemen, as we start our descent, please make sure your seat backs and tray tables are in their full upright position, your seat belt is securely fastened, and all carry-on luggage is stowed underneath the seat in front of you or in the overhead bins. Flight attendants, prepare the cabin. Thank you. We'll be landing shortly."

I fold my hands on my lap. J. B., who's been sitting sideways with his long legs stretched out in the aisle, pulls his feet in and slips them under the seat in front of him.

"I haven't been to the Bronx in nearly forty years," I say.

"Why did you leave?" he asks.

"There was nothing for me there anymore," I say. "Everyone was going back to the land, living in communes. It was the thing to do. My husband and I bought a simple one-room cabin on a tiny lake in the woods where we didn't have to lock our doors at night." I turn my head to the window and look down at the city below. The lump in my throat is the same size as the one I had the day we drove away from the Bronx and I turned around for one last look. What I told J. B. was my standard line whenever someone asked why we left. The real story is much more complicated.

J. B. gives me a curious look.

"Some people were glad to see the back of me when I left," I say.

He shrugs. "Sometimes things aren't always as they seem."

"And sometimes they are." I take a breath and then say, "I tried to make things better, but it was a lost cause. Or I was. I left the Bronx feeling like a failure."

"The world will never be perfect." J. B. says. He gives me that half grin of his that gets the message across without being judgmental. "And yet you keep trying. Like with Markus, you never give up." His smile is filled with respect, or maybe even admiration.

The captain's deep voice comes on the loudspeaker. "Cabin crew, please take your seats."

A girl about two years old hangs over the armrest of a seat in front of us. She opens her mouth and out comes a long wail. I cover my ears. The girl's mother speaks softly to her and hands her a piece of candy. I have no regrets about not having children. I wouldn't have been any good at it. I think Frank could have been a good father. He was good with Mentayer. I hope he found someone with children to marry.

"I never gave up on Mentayer," I muse out loud. "I never expected to fall in love with her. I did what I thought was right for her back then, but I didn't know it would mean losing her." A tear escapes and I wipe it away. Why did I let her go? Why didn't I fight for her? Was it because I was raised to be a good girl, to please people and make them happy? No, that wasn't all of it. I was raised to be responsible, too. The problem is, you can't always please people and be responsible at the same time. That was a painful lesson. If I'd known what the outcome would be, would I have done something different? That, I would never know.

The microphone squeals, cutting through my sadness about Mentayer and my never-ceasing guilt about her brother, Markus.

"Welcome to New York City," the flight attendant announces. "Please remain seated with your seat belts fastened until the aircraft has come to a halt at the gate and the captain has switched off the seat belt signs."

"When Mentayer finds out you're here," J. B. says, "she'll talk to you."

I appreciate his encouragement, but even though he's often right, I'm not at all convinced that he's right this time. "I should have contacted her a long time ago. Maybe then I'd know what happened to Markus."

"I think you already do, or at least you're afraid that you do."

"I hope I'm wrong," I say, "but this teacher, Anthony Frascatore"—goose bumps pop up on my arms at the sound of his name on my lips—"who taught across the hall from me, he abused students. He called it a get-tough approach to discipline. I know firsthand that he assaulted two boys, but no one would listen to me." I look out the window at the planes taxiing to and from the runway. "Frank thought I obsessed about Frascatore," I say, turning back to J. B. "Maybe I did. Maybe I still do, because ever since I read the

New York Times article about the boy's body, I haven't been able to get him out of my mind. Like a bomb in my gut has been lying dormant all these years waiting to explode."

We pick up our luggage, then take a cab from JFK to the boutique hotel in Greenwich Village near Washington Square Park that J. B. booked for us.

"I'm staying in New York until I know," I say. J. B. nods but doesn't say anything, so I ask him what he's thinking.

"I'm thinking that the first thing I want to do tomorrow is talk to Daniel Leacham. That will help me decide what to do next. Maybe go to the CSCH Corporation headquarters."

We slip into silence the rest of the way. Our reasons for coming to New York are not the same, so we might end up going different ways and following different leads. One thing we're both curious about, though, is the site where the body was discovered.

It's almost nine o'clock when the cab drops us off at the hotel. After checking into our rooms and agreeing to meet for breakfast, we say good-night.

My room is small and cramped but impeccable. Its quaint, artsy ambiance suits me. I open my suitcase and take out my toiletries and bring them to the bathroom. I shouldn't call Mentayer this late, but if I wait until morning I'll lie awake all night worrying about it, so I give it a try.

She answers the phone after the first ring. Her voice is pleasant. But when I tell her I'm in New York and would love to see her, she chills. "I'm afraid that won't be possible," she says.

"I'm sorry," I say. I want to break down right then and there but manage to hold myself together. This is my one chance to press her about her brother. "But maybe, I mean, I wonder if it might be possible for me to see Markus, though?"

"I haven't seen my brother since he was eight years old," she says after a silence that lasted an eternity. "I can't tell you where he is. All I can say is that he is fine. And now I must retire. I have a meeting early in the morning. It's a busy time at work. I'm afraid I must say good-night now."

So that's it. My worst fears have been realized. She resents me. She doesn't want to see me. She isn't going to tell me why she hasn't seen her brother all these years, or anything else. I've come all this way for nothing.

I drop my cell phone onto the desk next to a tourist magazine with a cover picture of the new World Trade Center, on which construction is soon to begin. The last time I was in New York, a year after the attack on the twin towers, I stood at ground zero with my hotel's complimentary face mask over my nose and mouth. I didn't cry then, but tears stream down my face now. Not because I missed seeing the twin towers during the ride from the airport, but because I didn't even notice they were gone.

I strip off my clothes, crawl under the covers, and curl into a ball on the double bed. All I want to do right now is go to sleep and never wake up. Is this what depression feels like, I wonder? Is this how Mentayer would feel if she could no longer believe that her brother was fine? Has she, in order to make her way in life, ruled out any other possibility?

It would be cruel of me to suggest to her that the body they found under the school might be Markus. If hope has kept her going all these years, then I have no right to shatter that hope. I won't pursue this with her any further. I can do it for myself, but not for her.

But then I wake up in the morning, and the sun's rays through the tall, narrow window next to my bed warm my face and infuse my mind with more questions. What if the body is identified, and it isn't Markus? Then what would have been the harm in pushing for answers? Mentayer could then still hold on to her hope. The problem, of course, is if the dead body *is* identified as Markus. And then what would happen to Mentayer? I think about the price she must have paid all these years to continue believing her brother was okay, all the expended energy and stifled emotions it must have cost her. Would it destroy her to know that he's dead, if that's what we learn, or would it free her? Would she be able to grieve and then move on? And in the end, would she be grateful for my help, or would she resent me for meddling in her business?

So here I am, at a fork in the road, a not unfamiliar place in which to find myself. The path of least resistance calls to me, tells me that if I don't pursue the truth, there's a chance Mentayer and I could renew our relationship. Then a critical voice comes into my head. It sounds so much like Frank's that it seems as if he's here with me now: *Why do you always have to choose the harder path, Sylvia? Why do you always insist on putting yourself in situations that chew you up and spit you out? Do you think that maybe, this once, you can let it go?*

I'm as irritated with Frank now as I was when we were married. My defiance takes over. It grabs me by the neck and refuses to let me walk away.

It won't let me give up, at least until the body is identified. I throw my legs over the side of the bed and sit up. "I can't help it," I say out loud. "I have to know. I can't stop. It's who I am."

It's a grand declaration, but it doesn't make the way forward any less daunting.

J. B. would tell me to find the first lead and follow it. Each lead will take me to the next one. Find that initial thread and pull on it; the other threads will start unraveling. Bonnie Goldmann comes to mind. Maybe she's that first thread. It's a long shot. I don't even know if she's still alive. But when I taught with her back in the sixties, she knew everyone worth knowing in the city, and I would bet that, if she is still alive, she still does.

A quick Internet search yields a long list of people whose last name is Goldmann, but there's one with an address and phone number that sound familiar. I can't believe my good fortune.

"Who did you say you were?" Bonnie says after I identify myself. She sounds old and confused.

"I'm sorry if I woke you," I say. "This is Sylvia... Sylvia Waters, a voice from the past." I wait a second or two and then add, "We taught together a long time ago, way back in the sixties. Maybe you don't remember me."

"Of course I do," she snaps. "Sylvia! I was surprised for a minute there. After all, you did disappear back in 1969. I never knew what happened to you."

"My husband and I moved back to the Midwest that summer," I say.

"Well," she says with a huff, "mighty nice of you to tell me."

"You and I weren't talking," I say.

"That was a hard time," she laments. "It was unfortunate. So many things to be sorry for... if you're into wallowing."

"I know, Bonnie. Believe me, I know."

"I must say," she says with a chuckle, "you were a gutsy little thing."

I laugh along with her. "I was clueless and too young to know it."

"Not so clueless. You nailed it about Anthony Frascatore."

"What did you say? What do you mean?" My eyes are about to pop out of my head. Could it be?

"I always figured Anthony for a hothead who didn't have a lick of sense, but you know his loyalty to the union went a long way with me. Yes, he was full of himself, even blew his own horn so loud he landed himself a big job at headquarters. But I never expected him to end up in prison. None of us did."

"Bonnie! Are you saying what I think you're saying?" My chest is heavy with anticipation. Was Frascatore convicted of killing Dion Brown after all? Never, in my wildest dreams, did I think that could happen.

"He got what he deserved," she says. "He betrayed us." She sighs, leaving me confused. What did she mean, he betrayed her?

"That was our money, after all, that he stole from the union coffers. Rumor was he needed it to support a drug habit. So, he spent a few years in prison, and it served him right. But I'm sure you knew all about that."

"Are you kidding?" I say, making no attempt to hide my disappointment. "This is the first I've heard of it."

"But here I am," Bonnie says, laughing, "going on and on as usual without even asking about you. Why are you calling me after all this time? I mean, it's good to hear from you and everything, but there must be a reason. I'm sure you aren't calling to make small talk."

"Do you remember Mentayer LeMeur?"

"Of course. Brilliant child. Quite unusual."

"Remember her brother, Markus?"

Bonnie lowers her voice. "Sylvia, when I read about that body they found under the school... well, I have to admit that I thought... Well, I thought about him."

"Me, too. That's why I came to New York," I say. "I have to know. The trouble is, I don't know anyone in the NYPD, and I was hoping maybe you knew someone who could help me."

"Let me see what I can do, Sylvia. Give me your number and I'll call you back." Bonnie pauses, then clears her throat. "You think Anthony killed him, don't you?"

"You know I do."

"Well," she says, "it's obvious I didn't know Anthony like I thought I did. I can't know what he was capable of. But if that body turns out to be Markus and he had anything to do with it, you bet I'd want to see them put him right back in prison, and throw away the key."

I thank her and hang up. Bonnie and I are on the same page about Frascatore at last. I look at my watch. It's time to go.

I meet J. B. in the basement restaurant for the hotel's continental breakfast of bagels and English muffins, a nice assortment of fresh fruit and cheese slices, and as much coffee as you can drink. Two things fascinate me about the restaurant: the walls covered with framed photographs of the famous people who have eaten here, and the view through the basement windows of people's legs and feet as they walk by on the sidewalk outside.

J. B. spoons raspberry jam on the glob of cream cheese already on top of his bagel and takes a bite. "I reached Daniel Leacham this morning," he says, licking his fingers, "and arranged a meeting this afternoon. Will you be seeing Mentayer today?"

I tell him about calling her last night, how she insisted Markus was fine but couldn't tell me where he is, and that she hadn't seen him since he was eight.

"Did she tell you why she hasn't seen him all that time?" J. B. asks.

"I didn't ask." I look away, glance out the window at the feet walking by. "She doesn't want to see me. She didn't even want to talk to me on the phone."

J. B.'s eyes, curious and observing, watch me put a slab of butter on my knife and slather it on my bagel. He picks up his cup and sips his coffee.

"I suppose there's a chance," I say, "that Markus was so scared he ran away and went into hiding. Maybe he's in trouble and she's protecting him."

J. B.'s eyes linger on me as he places his cup down on the table. "Or maybe she's lying," he says.

I bristle. "Well, if she is," I say, "I can't blame her. She doesn't want her brother to be dead."

J. B. takes another bite of his bagel, oblivious to my irritability. I stab at a piece of cantaloupe with my fork. I'm about to lift it to my mouth when my cell phone rings. I brighten as soon as I look at the caller ID. "It's Bonnie Goldmann," I say. "She taught at P.S. 457 with me. She may have a contact in the NYPD that I can call." I raise my free hand, cross my fingers.

"Hi, Bonnie. That was quick."

She starts talking without bothering to say hello. "My daughter works in the New York City medical examiner's office. I didn't want to tell you that until I checked with her. Anyway, she's agreed to see what she can find out about the body. She'll meet with you at one o'clock today." She gives me the address, which I jot down on a napkin. "No need to thank me, Sylvia. I owe you one."

But of course I do thank her, with my typical Midwestern niceness, babbling on about how grateful I am, how glad I am that she doesn't hate me and, of course, she owes me nothing. I hear Bonnie laugh in my ear, see J. B.'s grin across the table.

"Talk about contacts," I say after I put the phone away. "Bonnie's daughter works in the medical examiner's office." I look down at what I wrote on the napkin. "Dr. Jacqueline Goldmann. Today. One o'clock. It looks like it's not too far from here. Can you believe this? Bonnie's been living in the same apartment all these years. With rent control, she must be paying thirty dollars a month or some crazy cheap rent like that." I stop to take a breath, notice that J. B. is looking at his smartphone instead of me.

"Dr. Jacqueline Goldmann," he reads. "Supervisor in the Office of Chief Medical Examiner. Licensed to practice medicine. Certified forensic pathologist with twenty years of experience. Anatomical pathology. Neuropathology. Pediatric pathology. Looks like you hit the jackpot."

"If the body isn't identified as Markus," I say, "that boy was still someone else's brother, some mother's son, a member of someone else's family who never knew what happened to him, never even knew if he was dead or alive. And whoever the dead boy was, he could have been murdered, and if no one cares enough to investigate, the killer will get away with it. That's wrong. Just plain wrong."

"Are you trying to convince me that you're doing the right thing, or is it Sylvia who needs convincing?"

"It's a matter of fairness," I say. "Of justice. That's what it comes down to. That's what it always comes down to." I squirm. My passion reeks of self-justification. I'm uncomfortable about proceeding without telling Mentayer. What if I find out the body was Markus? What will I tell her then?

We sit for a while in silence. "Whatever happened wasn't your fault," J. B. says at last, with a sigh.

I say nothing, but reject what he says out of hand. Assigning blame is what I do, and whatever happened to Markus has to be someone's fault.

"I don't know the story or what you did or think you did or didn't do," J. B. says, "but I do know that you did your best."

"How do you know that?"

"Because it's true for all of us. If people could do better, they would. It's that simple."

I don't agree but remain silent. J. B. is often very wise, but I know that when Markus went missing, I didn't do my best. I started drinking instead. If I hadn't, it wouldn't have taken me thirty-eight years to find out what happened to him.

No, J. B. was wrong this time. I could have done better, and I didn't.

"I'm going to see if there's an Alcoholics Anonymous meeting somewhere near here," I say. "Are you willing to go to the medical examiner's office with me afterward?"

"I didn't know I wasn't invited," he says with a laugh.

We agree to meet for lunch, and I go off to a meeting near New York University where twenty-some alcoholics sit in a circle in a church basement and talk about acceptance. The past stares me in the face as I listen to people talk about accepting the things they cannot change. What about changing the things you cannot accept? Like not letting Markus's fate remain unknown. Like not letting his murderer get away with it. If he was murdered. I cross my arms over my chest and dig my heels into the coffee-stained carpet.

"I'm having one helluva time trying to discern what I can change and what I can't change," a twenty-something brown-skinned woman says.

Hallelujah, I say to myself. *At least she's trying, which is more than I can say for me.* A gray-haired white man speaks next. He starts by saying he's been in recovery for thirty years.

"I'm not the brightest light on the porch," he says. "I'm not wise enough to always know what I can or cannot change. So I guess that's what I need to accept. That I don't know."

That's it. That's what I should do.

When I leave the meeting, I'm still intense and anxious about what is to come, but something has shifted inside me. I make my way through the buzz of humanity in Washington Square Park knowing that I must do whatever is in front of me to be done, but that I'm not in charge of the outcome. However it turns out, it turns out.

J. B. meets me under the arch. We grab a quick lunch at a nearby restaurant, and then it takes us ten minutes to walk to the building of the Office of Chief Medical Examiner. Dr. Jacqueline Goldmann greets us wearing a white lab coat, a navy blue skirt, and sensible low-heeled shoes to match. She wears her red hair pulled back in a bun like her mother did at her age. She's so much like Bonnie in physical appearance and pattern of speech that it's like I've traveled back in time.

"Mom calls you a woman of courage," she says.

The warmth of a blush moves up my neck. "I've been called worse," I say, wondering what else Bonnie told her about me.

I introduce J. B. as a friend. As the two of them exchange a few pleasantries, I look around her office. It's bright and sunny, a striking contrast to the atrocities she must encounter every day when examining the corpses of people who died from criminal violence or other suspicious causes. One wall is a full bank of windows, the others a reserved azure blue color that conveys a sense of order and reliability. Framed diplomas from Princeton and Cornell, certificates and licenses from the state of New York, the American Board of Pathology, and an impressive number of awards and honors speak of ambition and accomplishment, many reasons for Bonnie to be proud of her daughter.

"Please, shall we." Dr. Goldmann picks up a manila folder from her desk and then points to a round table, in the middle of which sits a basswood plank carved with the words Science Serving Justice.

Dr. Goldmann rests her open palm on top of the folder. "Mom tells me you think you may know the identity of the boy whose body was found under that school in the Bronx. Is that right?"

"I have my suspicions," I say. "But I hope I'm wrong."

I stare at the folder, wishing her to open it and tell us. Dr. Goldmann raises one eyebrow, then opens the folder. She pulls out the top sheet of paper, a form of some kind. She scans the page and reads parts out loud by way of summary. "January 14, 2006... skeletal remains in the rubble of P.S. 457... initial examination indicated likely to be male, negroid—likely African American, that is, if the boy was from the Bronx—somewhere between seven and nine years of age. Based on the state of decomposition, estimated death was thirty to forty years ago. Back of the skull indicates a blow to the head or maybe a fall. Broken index finger on the left hand. Could be a defensive wound." Dr. Goldmann closes the folder, leans back in her chair. "That's it. Not much to go on, I'm afraid." She pauses, an expectant look on her face. "Maybe you know something that will help us?"

I lean toward her, open my hands on top of the table in a pleading gesture. "I was hoping... it's possible, though, isn't it?"

"If you're asking if it's possible to make an identification based on remains that are so old, the answer is yes, it is possible. We do have the capacity now to do high-sensitivity DNA testing of trace amounts of evidence."

J. B. sits back and crosses one leg over the other so his left ankle is resting on his right knee. "I understand from the *New York Times*," he says, his tone neutral, relaxed, "that the NYPD Forensic Investigations Division is conducting an investigation."

"In cases like this," Dr. Goldmann says, "the evidence is first turned over to us here in the Office of Chief Medical Examiner to identify the remains and determine possible cause of death. If we suspect foul play, then we turn the case over to the NYPD Division of Criminal Justice Services and, of course, continue to work with them during their investigation. In this case, neither the boy's identity nor the cause of death has been determined as yet. Any information you can provide would be much appreciated."

"What about the blow to the head?"

"Indeed. That raises some suspicions. An injury to the back of the skull can be caused by a purposeful blow but also by an accidental fall, or any other number of things that can't be ruled out."

I felt my back tense up. "You can rule out accidental death," I say.

Dr. Goldmann raises both eyebrows. I take it as encouragement and go on to explain.

"Another boy at that school died in 1968 from an injury to the back of his head. A teacher slammed him up against the wall. The boy's name was Dion Brown. The teacher's name was Frascatore. Anthony Frascatore." I hear the edginess creeping into my voice but I don't try to tone it down.

A look of concern comes over Dr. Goldmann's face. There's an uncomfortable pause. "I think we're getting ahead of ourselves here."

J. B. leans forward, his eyes drilling into her. I recognize the look. He's about to strike. "Think about where the body was found," he says. "In the school basement, no less. How does that happen? Seems like enough of a reason to investigate cause of death."

Dr. Goldmann nods, but in a cautious way. "Maybe. But it's impossible at this stage to determine whether the boy died at the scene or somewhere else." I can tell she's making sure her facial expression remains neutral. I wonder if she's trying to determine the best way to say something.

"I want to be clear," she says at last, "so as not to mislead you here. Even if, for whatever the reason, the case is turned over to the NYPD, chances are good it will be classified as a cold case after all this time."

"In other words," I say, "not a priority."

"I'm afraid that's right."

"Well, it *is* a priority for me. I have to know if that body is Markus LeMeur or not."

Dr. Goldmann flinches, then smiles, her eyes filled with sympathy. "Identification of the body has to be the first step, and I need your help with that. If you can get me Markus's dental records and some DNA samples from members of his family, I'll run the tests myself."

My shoulders droop. "Is there any other way?"

"Not really," she says with a shake of her head. "Although... the report did say that some of the boy's clothing was recovered. A pair of jeans and a T-shirt, one sneaker. I suppose if someone could describe what Markus was wearing the day he died, that could tell us something. But, of course, not with anywhere close to the same certainty as DNA testing."

I rack my brain, but for the life of me can't recall what Markus was wearing the last time I saw him. It's no use. I hold my head in my hands.

"Do you know anyone related to Markus?" Dr. Goldmann leans forward, concern on her face.

"His sister," I say with a frown. I rub my hands together. "But she, well, I don't think that would work." Not wanting to be disloyal to Mentayer, I don't mention that she insisted in our phone conversation that Markus was alive, even though she hasn't seen him since he was eight years old.

"Could she be ordered to submit a DNA sample?" J. B. asks.

I turn and glare at him. I can't believe he'd even suggest such a thing. There's no way I would ever allow anyone to force Mentayer to do anything, much less provide a DNA sample.

"Yes, if it was deemed essential for a murder investigation," Dr. Goldmann says. "But not without a court order. Are there other family members who might be willing to provide DNA samples?"

"There was an uncle and several cousins," I say, but I don't know how I could ask Markus's uncle or cousins to help without Mentayer finding out.

"If you bring me something to work with, I can help. I promised my mother, after all," she says with a wink.

"I'm not sure we can find them," I say with a shake of my head. "There has to be another way. When Markus disappeared in 1968, we filed several missing person reports with the police. Do you think the police keep reports like that? I mean, do you think they might have a list of any other boys who went missing during that time?" I wonder if she thinks I don't know what I'm talking about, and then barrel on through. "If they do have a list, maybe we could contact those missing boys' families and ask them to submit DNA samples. That way Mentayer and other family members would be asked along with all the others. Even if they refused, the results might confirm that the dead boy was one of the other boys and not Markus."

"Too labor intensive, I'm afraid," Dr. Goldmann says. "It would be unrealistic to think we could get the police to do something like that without a compelling reason. I'm sorry, Sylvia, but this is as cold a case as you can get. And without the family pushing for answers, well... "

I open my mouth, ready to argue. Maybe I can make a case for how important this is. But J. B. beats me to it.

"As a journalist," he says, "I'm curious about something. Why weren't all the details about the condition of the body that you shared with us made public? If they were, it seems to me someone might come forward with information that could help you make an identification. Maybe even help determine the cause of death."

Dr. Goldmann frowns. She pushes her chair back and abruptly stands up. "I didn't realize you were a reporter," she says. She glances at me like she's disappointed. I jump in to say I'm sorry and to explain but J. B. cuts me off.

"I'm not here as a reporter, Dr. Goldmann. I'm here as Sylvia's friend. But I still think like a journalist, I'm afraid, and the journalist in me wonders why a month went by after the body was discovered before there was anything in the newspaper about it at all."

Dr. Goldmann sits back down. She starts to speak and then hesitates, looks from J. B. to me. "Off the record?"

"Understood," J. B. says with a sharp nod.

"Nothing I've told you today or am about to tell you goes any further than this room." Dr. Goldmann pauses, looks at me, and adds, "Not even to my mother."

I nod, then nod again to reassure her. My foot starts tapping, my anticipation needing an outlet. A surge of hope runs through me. What does she know that she hasn't already told us? For a split second I wonder if she already knows the identity of the body. But, no—if it were Markus, she would have told me.

"We will both treat this entire conversation with the utmost confidence," J. B. says. He sits down.

Dr. Goldmann pulls a piece of paper from the folder. Her eyes are on me, seeking reassurance perhaps. I nod, and she turns her gaze to J. B.

"You have my word," he says.

"I want the body to be identified as much as you do," she says, "believe me. I want to help. That's why I told you everything I know." She looks down at the paper, and after a long, drawn-out silence, she says, "Except this memo." She reads it out loud: "'On orders of the police commissioner, no information about this case is to be released to the press without his written agreement.'"

She slips the paper back into the folder and rests her elbows on top of it. "I shared information with you in good faith. I did not know that you were the press, Mr. Harrell. I need your word that you will not treat any of what's been said today in any professional capacity whatsoever."

"You can trust me, doctor." J. B. stands up, reaches down to shake her hand.

"I do want to get to the bottom of this," she says. "I hope we can."

"I didn't mean to mislead you," I say when we're all standing and ready to say good-bye. Dr. Goldmann reaches out and pulls me into an embrace that feels warm and forgiving.

"Call if you have any questions," she says as we walk out of her office.

We stand on the sidewalk in front of the building for a few minutes to talk about what we've learned. I'm feeling discouraged and pessimistic about whether the body will ever be identified, but J. B.'s eyes radiate a new excitement. "A gag order from the top of the NYPD? This is getting interesting. I wonder what Daniel Leacham will have to say."

SEVEN

Summer 1968

Ten days after Dion Brown died, Anthony Frascatore was suspended pending an investigation. I was confident that he would be charged with murder. At first. But then two months passed with no word. Now it was June, the last day of school, and still no official determination had been made as to the cause of Dion's death. After a tearful good-bye with my students, I stopped to ask the principal to call me during the summer if she heard anything.

Miss Huskings waved me into her office. She sat, as usual, behind her desk like a lump of clay, but her face was different. There were fewer indentations around her mouth and her lips were turned more upward than usual.

"Good timing, Mrs. Waters. This police report was messengered to me this morning."

I stood across from her desk and stared at the official-looking document lying open on her desk. I gripped the back of a chair as a surge of adrenaline shot through my veins. The day was here at last. I was about to hear the words I'd been waiting so long to hear: *Anthony Frascatore has been charged with murder in the death of Dion Brown.*

"Please, Mrs. Waters, sit down." I shook my head no, but she raised her eyebrows and waited until I complied.

"It says here that Dion Brown's death was determined to be the result of a subdural hematoma caused by an injury to his head."

I didn't realize that I'd stopped breathing until my chest started to fill with air again. I blew it out, a long, slow exhale, absorbing the news. This was confirmation. It was official.

"However," Miss Huskings added, "there was no evidence from the autopsy that the injury was inflicted on the day of the boy's death. In fact, the medical examiner determined that his death was caused by"—she looks down and reads from the report—"slowly leaking blood that formed a hematoma that pressed on his brain tissue after he was injured, and that the symptoms had gone undetected for at least several days, maybe weeks."

"Mr. Frascatore must have hurt Dion more than once then," I said.

Miss Huskings let the report drop onto her desk. The impatient move matched her scrunched eyebrows and the irritation in her voice. "I'm afraid, Mrs. Waters, that you have jumped to a conclusion for which there is no evidence."

I scooted to the edge of the chair and thrust out my chin. "Miss Huskings, I saw what Anthony Frascatore did to Dion. I saw him slam another student into the wall the same way. He did it to students all the time. I told them that in my statement."

"I have the transcript of your testimony right here, Mrs. Waters. It concluded that you heard a sound out in the hall and made an *assumption* that it was caused by Anthony slamming Dion's head against the wall. You never saw him do it."

I gripped my knees until my knuckles started turning white. Did this mean the police didn't believe me? They concluded that I didn't see anything? They discounted my testimony?

"I'm going to read this to you." Miss Huskings's eyes rested on me to make sure I was listening. "'No one directly witnessed any physical harm being done to Dion Brown that could have caused a brain injury, nor were any new injuries sustained on the day he died.'" She stopped reading and looked up. "So, you can see, Anthony Frascatore cannot be held responsible for Dion Brown's death."

I heard the click of the principal's cigarette lighter. The sound of her inhaling. The smell of smoke as she blew it out. Snippets of her words receded into the background. There were crashing noises and scattered images in my head. Frascatore's shouts. The thud of Dion's head hitting the wall.

"Anthony has been reinstated, Mrs. Waters."

At the sound of those words, a pain as sharp as the stings from a swarm of yellow jackets shot through me. This wasn't what was supposed to happen. If you did the right thing no matter how difficult, if you spoke up, if you told the truth, justice would prevail. That was how it was supposed to work. That was the natural order of things. But now the ribbon of life had been cut. I was left disconnected. The path forward was unclear. My moral compass was gone.

"Mrs. Waters?" Miss Huskings's voice cut through the humming white noise in my head.

My jaw quivered. "It doesn't matter to you how we treat our students, does it."

"Of course it matters, Mrs. Waters. About that, you and I have always been in complete agreement." Her voice was calm, the voice of someone trying to pacify a child.

"Then why isn't Mr. Frascatore in jail?"

"Believe me," Miss Huskings said with a huff, "I am the first one to hold people accountable if they cross the line."

I slammed my hands on her desk. A holder of pens and pencils flew into the air and crashed onto the floor. "If? *If* people cross the line? If what Mr. Anthony Frascatore did wasn't crossing it, then where is your line?"

"That is where we diverge, Mrs. Waters." She sighed, the long, raspy sigh of someone trying to be patient. "Holding a student in place may be an acceptable means of restraint to some, although it's clear that would be crossing your line. As a matter of fact, such conflicting opinions about discipline are at the core of the escalating tensions dividing the teachers right now."

"I know what I saw." I spat out the words. "And it wasn't about discipline. Dion wasn't even in Mr. Frascatore's class."

Miss Huskings took a puff of her cigarette, blew out the smoke. "Anthony stopped the boy because he was in the hall without a pass. The timing of that interaction with the consequences of an earlier injury was an unfortunate coincidence."

Hadn't anyone considered the possibility that the earlier injury might have been caused by Frascatore? If it hadn't been him, then who had hurt Dion? No, it had to be Frascatore. He'd gotten away with murder. There would be no justice for Dion Brown.

"I know the conclusions aren't what you expected or wanted, Mrs. Waters." A long pause, another puff of her cigarette, another perfect smoke ring. "But sometimes we have to accept the justice we get, not the justice we want."

I stood up and almost knocked the chair over, then turned to leave.

"One more thing, Mrs. Waters."

I wiped the moisture from my brow and looked back at her over my shoulder.

"If you happen to talk to Anthony, I hope you will try to be nice? I know this has been a difficult time for you, but it has been an even more difficult time for him."

I stared at her, my mouth hanging open. Be nice? How dare she ask that of me? I stomped out the door, out the main office, down the stairs. A cluster of teachers had gathered at the main entrance, heads huddled in a circle, their voices animated, looks of relief on their faces. I spotted Bonnie right in the middle. They saw me and a hush came over them. I stopped, in a daze and out of breath.

"We were talking about Anthony," Bonnie said.

"Bad news travels fast," I mumbled. Then I started walking away.

"It was a fair process," I heard one of the teachers say.

I turned to face them, my hands clenched into fists. "Anthony Frascatore is guilty as hell."

"Come on, it was a thorough investigation," another teacher said. I knew her name but for the life of me couldn't, at that moment, remember who she was, even what grade she taught. There was no room in my head for anything but Dion Brown's fear-filled eyes, my students' faces when I told them he was dead, the sound of Mentayer saying, "It's okay, Ms. Sylvia, we know you tried."

I walked away, my legs and feet as heavy as if I were dragging them through thick mud. Angry voices, a few snorts, followed me.

"It was a false accusation."

"So what else is new already?"

"Yeah, we get blamed for everything."

I swiveled around, hands on my hips, and screamed, "A boy is dead!"

They fell mute and stared at me. They thought I was crazy.

I lowered my voice. "A. Child. Died." It was a choke, a sob, a knife cutting into their silence. I turned around and resumed walking.

"Kids die around here all the time," someone said to my back.

"That's harsh," came Bonnie's gentle rebuke.

"It's reality." Those were the last words I heard.

I didn't know how I managed to get home. I ran. I stumbled and almost fell several times. Frank was out of town at a seminary retreat, so once I was home there was no one to bear witness to my deterioration. Over the next several days, no one saw me lying in bed except when I had to eat or go to the bathroom. No one saw me choking on glasses of horrible-tasting bourbon in order to sleep. No one saw me staring up at the ceiling in between bouts of sleeping the sleep of the dead.

Day and night merged. I lost all track of time. I burst into tears whenever I thought about the day I'd told my students Dion Brown was dead. My students, who had already experienced more of the cruelties of life at their young ages than I ever would. Never before had I been filled with such despair and rage. No matter what I'd done to get justice for Dion, nothing had worked. Nothing had changed. Dion was still dead, and Frascatore would still be teaching in the fall. Some of my students might even end up in his class. Never before had I felt so angry and yet so small and insignificant, so powerless.

The outside world ceased to exist for me until one day, when I was in the kitchen, scooping the last bit of peanut butter and jelly from the commodity food cans our neighbor had shared with Frank and me, the phone rang. It was Mentayer. In a miraculous, almost instantaneous way, the sound of her voice brought me back to life, sent the blood of hope rushing through my veins again.

"Grandma's sick, Ms. Sylvia. They took her to the hospital in an ambulance. She told me to call you if anything happened to her."

"What happened?" I asked. "Did she have a heart attack? Mentayer? Are you still there?"

"Hello, Mrs. Waters." A woman whose voice I didn't recognize came on the line, maybe a nurse, maybe someone else from the hospital. "My name is Janet Keens," she said. "I live across the hall from the LeMeurs. Grandma had a stroke last night. I called the hospital and they say it's not looking good. She can't move. Can't even talk."

I dropped down onto a chair, the news jolting me back to reality. It was summer. School was out. Mentayer was no longer in my class, yet here she was, calling me to tell me about her grandmother.

"Mentayer and Markus are with me," I heard the woman saying, "but I'm leaving tomorrow to go to live with my daughter in Chicago. There's an uncle who lives not too far from here with his wife and four sons. They're all squeezed in a one-bedroom apartment, but he says Markus can sleep on the floor. It's not the place for a girl."

"Mentayer can stay with us," I said without even thinking twice about it.

"Hold on," the neighbor said. There were muffled voices in the background, then a shriek and Mentayer's excited voice, loud and clear. "Can I go there now? Ask her if she's coming to get me. Ask her what I should bring."

After that, everything changed. Mentayer's presence yanked the anger from my wound and replaced my despair with a healing balm of hope. The girl's energy—headstrong, impatient, and curious—was contagious. Her goofy smile and disarming fondness for the world was downright staggering. When Frank came home from his retreat and found her staying with us, he wasn't thrilled at first. But it wasn't long before she endeared herself to him. She even managed to turn him soft, something I'd never been able to do—not that I'd tried. She became the child we could never have.

Mentayer worried a lot about her grandmother. And she worried almost as much about Markus. She called him every day, sometimes twice a day. She was as jittery after talking to him as she was when she came back from visiting her grandmother in the hospital. I asked her what was wrong.

"My brother's being weird," she said.

"He may be worried about Grandma," I said.

"It's not that," she said. "He was being weird even before Grandma stroked. It's worse now is all. He got quiet. And you know, Ms. Sylvia, being quiet is not normal for him. He doesn't want to go out to play. He doesn't do anything."

Markus was an innocent boy, the sweet-looking kind that was vulnerable to being picked on. "Did he ever come home hurt," I asked.

"He broke his finger once," Mentayer said, "from playing baseball."

"Have you asked him if anything's wrong?"

"I ask him all the time. So did Grandma, when she could still talk. Every time he says the same thing, that nothing's wrong. He's being a brat."

I didn't like the idea of Markus staying indoors in his uncle's crowded apartment all the time with a bunch of little kids and with little, if any, adult supervision. So I suggested to Mentayer that we include her brother in our daily field trips. She jumped at the idea, and so did he. And so, after that, we picked up Markus every morning at his uncle's, and then the three of us set out to explore the city. We took the bus to the Cloisters, rode the Staten Island Ferry, listened to the musicians in Washington Square Park, took books out of the main branch library in the grand Beaux-Arts building in Manhattan, went to art museums, stared at the tourists in Times Square and the animals in the Bronx zoo, took a boat cruise around Manhattan, and saw the United Nations Headquarters and Johnny Carson's apartment high atop United Nations Plaza.

Everything seemed to be fine until one day, when summer was almost over and fall loomed, Markus grabbed my hand and looked up at me with eyes so filled with anxiety it alarmed me. "I get to be in your third-grade class, don't I?"

"Indeed you do," I said, giving him a hug. "Indeed you do."

"Okay," he said, with a look of such relief it gave me pause.

"Is everything all right, Markus?"

"Yes," he said with a smile. "I'm fine."

But the pleading I'd heard in his voice continued to haunt me. I couldn't shake the idea that something wasn't right, that there must be a reason Mentayer had been so worried about him. Every day we were together, I studied him, asked him if he was okay. And every day he said he was fine. But I couldn't shake the feeling. Something was wrong.

EIGHT

April 2006

J. B. and I stop for coffee at a small place a few doors down from the medical examiner's office. After Dr. Goldmann's revelation about the police commissioner's gag order, I don't want to wait to hear what J. B.'s reporter friend has to say about it before putting pressure on the police to do something. "Time to take action," I say as I yank out my cell phone and call 911.

J. B. shakes his head, a look of skepticism on his face. I don't care if he thinks it's futile. Something's fishy, and I aim to find out what it is.

"No, this is not an emergency," I say when someone answers, "but I need to speak to a detective about a murder in the Bronx. I have a lead. Yes, I'll wait." I turn on the speakerphone and lay my cell on the table. I've already finished eating my croissant and am on my second cup of coffee by the time someone comes back on the line.

"Detective Gretchen Crannower speaking."

Her voice is clipped and precise. I talk fast, explain who I am, that I've come to New York to find out about the body that was found a few months ago under the school where I used to teach, that if the boy is who I think he is, then I know who killed him. I end by saying I've received some information from a reliable source (I don't mention the medical examiner's office) about the boy's death that is important to solving the case. I end by asking when the body will be identified.

"This boy," Detective Crannower says, her voice going up in a question, "when did you say he died?"

"Nineteen sixty-eight. In the fall."

Several seconds of silence follow. "Could you be more specific," she says at last. I hear the sound of rustling papers in the background. "It was a long time ago. I don't—"

"I have a lead," I interrupt. "A boy who was a student at that school went missing back then. I think it might be him."

"I understand why you might make an assumption like that, ma'am, but, with all due respect, that's pretty skimpy evidence and—"

"And, yes, I know, it was a long time ago," I interject, "but could you let me know what's being done to identify the body? If it turns out to be him, then my evidence would help your investigation."

The detective emits into the phone what sounds to me like a groan. "I hate to disappoint you, ma'am, but I have to be honest. There aren't enough of us detectives here in the Bronx to keep up with current crimes, much less something that happened decades ago that could have been an accident as easily as a crime. Our resources are already squeezed to the max. My caseload is twice the size it should be."

"So you're saying you won't do anything?" I lean closer to the phone in the middle of the table and raise my voice. "A boy is dead and so what? Is that it?"

Detective Crannower sighs and tells me to give her my name and phone number and she'll let me know if there's any news. Before saying good-bye, I tell her that I will be calling her again with any news I might have, too.

"Don't knock me for trying," I say to J. B. as I open my purse and drop the phone back into it.

He leans back in his chair, smiling. "Never. In fact, I did something futile myself. I made a cold call to CSCH earlier. I talked to this woman who said she was on the corporate board. She was adamant that no child should be forced to go to what she called government schools and that everyone should be given vouchers so they'd have a choice. Then she went on and on about how schools are God's kingdom on earth and how she wants to make all our public schools into for-profit, religious charter schools."

My hand flies up to my mouth. "What? That's a violation of the separation of church and state. Is CSCH using public funds to teach religion?"

"She was too smart to say that if they are."

I cringe. Talk about vouchers and school choice always makes me squirm. It reminds me that I once thought it might be a good idea. J. B. notices my discomfort and asks me if something is wrong.

"When I was in the Bronx," I say, "I thought that if parents could enroll their children in the public school of their choice with a voucher, then schools would have to compete for students, and that would force them to either improve or close. How naive was that?"

"Cut yourself a break, Sylvia. Wasn't it Albert Shanker, the head of the UFT, who introduced the idea of charter schools in the first place?"

"It was, actually. He believed it was the children whose parents could least afford high-quality education that would benefit most from charter schools. Affluent children would continue to have their private schools. I shared his vision of schools with unionized teachers. I thought if they were empowered by more creative freedom and student bodies that were diverse, the schools would improve." I let out a groan. "But then someone came up with the brilliant idea of funding charter schools with public money and making a profit off them. That changed everything. And now, to put religion into the mix, well, it's all too much."

J. B. glances at his watch. "Time to meet with Daniel Leacham," he says.

"So, did you ask that CSCH board member about the dead body at CSCH's construction site?" I ask as we stand up to leave.

He shakes his head. "No point in asking a question if all you're going to get is more spin." He drops a couple of dollars on the table. "I think Leacham will prove to be a much more reliable source of information about that."

When we first walk into the basement dive bar, not far from our hotel in Greenwich Village, it takes a few minutes for my eyes to adjust to the darkness inside, and even longer to acclimate to the unpleasant musty smell. Memories of my drinking days flood through me. The smell of stale beer both repels and intrigues me. People come in and go out of the dark bar, walk back and forth; some stagger, already forgetting their work day; some nurse cocktails as if they're in a fancy hotel lounge instead of a bleak, cave-like room. Toward the end of my drinking days, there were many nights when I didn't know how I got home. I'm not that person anymore, but I must never forget that I could be that person again.

J. B. spots a man in a booth toward the front of the long, narrow room and heads toward him at much too fast a clip for me. I stumble along behind, stub my toe on the leg of a chair. A man reaches out to steady me. He gives me an indulgent smile. I'm sure he thinks I'm drunk. I smile and thank him.

J. B. and Daniel Leacham are exchanging pleasantries when I reach the booth. Leacham sees me and tips his beer bottle in greeting.

I'm spellbound. His presence is, to me, as imposing as that of an African king. His mature yet wrinkle-free brown face suggests a man in his forties, the wire-rimmed glasses resting on his chiseled nose the trademark of an intellectual, and the casual tip of his head and brief but bright flash of a smile, confidence. His casual blue suit fits as if he'd been born wearing it, a striped shirt open at the neck the indication of a man comfortable with himself.

"I've always admired your work," J. B. says.

A shrug, a flash of boredom. A sign of arrogance? Could it be that this otherwise perfect-appearing man, this prizewinning journalist, is full of himself? I'm unsettled by the thought and find myself blurting out one question after another without a breath in between. I can't seem to help myself.

"Will you be doing a follow-up story to the first one you wrote? Why hasn't the body been identified yet? Or has it? Have you talked to the police? Did you contact anyone in the medical examiner's office? Why hasn't there been any other information in the paper?"

Daniel Leacham gulps down the rest of his beer. He holds the empty bottle up and signals for another one. "The police are never forthcoming," he says in an offhanded way that suggests he thinks I should already know that. "They have their own secrets," he then adds. "Their own sordid history of police brutality back then."

"Are you suggesting the police might have been involved? Is there something you know?"

He shrugs me off. "I'm busy working on something else right now."

J. B. leans forward with his hands resting on the table, the man-on-hunt gleam in his eyes. "More stories about CSCH, by any chance?"

Leacham stares off into space as if trying to decide what to say. The waitress sets another beer in front of him. Her familiar smile suggests that he's one of her regulars. Then she asks us if we'd like anything.

I order a Diet Coke. J. B. shakes his head in a distracted way.

"Don't misunderstand," he says as soon as the waitress leaves. "I'm not after any journalistic secrets. I'm interested in CSCH as part of a series I'm working on about charter schools."

"I think I might know the identity of the dead boy whose body was found at CSCH's construction site," I interject.

Leacham raises his left eyebrow and brings the bottle of beer up to his lips. I want to tell him more about Markus, about teaching at P.S. 457, about what I fear might have happened to him. But all of a sudden I'm tongue-tied.

"I would think," J. B. says, plunging into the void, "that news of a dead boy might be seen by CSCH as bad publicity for them." He makes it sound like he's considering the idea for the first time.

Leacham gulps his beer, sets the bottle down with a bang. "I wouldn't know."

"I wonder," J. B. persists, "if that's why there hasn't been any more news coverage about it."

I'm surprised when Leacham twists his lips in a lopsided and bitter way. "I wouldn't put anything past CSCH," he says. "All they care about is getting rich off poor kids. Not a lick of conscience in the mix."

My own anger toward CSCH is stirred up. I'm tempted to spew out all my venom about what the corporation is doing in Monrow City, how they're conning poor people into believing they care about their kids. But I restrain myself. Satisfying as such commiseration might be, I want to focus on the dead body, not on CSCH.

"Markus LeMeur," I say. "That's who I think the dead boy was."

"It's all about money with CSCH," Leacham says, as if he hasn't heard me. "Greedy bastards. They talk a good game about the kids and education, but don't be fooled by that. All they care about is the bottom line." And then he's off and running, with a string of invectives, his speech speeding up and slurring a bit more with each gulp of beer. It reminds me of how I used to go off on tangents when I was drinking, thinking in my drunken stupor that I was a brilliant conversationalist and that everyone was enamored with me.

"Bunch of scoundrels," Leacham says. "Nothing but a bunch of scoundrels."

J. B., who brought his briefcase along for this meeting, reaches into it now and pulls out a pad of legal-sized paper. He slides it across the table. "Any scoundrels in particular? Anyone on this list of CSCH investors?"

Leacham runs his finger down the list. "A Wall Street who's who, isn't it. CEOs of major foundations... hedge fund billionaires... Wall Street bank executives... wealthy real estate developers." He strikes at the names with his forefinger, pausing in between for emphasis. "This guy's an investment company manager, but he used to be a public school teacher and union organizer. Here's one whose company has contracts to manage CSCH's schools. This one's on the advisory board of the CSCH Corporation *and* he's the CEO of a real estate investment firm that contracts with CSCH to manage some of its buildings. Talk about conflict of interest. Did you know that financiers double the returns on their charter school investments within seven years? Then they filter their money through large nonprofit organizations to look legit. Charter schools are the most high-demand and most profitable product in the real estate sector right now. You want to know why? Because they get a huge federal tax credit, that's why."

His words are music to my ears. I find myself humming along with his diatribes, dancing to the sharp movements and wild rhythms of his fury. He's singing my song.

He takes another gulp of beer. "It's all legal, of course," he says in a more subdued voice. "You can't blame them. Who wouldn't jump at the chance to make windfall profits like that? And why not be strategic about where you build your school so you can get an additional federal tax break for financing new construction in an underserved community? Don't think for a minute they're building a school in that section of the Bronx because they care about the kids there. It's all about exploitation of the poor for profit. Nothing but."

"I'd like to interview some of these investors," J. B. says. "Who do you suggest I talk to?"

Leacham pauses, then places his finger on one name on the list in particular. "Clarke Craine," he says. "You might start with him."

J. B. gets on his phone. He turns away from us and covers one ear with his hand to block out the noise.

"Does the name Anthony Frascatore ring a bell for you?" I ask Leacham.

He sucks in his breath. "Yeah, he's a big factor. A big talker. Never know what he might say."

"What do you mean?" I ask. "Have you talked to Frascatore?"

Leacham waves me away and motions to the waitress.

J. B. slips his phone back in his pocket and says we have an appointment to see Clarke Craine first thing in the morning. Then he stands up and says it's time to leave. He leans down and takes my hand, pulls me up from the booth.

"So where are we going?" I ask.

"To the Jefferson Market Library. Craine is doing a book reading there right now. I thought we could check him out."

I press my palms on the table and lean toward Leacham. "Can we talk more later?"

He leans back in the booth and closes his eyes, waves me away. J. B. cups my elbow in his hand and steers me toward the door and out the exit. There's a taxi at the curb.

"Daniel Leacham knows something," I say as the taxi makes its way through heavy traffic. "We have to see him again. I want to find out what he knows about Frascatore."

"And I want to find out why he has such a huge beef against CSCH," J. B. says.

We get out of the taxi in front of the Jefferson Market Library. The early evening sky is a grayish blue with hints of light behind the scattered clouds, the air cool with a pleasant breeze that is a refreshing change from the stuffy, smoke-filled dive bar from which we've come. We hurry up the steps, passing a plaque by the door that says the building is a New York City landmark, erected between 1875 and 1877. It was a courthouse that was later converted into a public library that opened in 1967. The same year Frank and I moved to the Bronx. I wish it had been one of the places I'd thought to explore with Mentayer and Markus the summer we toured the city.

Inside, my breath is taken away by the beauty of the soaring stained glass windows and spiral stairs. I can taste the history of the place, smell the books. There's a poster on an easel by the entrance about Clarke Craine's reading from his book, *Why Good People Make Good Money: Good Works Are Good Business*, at six o'clock. There's a photograph of Craine on the poster, a headshot—his face, smooth and devoid of wrinkles; his teeth, white and straight; his hair, coiffed, not a strand out of place.

"Photoshopped," I whisper to J. B. He smiles.

The reading room is full except for two empty seats in the back. We slip into them unnoticed. Craine stands behind a lectern with a hardcover copy of his book on display in front of him. He's wearing a classic gray herringbone suit tailored to accommodate an age-thickened waist, and a crisp white shirt with a red striped tie. Soon he moves away from the lectern and invites questions from the audience. With his chest pumped up, he anticipates and answers questions before they're even asked. It's obvious that he's a man who likes to hear the sound of his own voice. Self-assured to the point of smugness, in my opinion.

I glean snippets of information about him from the discussion. He spent time in Cambodia and in several African countries working on development projects. He is engaged in efforts to develop low-income communities in the United States. With each experience he recounts, he emphasizes the message of his book: It's good to make money. You can make money by doing the right thing. It's wise to invest in worthy projects that will make you money, a lot of money, while also doing a lot of good.

We leave before the session ends.

"He sure seems full of himself," I say after we exit the library. "But he's done some good things, so maybe he isn't such a bad guy. I'm kind of looking forward to our interview with him."

J. B. rolls his eyes and shrugs.

The next morning we go to Clarke Craine's office on the tenth floor of a building in the financial district. Nothing in his office, no photograph or memento from the projects or countries he talked about last night, reflects the man he'd presented himself as. Now my impression of him, based on the profusion of gold in his office—vases and other art objects, the pen and business card holders on his desk, gold-framed original works of art; even the legs of the coffee table are gold-plated—plus all the business journals and success symbols on display, is that Craine is a man for whom winning and making money are the most important things in life, and maybe the only things that matter.

"Thank you for agreeing to be interviewed on such short notice," J. B. says as the two of them shake hands. "As I mentioned on the phone, my series on charter schools will be published in the *Monrow City Tribune*." He tips his head in my direction. "I brought our photographer along to get a candid shot of you for the story, if you don't mind."

Craine glances at me and blinks. I sit in a chair back by the wall with my cheap camera in my folded arms and try to make myself invisible. Maybe the plan to pass me off as a professional photographer wasn't such a good idea after all.

"Please, do sit down, Mr. Harrell," Craine says, pointing to the leather couch with one hand and picking up his phone with the other. "Give me a minute to give my secretary some instructions for the day."

As I scan the bookshelf next to the couch, an old black-and-white photograph grabs my attention. It's a picture of two young men, maybe in their twenties or early thirties—boys posing as men—standing arm in arm, hanging on to each other, in front of a school.

My stomach does a flip. I strain my eyes to see the shorter, disheveled-looking man. His handlebar mustache is familiar as is the dingy shirt hanging out on one side of his pants. It's Frascatore.

I study the straight white teeth and slick, combed-back hair of the taller man, a younger version of Craine. I reach in my purse for a pen and piece of paper. My handwriting is wobbly, but I manage to write a note to J. B., then step over to the back of the couch and hand it to him. He shows no reaction as he reads it. He slips it into his jacket pocket.

Craine stares at me, his eyes on me even as he puts the phone down and lowers himself into a chair across from J. B. on the couch. I squirm. His grayish-blond hairstyle, a pompous pompadour, may be impressive, but it's playing second fiddle to those piercing green eyes right now.

"Mr. Craine," J. B. says. "I'm interested in your perspective, as a CSCH investor, about the corporation's takeover of the Monrow City public schools."

Craine's eyes leave me and trail back to the couch. "I've read the research, Mr. Harrell, as I'm sure you have as well, and the facts speak for themselves. Your mayor is making a wise decision."

"I understand that you're one of CSCH's biggest stakeholders," J. B. says.

"Charter schools are my proudest investments," he says. "My real estate portfolio is quite diverse—multiplex theaters and retail complexes, worldwide recreational investments, a range of corporate buildings and apartment buildings around the globe. But I won't kid you, Mr. Harrell. Charter school properties are the best investments. No rent price capping and few regulations. They're the best deal going these days, *and* they do the most good."

"So," J. B. says with a broad smile, "charter schools are good business."

"Nothing wrong with that. I'm a businessman, Mr. Harrell. A successful businessman, if I say so myself. And I know a stable, recession-resistant investment when I see one. My job is to make a profit. That's what I do. And I do it well. Better than most, as a matter of fact."

He rests his right foot on his upper left thigh, and the proud gleam in his eye is reflected in the glow of his polished shoe. "Now, I know, Mr. Harrell, that there are critics who claim that profit is the reason investors like me are interested in education. You want to know the first thing I say to those critics? I say, come on. Making money's the American way. It's what makes this country great. But the second thing I say to those critics is that CSCH does more than make money. It does good. It makes disadvantaged children into productive and successful members of society." He pauses, and then with a smile and a wink asks, "Do you have children, Mr. Harrell?"

"No, I don't."

"Well, let me tell you, if you did, they'd be damn lucky to have the chance to go to a CSCH school. Damn lucky. You do know who's going to benefit the most when CSCH takes over those lousy public schools of yours, don't you? American Indian kids, that's who. You of all people understand that. Be sure to put that in your story. Make it personal. People like it when stories are personal."

I roll my eyes. I've seen this happen before. People make stupid comments or ask dumb questions about J. B.'s American Indian identity, and he doesn't even bat an eye. I'm the one who flinches every time.

After a few seconds, J. B. moves his hands up to his neck and straightens his tie. Then he tugs on the collar of his exclusive Armani shirt and pats the lapel of the jacket of his tailored Brooks Brothers suit as if to point out that his is as stylish as Craine's herringbone. Whether this is a conscious or unconscious act, it throws into relief an image of J. B. as someone who doesn't have to grapple with his past or struggle to know who he is.

A few more seconds pass, and then a gleam creeps into J. B.'s eyes. Something is about to happen. "CSCH claims, as you know, Mr. Craine," he says, "that its schools outperform traditional public schools. Tell me, how do they do that? What's the secret?"

"It's quite obvious, is it not, Mr. Harrell?" Craine uncrosses his legs and sits up straight, his arms outstretched. He presses his palms against each other so it looks like he's praying to the pricey antique gold vase in front of him. "It's simple. You apply market principles. You break up the public school monopoly and make education competitive instead. Voila, the quality of the product increases." I place my hand on my forehead, remembering how I once thought that might work, too.

"Charter schools," Craine says, his voice growing in animation, "are both a viable alternative to our failing public school systems and, at the same time, the highest growth sector in the portfolios of investors like me. It's a win-win. Classic! Win-win!" He slaps his knees and laughs, falls back in his chair.

J. B. nods his approval. I wonder if he's forgotten about the photograph. If it had been up to me, as soon as I saw the picture, I would have pounced on it. I would have pontificated about Frascatore, accused Craine of who knows what. In other words, I would have blown it. It's a good thing J. B.'s in charge of this interview and I'm not. He has this uncanny ability to know how and when to confront, when to retreat, when to employ trickery, even when to lie if necessary. Having been trained in social work, a profession that frowns on manipulating people, I often find it disconcerting to witness how well it works for him.

He glances around the office now with slow, casual movements. What is he doing? I focus on the worn leather of my sandals. The dryness in my mouth. A cramp in my foot. At long last, J. B.'s eyes move to his left and settle on the black-and-white photo on the bookshelf. I wait, even though it's killing me. I think about what I've learned from him, that hope resides in the steady progression of one lead after another, his shining light of faith in recognizing and knowing how to follow each lead.

I unclench my fists. J. B.'s on it. He knows what he's doing.

"Were you a teacher, Mr. Craine?" he says. "Isn't that you in that picture? Looks like it was taken in front of a school."

"That's me with my buddy Tony. We grew up together. He taught public school for many years, but I was more interested in the business world, if you know what I mean. Tony was a strong union guy until he saw the light. No one better to ask than him if you want to understand why the union is against charter schools. He'll tell you in a nutshell. Or, I can save you the effort and tell you myself. Unions are about protecting teachers, and charter schools are about protecting children. Tony worked at union headquarters for a while. He told me what his boss, Al Shanker, said, and this is a direct quote, trust me, I did not make this up. He said, 'When schoolchildren start paying union dues, that's when I'll start representing the interests of schoolchildren.' That about sums it up, don't you agree, Mr. Harrell?"

I recoil, push my body back in the chair. It's been proven Shanker never actually said that, but really, what bothers me most about Craine's anti-union stance is it reminds me too much of my own self-righteous criticism of the teachers' union years ago. Sometimes I wonder if my actions contributed to a weakening of teachers' rights and helped bring about the charter school movement, but it's too disturbing a view of myself to dwell on.

"So where's your friend Tony now," J. B. asks.

"He's working for CSCH, thanks to me. He's incorporating his ideas about no excuses discipline into its mission. Zero tolerance is his motto. He's a wonderful asset for CSCH, if I do say so myself. It's good to bring the old guard in. They know what worked and what didn't, so we don't have to repeat the same mistakes."

Listening to him leaves me light-headed. I can't believe Craine, with all his talk about doing good and improving education, would bring in someone like Frascatore. *He* didn't care about his students. He abused them.

Craine glances at me, then sits back and reaches into his shirt pocket. He draws out two small Tootsie Rolls and unwraps them. He pops them into his mouth and starts chewing, smacking his lips like a four-year-old. My mouth tingles with nausea. I look out the big window along one wall and see the windows of other buildings, stacked next to and on top of each other. Each one opens into its own unfolding scenario of secrets, its own dramas, its own discoveries. Like the mystery of Craine and Frascatore in the photograph, still to be unfolded.

"Your involvement with CSCH seems to go beyond investing, Mr. Craine," J. B. says, changing the subject.

Craine looks at him sideways and shrugs. J. B. gives him a half smile and then turns somber. "Too bad, isn't it, about that dead body they found at CSCH's construction site in the Bronx," he says.

"Yes, a terrible thing, Mr. Harrell."

"Does anyone know what happened," J. B. says, "or who the boy was?"

Craine shakes his head, lowers his eyes, stares at the floor.

"I don't suppose finding a dead student where your school is going to be built can be good publicity for the CSCH Corporation."

"No, not good." Craine slaps his palms together. "Not good at all. Terrible, in fact. That's a bad neighborhood, you know, in that part of the Bronx. No revitalization going on there like in other parts of the borough. The community is already demoralized. The last thing those people need is another tragedy, more proof of their failure. No, what they need, Mr. Harrell, is hope. And that's what CSCH offers them. Hope. CSCH wants to present a positive image to the community as a good place for parents to send their kids to school. The worst thing to do is scare them off. We want the new school to be a source of pride, of optimism and hope."

He leans forward, his lips now twisted in a sneer. "And, let's face it, whenever there's any bad publicity, all those crazy activist characters come out of the woodwork. It's another opportunity for them to try to plant doubts about charter schools in people's heads. They swoop in to spew their lies and misinformation. If you ask me, it's the union behind that stuff. Course, you can never prove it."

"Hmm. So maybe... " J. B. pauses. He knits his eyebrows together like he's deep in thought. "I mean, I guess that must be why the police commissioner issued a gag order forbidding the release of any information to the press."

At the faux look of innocence on J. B.'s face, I have to look down and fidget with my camera to stop myself from laughing out loud.

"The commissioner's doing his job," Craine says.

J. B. powers through the defensiveness in Craine's voice. "But it seems to me that if the public were given more information, someone might come forward with evidence that would help to identify the body."

"The commissioner's a reasonable man," Craine says.

"Well, I must say that's encouraging," J. B. says. "I was hoping to convince him to lift the gag order when I meet with him. Maybe, since you know him, you have some advice about how I might approach the subject?"

"Did I say I knew him?" Craine sputters. His face turns pink, then red, bordering on purple. "All I said was he has a reputation for being reasonable."

J. B. raises both hands in surrender and flashes Craine a conciliatory smile. "Sorry, I misunderstood. I guess I'll have to wait and see what he says.

I plan to write an article about it either way." He stands up, reaches out to shake hands. "Thank you for your time, Mr. Craine. It's been enlightening."

J. B. heads for the door and I stagger behind. We get on the elevator and the door closes. I hold up the camera and mumble something about forgetting to take a picture. "No need," J. B. says with a smile. "Mission accomplished."

When we reach the first floor and step out into the lobby, I fall back against the wall. "What are the odds," I say, "that Frascatore and this stranger, this Craine guy, who Leacham suggested you interview out of the blue, grew up together? What are the odds that Frascatore works at CSCH? And that Craine got him the job? What's with all these connections?"

I know what he's going to say and say it along with him.

"There are no coincidences."

"I didn't know you had an appointment with the police commissioner," I say.

He scrunches up his face and grins.

"Well," I say, laughing, "I guess if I believed that, then maybe Craine did, too."

"Let's hope so. But he was a step ahead the whole time. He was playing chess with me."

"So now what?"

"Now we wait. But I have a hunch we won't have to wait long. I'll bet Craine's on the phone with NYPD right now, trying to figure out how to stop me from writing that article."

NINE

Fall 1968

"Good morning, Ms. Sylvia."

My students' greetings were loud and enthusiastic, but none more so than that from Mentayer's brother, Markus. His voice rose above all the rest. I bounced on my feet and smiled at him, a brief recognition of our time together over the summer, but resisted an urge to wink—didn't want to show him any preferential treatment. In my arms I cradled a notebook filled with lesson plans for the year, each month plotted out in meticulous detail. I breathed in the contagious aroma of first-day excitement emanating from the mass of morning-shift students in the gymnasium.

My name was posted on the wall as *Ms. Sylvia, Third Grade, Section 8*. Ms. Sylvia, not Mrs. Waters. Having my name written the way I wanted didn't make me a veteran. It was, after all, only my second year of teaching at P.S. 457. Last year's challenges had shifted my perspective and diminished some of my idealism, but my passion was intact and my commitment stronger than ever.

Bonnie Goldmann, to my left, was in deep conversation with another teacher. The two of them glanced in my direction. A few strands of reddish-blond hair escaped the chignon at the back of Bonnie's head. I wondered if they were talking about me. I hadn't talked to Bonnie since the day Frascatore was absolved of any responsibility for Dion Brown's death and I had insisted he was guilty in front of her friends. When she turned and took a step toward me, I stiffened, braced myself for the worst.

"Welcome back," she said, reaching out to give me a warm hug.

"You too," I said, with a relief so strong it felt physical.

"I thought we were going to do something fun over the summer," she said. "What happened?"

"Mentayer LeMeur's been staying with me and Frank," I said. "Her grandmother had a stroke a few months ago. It's been a delight having her, but it's pretty much consumed me. I swear that child's mind is on the loose all the time. And funny? She even gets Frank going."

"Make you want to have one of your own?" She winked, that conspiratorial gesture often delivered by women whose childbearing years were behind them.

"Are you kidding?" I said. "I wish babies came ready-made like Mentayer, but they don't."

I didn't tell her the truth, that Frank and I weren't able to have children of our own. There was another truth, too, which I never admitted to anyone but myself. I was afraid that if I had children of my own, they would eat me alive. I'd offer myself to them on a plate like I did with my students, and because they were my progeny, they'd feel entitled to demand seconds and even thirds.

"So, you're back, Mrs. Waters."

My skin flinched and I took a step back. *Go ahead and look at me like that,* I said to Frascatore in my head. *I'm going to have to put up with you for another year, too.*

He looked different. His handlebar mustache was gone, revealing an almost nonexistent chin that gave him a turtle-like appearance. He'd put on extra pounds, too. He looked older and he sagged, but he didn't look defeated. A jagged pain pierced my gut: it was a moral injury I'd suffered, after witnessing him abuse students and failing to stop it. I placed my free hand over my chest, and my notebook slipped from my arms and onto the floor. Frascatore grunted as he bent down and picked it up.

"So you're going to give it another go," he said as he handed it over, like he was gifting me with a grudge.

"Why wouldn't I?"

He shrugged. "One year's usually enough for newbies," he said, dropping his shoulders back down. "Even the old-timers are leaving. It's getting tougher and tougher to teach. The students... " His voice trailed off and his eyes rolled up in his head.

I bit my tongue and sucked in my breath. *You know that I know, don't you? You think you got away with it, but I'm not done with you. Mark my words: you will never lay hands on another child.*

"What do you say, Anthony?" Bonnie's teasing voice, loud enough to be heard over the gymnasium din, sliced into my silent threat. "So we're starting school two days late this year. I guess that's an improvement."

"We still wouldn't be here," he said, "if the Board of Education hadn't got smart and promised to reinstate the teachers that were fired by the community board in Ocean Hill—Brownsville... without due process, as you well know."

The arrogant, knife-edged sarcasm in his voice set my teeth on edge. But unlike last year, now I understood the union's opposition to the community control experiment, and I knew he was lying. "As *you* well know," I said, "those teachers were transferred, not fired. And, as you well know, teachers are transferred in the system all the time."

"That's what you think?" he said with a snort. "You think fifty-eight thousand teachers walked out to protest some normal transfers?"

"Those teachers were undermining the community control experiment."

"As well they should," Frascatore said. "As well we all should."

I felt my cheeks burn red. I clenched my fists and turned toward Frascatore's new batch of fourth-grade students. They were standing at attention in a straight line before him. I studied their anxious faces, and when I found none of my last year's students among them, I relaxed my hands. I made a mental note to thank Miss Huskings for honoring my request.

Bonnie gripped my elbow and pulled me off to the side. "Look, we're here now," she said in a low voice. "No need to stir things up. It's over."

"I can't believe he's still our union rep," I said under my breath.

Bonnie dismissed Frascatore with a wave of her hand and said I should ignore him. Her advice, however, only triggered my anger from the conversation I'd had with Frank that morning.

"He's nothing," he had said as we were getting out of bed.

"Who's nothing?"

"That Frascatore guy."

"If he's nothing, why mention him?"

"What I mean, hon, is now that you're starting a new school year, it might be best if you tried to ignore him."

"Well, Frank, I guess that's your answer to everything."

He turned away with a hurt look on his face. Another sticky layer of residual contempt had been added to our relationship.

"I don't let him get to me," I heard Bonnie say. "You shouldn't either."

I pursed my lips and nodded. I didn't want to alienate the one person in the school I could talk to, the one person who would talk to me.

I had always put myself on the margin like this, the result of growing up sheltered in a small Midwestern town. The first time I felt inadequate was on a high school field trip to the big city. I'd never eaten at a Chinese restaurant before, so when the waitress brought us finger bowls, I asked what the soup was. Everyone laughed at me. No wonder I found it both flattering and baffling that a sophisticated New Yorker like Bonnie, who seemed to be in the center of everything, wanted to be my friend.

"I'm surprised that... "

Bonnie laughed, her signature belly laugh, and I stopped stammering.

"Come on, Sylvia, being surprised by Anthony's stubbornness is like landing in a monastery and then being surprised that it's quiet."

I jerked my head in Frascatore's direction. "What I'm surprised about," I said in a lowered voice, "is that he wasn't transferred to another school."

The seven o'clock bell rang with an ear-splitting clang. Then the gymnasium fell silent and Bonnie rushed off with a wave. I turned my attention to my new students. Their eager smiles and bright eyes poured over me like a wave of hope. I made a silent pledge to them. *I promise to say yes to every effort to affirm your potential and to say no to any effort, whatever the source, to squelch it.*

The new school year seemed to be off to a good start. Until two days later. I was in the bedroom getting dressed when the news was confirmed on the radio.

"For the second time this year, New York City's public school teachers are walking out as the battle over community control of schools escalates to another level," the newscaster said. "The dispute goes back to last spring, when several teachers were transferred out of the Ocean Hill—Brownsville district schools by the experimental community school board there. The teachers' union claims that the teachers were fired, not transferred, and without cause and has insisted they be reinstated. The New York City Board of Education promised to overrule the community board and reinstate the teachers. But today, UFT president Albert Shanker said that because the Board of Education failed to keep its promise, the teachers had no choice but to go out on strike again. Schools will be closed until further notice. Parents should stay tuned to this station for daily information."

I plopped down on the edge of the bed with my head in my hands. "Here we go again," I moaned. "So much for hoping everything could be settled."

Frank sat next to me, our shoulders touching. "So, what are the teachers at school saying?"

"Nothing. I mean, how would I know? I've been busy. Teaching." I bit my tongue. *What is it with me,* I asked myself, *always assuming his questions are disguised criticisms?*

Maybe because they are, I answered myself.

"Didn't you vote on it or anything?"

"I don't know, Frank. I'd hoped it could be settled. That's all I know." I stood up. "I better go tell Mentayer."

The sheets and blankets were in a neatly folded pile on the living room couch. Mentayer, already dressed, was sitting at the kitchen table eating a bowl of Cheerios with slices of banana on top.

"I'm all ready, Ms. Sylvia," she said with her mouth full.

Warmth radiated through my chest as I leaned down and kissed her forehead. "The teachers are striking again," I said. "It was on the radio."

"Why?"

"God only knows."

"So are we going to school?"

"I don't know."

Frank stood in the doorway, watching. Mentayer looked up at him with questioning eyes. He shrugged his shoulders. The two of them watched, their eyebrows raised, as I dialed the phone with jolting tugs of my index finger.

"Bonnie," I said. "What's going on? What do you know?"

"What do I know? I know Shanker's an idiot." Bonnie's voice on the other end of the line was loud enough to be heard across the room. "What he thinks this is going to accomplish is beyond me. He's obsessed about anything to do with the community control experiment. He's determined to stop it. He doesn't want it to catch on and spread to other communities across the city. The fool doesn't realize what a big mistake it is to pit us teachers against the parents."

"Well, today's Friday," I said, "so they have the weekend to work things out."

"No one thinks that's going to happen. Shanker's prepared to hold out for as long as it takes."

"As long as it takes to do what?" I said.

"I wish I knew, Sylvia. Maybe until the Board of Education keeps its promise and reinstates those teachers. Maybe not until the community control experiment is ended. I hope it doesn't come to that, but I wouldn't put it past Shanker."

"My students can't read," I said. "They're in third grade and they can't read. They can't afford to miss school."

"Neither can mine, Sylvia."

I dropped onto a chair across from Mentayer at the kitchen table. "What can we do?"

"Nothing to do but wait," Bonnie said.

I stared out the window. Then it came to me. I straightened my back and shot up from the chair. "What if we could find a way for our students to be in school and for us to teach without violating the strike? Would you do it?"

"Scabbing without scabbing?" Bonnie said. "There's no way to do that."

"Maybe there is. I'll call you later." I hung up the phone and pushed my chair back with such force that it almost tipped over. "Let's go," I said, heading for the door.

"Where?" Frank asked.

"What about our stuff?" Mentayer asked.

"We're only going across the street," I said, with a glance at the bag of books and papers on the table.

I grabbed Mentayer's hand and pulled her out the door. I raced down the steps so fast the poor child had to struggle to keep up. Frank locked up the apartment, then followed behind. Pastor Paul, an early riser, was already in his office. His face lit up when he saw the three of us standing in the doorway.

"Hur står det till?" he said. "And to what do I owe this pleasure?" He gathered up the mess of books and papers that were scattered on his couch, glanced around the room, searching for an open space on which to deposit them, then gave up and plopped them down on the floor next to his desk.

The three of us sank into the springs of his threadbare couch, shoulders pressed against shoulders.

"It's about the teachers' strike," I said.

"I heard." Pastor Paul sat down behind his desk with a shake of his head.

"The students can't afford to miss any more school," I said. "They were kept out for two weeks last year, and we're already late getting started this year. And what about their parents? What are they supposed to do with their kids? They have to go to work." I paused, let my words sink in. The fabric of the lives of my students' families was already worn thin; another strike could tear it apart. I pressed my palms into my upper thighs. "I stayed out last year, but I won't abandon my students this time. Not again."

"Yay, we're going to school," Mentayer said, her face brightening.

"Is that what you're thinking?" Frank said with a scowl.

I glared at him. Mentayer's eyes widened. She looked from me to Frank, back to me, then to the minister.

"I'd say Ms. Sylvia is up to something," Pastor Paul said to her with a wink. "What do you think?"

Mentayer nodded, her mouth curled up. She moved to the edge of the couch and twisted her body toward me.

"What would you think," I said to Pastor Paul, "if Bonnie and I taught our classes here in the church? That way our students wouldn't have to miss school, and we wouldn't have to cross the picket line."

He sat back in his chair and patted his stomach like he always did after eating a satisfying meal. "What'd I tell you," he said, winking at Mentayer again. Then he paused, turned serious. "Well, let's see. We use the two meeting rooms in the basement for Sunday school, but they sit empty the rest of the week."

"We shouldn't need them for more than a week or two," I said.

"Consider them yours for the duration of the strike," he said. "It'll take some work to get them ready. I'll get my boys to help. It'll keep them busy during the strike."

And so plans were set in motion to convert the two rooms in the church basement into third-grade classrooms. Everyone pitched in. Frank and Mentayer. Jake and Ronnie Winston. Once Bonnie was convinced that teaching in the church wasn't the same as scabbing, she got her husband, Joe, to help, too. Pastor Paul popped in to deliver words of encouragement in between preparing his Sunday sermon and making house calls. His wife, Linnea, made sure we had plenty to eat all weekend. We designed learning spaces with tables from the large common room. Frank and a couple of the church women procured and filled the rooms with books and supplies.

Most of the day Saturday it rained. I was putting the finishing touches on a bulletin board display when Frank walked in with a box of books. His shoelaces were trailing on the floor, his socks soaked, and the bottoms of his jeans muddy. He bent over to put the box on the floor and looked up at me with a grin that felt like a hug. Then Mentayer dropped to the floor and started rummaging through books as if in search of her favorite candy. Frank and I laughed. I couldn't remember a time when we'd shared such a happy moment.

On Sunday, Bonnie and I called the parents and caretakers of our students and visited the apartments of those we couldn't reach by phone. By the end of the day, they all knew that our classes were going to be held at the church during the strike.

On Monday morning, the sky was a clear blue with a warm sun filled with promise. Only a handful of mothers showed up at the church with their children that first day. But soon word got out that there was no need to be skeptical. After a few days, most of our students were coming to school, along with several parents who volunteered to help.

We held class from eight in the morning until four in the afternoon, a full day. I wore jeans to school and sat on the floor with my students. The women of the church fed them orange juice and apple slices, cheese and crackers, peanut butter and jelly sandwiches, and milk. Ronnie Winston played the piano and his brother Jake the guitar, and the students sang and danced to songs that were new to them. The parents showered them with hugs, put Band-Aids on skinned knees, organized games during recess, became their reading buddies, and did whatever else was needed.

It was an environment in which everyone seemed to thrive, Mentayer more than any. After finishing the assignments I prepared for her, she helped the younger students with theirs. She made up corny stories and acted out wacky characters. She bowed, a goofy grin on her face, as the younger kids squealed with delight after each of her deadpan performances. She proved to be a patient tutor, particularly with those for whom English was a second language. But with her brother she was different. She was relentless with him, pushing him to excel like she was Grandma incarnate. And Markus, ever eager to please, proved that his precocious intelligence was every bit a match for his sister's.

The students were learning. So were their parents. Everyone was happy. Except for Bonnie. At the end of one day, she stood in the doorway watching me clean up. The look on her face was dark, downright gloomy.

"You're having a wonderful time, aren't you, Sylvia?"

I stopped what I was doing and looked at her. Her eyes looked so sad I felt self-conscious about how much I'd been enjoying myself.

"Do you ever wonder about the others?" she said.

I frowned, let out a long sigh. I didn't want to think about the children who were not in our classes, the ones left behind to languish without any options. It was too much akin to saving some lives and leaving others to be extinguished.

"It's better to save some than none," I mutter. "Doing this is better than doing nothing."

"The teachers are saying we're undermining the union," she said.

My eyes flashed, my words a swift, knee-jerk reaction. "What about the kids? Isn't the union undermining them?"

"My friends think what I'm doing is disloyal," she said. "I try not to get into it with them."

"It wouldn't do any good anyway," I said.

"Don't, Sylvia."

"Don't what?"

"Don't assume they don't care about the students."

My body tensed. I *was* assuming that.

"They feel stuck," she said. "They're conflicted."

I pursed my lips. "We're caught in the crosshairs, too, you know. We're trying to compromise. We're trying to support the union and our students at the same time. Do they not think that's possible?"

Bonnie shifted her weight from one foot to the other. She placed her hands on her hips, poised for a fight. "Anthony says we're putting the rights of students and their parents *above* the rights of teachers. He says the strike is about the rights of teachers not to be fired without cause. He thinks that by supporting teachers' rights, we're also supporting the students."

A volcano erupted in my stomach. "What? You've been talking to Mr. Frascatore?"

"I don't call him. He calls me. He thinks you're a bad influence on me." She chuckles. "He says you set yourself up as a moral judge. Says you think you're more righteous than anyone else because you're married to a preacher."

I sniffed, flared my nostrils. "Well, you know what? I don't give a rat's ass what that murderer thinks of me."

Agitated lines sprang up on Bonnie's forehead. I got the message. It was okay for me to disagree with Frascatore, to argue and fight with him, to joke about him and even ignore him, but it was *not* okay to call him a murderer.

"I'm sorry, Bonnie. That was out of line."

"I shouldn't have told you what Anthony said."

"Well, you know what? He's right about one thing," I said. "I *do* think that what we're doing is the moral thing to do."

She smiled. I smiled back. "Better be careful," she said with a shake of her head, "or your virtuousness could get you in trouble."

That night I realized how fortuitous her comment had been. Mentayer, Frank, and I were sitting down to eat the rice-and-bean burritos I'd picked up at the bodega around the corner when the phone rang.

"Mrs. Waters?" I didn't recognize the woman's voice.

"Yes?"

"This is Dr. Alexander, your district superintendent. I understand you've been teaching during the strike."

I braced myself. I had never considered the possibility that we might get in trouble for what we were doing. "Is that a problem? I'm not holding my class in the school."

"No, no, no problem at all," Dr. Alexander assured me. "I'm sure you know that most of the principals have now walked out in sympathy with the teachers."

I told her I hadn't heard the news. But why, I wondered, was she calling to tell me that? Why me, of all people, when she'd never even met me? I opened my mouth to ask, but then closed it. Better to give the district superintendent a chance to explain the purpose of her call.

"I think the strike is going to last a long time," Dr. Alexander continued. "I'm worried about our students. They can't afford to miss any more school. That's why I'm calling."

"That's why I'm still teaching," I said.

"Yes," the superintendent said, "and that's why I'm calling you. I'm committed to keeping all the schools in my district open. I want you to be acting principal of P.S. 457. You can start on Monday. I'll send a messenger over right away with the appointment letter."

I mouthed a silent "you've got to be kidding" scream. I fell back in the chair, its hard wood not so much supporting me as keeping me from plummeting to the floor. Mentayer and Frank watched with questioning eyes.

"Mrs. Waters?"

"Yes, I'm still here. Uh, I, uh. I think I need time to think about this, Dr. Alexander."

"Of course. Call me this weekend. Here's my home phone number."

I pointed to a pencil and piece of paper on the counter. Frank picked them up and started to hand them to me. I shook my head and motioned for him to write down the numbers. I repeated them out loud, twice, to make sure I got them right. After hanging up, I sat at the table stunned, the receiver frozen in my hand.

Frank tapped my shoulder. "Sylvia? What was that all about?"

"The district superintendent wants to reopen the school with me as acting principal."

Frank's eyes widened. Our eyes locked. There was a knock on the door, yet he held his gaze. Mentayer ran to see who it was, and when she came back with Teresa Grant, our upstairs neighbor, he still had his eyes on me.

"I told Miss Teresa that you were going to be our principal, Ms. Sylvia." Mentayer's eyes were filled with pride and excitement. "Allie and I get to go to school again starting Monday."

Teresa stood in the doorway with her hands on her hips and her eyebrows raised like flags over brown eyes that showed no surprise at all. Frank, who was still staring at me, didn't notice or admire, as I did, Teresa's red and white striped jumpsuit with its low-cut bodice, spaghetti straps, and wide pant legs—an outfit much too bold for me to consider for myself.

"Why you, Sylvia?" Frank asked. "Why did she have to ask you?"

"She must have heard that I'm teaching during the strike."

"So is Bonnie."

"Bonnie wouldn't do it."

Teresa patted my shoulder. "And she knew you would," she said.

"How could she know that? She doesn't even know me."

Frank scowled. "Sylvia will not cross the picket line. That's why she's teaching her class in the church. So she doesn't have to."

Teresa raised her chin up and looked straight into me. "If you open the school, Sylvia, all the other kids will get to learn, too. Not just yours."

I dropped my face in my hands and groaned. Teresa knew me all too well.

My relationship with her had been slow to develop. We were different in so many ways. She was in her thirties and I was in my early twenties. She was black and I was white. She had a daughter and I was childless. She was happy in her marriage and I wasn't happy in mine. She was a native New Yorker and I was a Midwesterner.

She was an insider and I was an outsider.

Teresa was a revered advocate in the community to whom people flocked for help. She was suspicious about my motivations for coming to the Bronx, pegged me as naive, and didn't expect us to stay long. But when Mentayer moved in over the summer, she and Teresa's daughter Allie hit it off, became the best of friends. One day, when the two of them were drawing pictures at the kitchen table, Allie laid her arm against mine and told me she felt sorry for me because my skin had no color. Teresa claimed that was the day she decided she could be friends with me, when I told her daughter I would give anything to have beautiful brown skin like hers.

"There aren't enough teachers available to cover all the classes," Frank said. He sounded reasonable, but the way he crossed his arms told another story.

"Don't worry, we'll find them," Teresa said. "Plenty of substitute teachers and some regular teachers, too, are against the strike because they support community control. Parents will help, too. It'll give them a chance to get involved in their kids' school. Which *is* the point, isn't it?"

I glanced at Frank. He and I had talked the other day about how wonderful it was that so many parents were helping with the classes at the church. He even referred to it as a small version of community control in action. And here was Teresa envisioning the same thing for P.S. 457 as a whole. Maybe she was right. Maybe it was possible.

"You can only do so much," Frank said, his eyes pleading with me.

I looked down at the table. Maybe it was true that I could only do so much, but wasn't that the case for everyone? But Frank knew my problem was that I never seemed to know what my limits were until I dropped from exhaustion or something else forced me to pull back.

"Don't you think you're doing enough already?" he added.

I shook my head. Of course I didn't think I was doing enough. I never did. So much needed to be done.

I stared out the window at the evidence. The hundreds of holes dotting the church's round stained glass window. The overcrowded apartment buildings, connected by clothes drying on lines stretched between them. The wind-borne debris escaping the garbage cans and making its way down the sidewalk. Maybe I never knew how much was enough because nothing ever was. There was always more that needed to be done.

"She won't be doing it alone," I heard Teresa tell Frank in a scolding voice.

Three sets of eyes behind me were reflected in the kitchen window. Frank's were filled with concern, Teresa's with optimism, Mentayer's with childlike pride. I didn't know what to think, what to do. I did know that not knowing what to do would make me crazy until I made a decision. Indecisiveness had always been a curse to me. With Frank it was the opposite. He preferred to sit in limbo forever without settling on what to do or what to think. His anxiety came from making a decision, mine came from not making one. No wonder we didn't get along.

"There must be a reason she asked me," I said.

"She asked you because it's what you're supposed to do," Teresa said.

"I should call Bonnie," I said. But then I changed my mind. She would never consider crossing the picket line. She was in the inner circle, whose membership was based on tenure, affability, position, and a host of other nebulous, undefined qualifications, one of which, I suspected, was being a native New Yorker. Those in the inner circle had an unspoken alliance against the administration. They shared a common language, and they were granted permission to speak out in a way those outside the circle were not. Bonnie had already risked her membership in the inner circle when she aligned herself with me. If she crossed the picket line, she would be expelled. I, on the other hand, had nothing to lose.

I heard Teresa and Frank arguing in the background. "Not all union members support the strike," Teresa said. "The media's making a big deal about how the black teachers are against the strike and the Jewish teachers support it, but a lot of Jewish teachers oppose it. They have a commitment to teaching black students."

"Well, the NAACP supports the strike," Frank said. "And Bayard Rustin and A. Philip Randolph came out in favor of it."

"And they should be ashamed of themselves."

"They're pro-union."

"The black and Puerto Rican union members who signed a statement saying they support Ocean Hill—Brownsville and oppose the strike are pro-union, too."

Teresa's voice was rising, her impatience showing. "Members of the African-American Teachers Association signed it, and they're all still strong union members. It's beyond me, though, how they can be, after what the union did to them last February." Teresa flicked her chin up for emphasis, indicating that she'd uttered the last definitive word on the subject.

"What did the union do to them?" Frank asked.

Teresa huffed. "I'm not surprised you don't know. Not many white people do. Some ATA members in Ocean Hill—Brownsville helped produce a tribute to Malcolm X, and the union demanded they be disciplined. And they were. Imagine! The union had its own members disciplined. That's how the UFT is undermining the community control experiment."

"But, Teresa, do you think community control is feasible, or is it more of a romantic idea?"

I scowled. Why couldn't Frank come out and give his opinion? Why make it into a question?

"Community control is already a reality, Frank." Teresa sounded as exasperated as I was. "And it's successful, too, I might add."

"What about last spring, when the Ocean Hill—Brownsville community board tried to get more control over personnel, finance, and curriculum? They failed, remember?"

Frank's question was a taunt. Teresa poked her forefinger in front of his face. "Don't forget what happened after. The community board called for a boycott and got rid of thirteen teachers and six administrators who were undermining their power."

"And then the Board of Education reinstated them," Frank shot back.

Teresa's chin shot up. "And," she said, "the community board refused to take them back."

"Which is why the union accused the Board of Education of not keeping its promise." Frank sat back and let out a long, pessimistic sigh. "Which is why the teachers are now out on strike. Which is why all the schools are closed."

Teresa flashed him a victory smile. "But the Ocean Hill—Brownsville schools are still open. Parents from all over the city are sending their kids to those schools. Like they were doing before the strike."

Frank raised his hands in surrender. "I don't want my wife getting in over her head."

I took that as an insult at first. Did Frank think I didn't have enough sense to stop myself? If that was what he thought, well, maybe he was right. Still. But later, when I was alone in the kitchen, I thought about what he said and realized he really was right. I was twenty-five years old, too young to do what the district superintendent was asking of me. I stood up and opened the kitchen window. Gusts of humid air, outside noises, and rancid smells of garbage and dog poop permeated the room. I was doing enough by living here and being enveloped by the neighborhood. I was doing enough by teaching my class in the church. A surge of relief came over me, the familiar release from anxiety that always came when I made a decision. I drew a happy face in the thin layer of soot on the windowsill.

Just then, the phone rang. Thinking it was Dr. Alexander, I was prepared to tell her I had made a decision, that I would not be acting principal of P.S. 457. But when I picked up the receiver and heard the voice on the other end, I froze.

"Hello, Sylvia. This is Anthony calling."

Frascatore's voice, while familiar, had an almost-respectful tone in it that sent a chill across my shoulders, down my arms, and into my hands. Why was he calling? How did he get my phone number? Was he going to berate me for teaching during the strike?

"Yes?" I said, with an involuntary shiver.

"I hear you were asked to be acting principal."

How did he know that? Was I the last person to know that Dr. Alexander was going to call? Teresa had to have known before she came to our apartment. That would explain her lack of surprise when Mentayer announced the news. So Frascatore knew about it, too. Was I a puppet, and if so, whose hands were pulling the strings?

"Have you decided what you're going to do, Sylvia?"

"No, I haven't." I didn't tell him I'd made a decision not to do it. Let him sweat. Let him think the school was going to be reopened.

"I know you're concerned about the students missing so much school, Sylvia. And I respect that, believe me."

Sure you do. I tightened my grip on the receiver. There was nothing I hated more than someone like him professing to have the inside scoop on my feelings. But what I hated most was that he was right. I *was* concerned about the students. Unlike him. I decided if he dared to claim that he cared about them, too, I would slam the phone down so hard it would make him lose his hearing.

"But you need to look at the bigger picture," he said.

I fidgeted with the telephone cord. How many times had I said to myself, *Don't get so involved, Sylvia, that you lose sight of the bigger picture.* How many other times had I said the opposite? *Don't focus too much on the bigger picture, Sylvia, or actual people and events will float away and get lost.* I hated it that Frascatore was reminding me of my own struggle to find the right balance.

"Unions can't survive unless their members are united," he went on. "We have disagreements within the rank and file, but we can't let those differences divide us. We need to stand together. I know you understand that."

I blew out my breath into the receiver. I hated hearing my own beliefs coming from the likes of him. I hated it even more that he was making me think maybe I *should* take a step back and think about the bigger picture, consider the union movement over the long term. But what was the price of unity? And when was that price too high? What if the union was wrong? How far should my support go then?

I thought about when I first signed up as a UFT member. I was proud to be in a union affiliated with the American Federation of Teachers, with its record of fighting for civil rights since the early 1900s. But wasn't the union violating that history now? Wasn't community control of one's own school a civil rights issue?

I might not have been saying much to Frascatore, but he sure was making me think. I didn't want him to know that.

"The union has always encouraged parental involvement," Frascatore said, "but we've seen what happens when you let a whole community get control of the system. It turns around and fires teachers at will, for no reason. Protecting teachers from that is why we needed a union in the first place."

"You know those teachers were transferred, not fired," I said through gritted teeth. "And there were legitimate reasons. They were undercutting the community control experiment. I'll bet there were other reasons, too."

"You know, Sylvia"—Frascatore's voice was so calm it spooked me, and I braced myself—"I admire your commitment to reforming our educational system."

My lips made a loud and disgusting hissing noise. He pressed on as if he hadn't noticed.

"I appreciate where you're coming from, Sylvia, but teachers have to be free to teach. They can't be looking over their shoulders all the time afraid of being fired. And the union cares about alleviating injustice as much as you do; in fact, that's what this strike is about. You and I are on the same page."

I almost laughed out loud. Was he saying that fighting for teachers' rights at the expense of the community's rights was a way to alleviate injustices in the school system?

"If it's about the discipline issue, Sylvia—"

"It's not." My tone was quick and sharp. *Do not try to make the death of Dion Brown at your hands an issue of teachers' rights,* I wanted to say. *Do not go there.*

"Okay, then, here's the thing, Sylvia. If we fail the teachers, we fail the students, too. You understand what I'm saying?"

"No, the two are not the same," I said. "Not the same at all. You think not supporting the strike is failing the teachers. I think supporting the strike is failing the students. You think supporting the union and opposing community control are one and the same. You don't think I can support both the union *and* community control, but I do." I stopped, out of breath. I was caught between two opposite and incompatible poles. Teaching my class in the church didn't solve the problem of being caught in the middle— between supporting the union and supporting the community—but it did alleviate some of my discomfort about it.

Frascatore lowered his voice. "I'm going to be frank with you, Sylvia. It's well-known that Dr. Alexander has it in for white teachers."

My body went stiff. I stopped breathing.

"If you know what I mean."

I slammed the phone down without saying good-bye. "I know exactly what you mean," I said as I pummeled the top of the table with my fists. A rush of blood moved through my body, transforming my anger into hard-edged determination and making my back straight as an arrow. Frank ran into the kitchen to see what had happened. He stood in the doorway, staring at me.

"I'm going to do it," I said, shooting him a "do not mess with me" look. "I'm going to open the school."

He leaned back against the doorjamb with his eyes closed, his head bowed and his palms squeezed together. "I pray to God," he said in a whisper, "that you won't live to regret it."

TEN

Fall 1968

On my first morning as acting principal, P.S. 457 stood like a ghost against the rising dawn and dimming streetlights. As I unlocked the back door, I could have sworn I heard phantom voices of children inside the vacant building.

I made my way up the dimly lit staircase to the main office, then searched along the wall to the left of the door for the light switch. I stepped into the principal's office, an inner sanctum with mysteries to which I would now be privy. I reached into my nylon backpack for the official letter of appointment from Dr. Alexander and placed it face up on top of Miss Huskings's desk, a reminder that it wasn't so much my choice to be here as that I had been chosen.

At seven thirty, a crowd of picketers appeared outside the window shouting "Scab" and "Traitor" in loud voices. They hissed and booed at the substitute teachers braving their way toward the entrance.

Dr. Alexander had sent teachers already? I'd expected them tomorrow maybe, but not today, not my first day on the job. Why hadn't she told me? And how had Frascatore known they were coming when I hadn't?

The substitute teachers huddled by the front door, looking in. I dashed from my office and flew down the stairs to unlock the door. One by one they filed in.

"Welcome," I said, out of breath as I held the door open for them. "Thank you for coming. Welcome. Thank you. Thank you. Welcome."

The last one in was my upstairs neighbor Teresa. She joined the others in the vestibule, a huge "didn't I tell you we'd do it" smile on her face. I walked up a couple of steps then turned. A silent army of twenty-eight— nonunion teachers plus a few union members from other schools, none from P.S. 457—looked at me, waiting for their marching orders.

"Okay, well." My voice shook. "Good morning and thank you for coming." I cleared my throat. "My name is Sylvia Waters, and I will be acting principal of P.S. 457 for the remainder of the strike. We will reopen the school tomorrow. That gives us today to get ready. We'll meet in the auditorium to get organized. It's one flight up. Oh, and please, call me Ms. Sylvia." The echo of my voice in the open, high-ceilinged atrium gave no hint of the vulnerability I felt inside.

The teachers trooped up the stairs as one body with different faces. Some with eyes shifting from side to side. Some looking straight ahead, chins up. Others with faces lowered. While they were getting settled in the front rows of the auditorium, I resurrected the to-do list I'd made in my head during the night. Then I stood before them and gave instructions, delegated tasks, assigned them to their classes and rooms, and sent them off to get ready for the next day.

At four o'clock, we gathered again in the auditorium. "It looks like we're as ready as we can be," I said. "You've had time to prepare for your classes. Parents have been notified that school will reopen tomorrow. Parent volunteers have been assigned as teachers' aides for most of the classrooms. If you don't have one yet for your class, don't worry, I'm sure we'll get more in the coming days. The lunchroom staff was called back, and they've ordered enough food to feed up to six hundred students this week. We did it. *You* did it." Everyone clapped.

"Now go on home and get a good night's sleep. I'll see you all at seven thirty in the morning."

The next morning, Frank drove me to school at dawn and then went back home to wake Mentayer. The two of them picked up Markus from his uncle's apartment in time to get to school by eight thirty. This became our regular routine during the strike.

That morning, the picketers gathered outside my office window, their numbers growing by the minute. By the time the teachers and parent volunteers arrived, well over a hundred raucous union members were there to greet them. Many of their faces were familiar. Some of them I knew, a few well enough to exchange pleasantries with, but none well enough to engage in conversation; thankfully, Bonnie wasn't there. Tensions were high. The shouts and name-calling grew louder, more strident, with each teacher that crossed the picket line. Most exchanges were verbal, a few involved pushing and shoving. But when a couple dozen parent volunteers, led by Teresa with head held high, strode en masse toward the entrance, the picketers fell back and let them pass in silence.

Students began arriving an hour later. Parents, grandparents, and other caretakers gripped their children's hands, put arms around shoulders, as they walked past the chanting picketers, keeping a wide berth from the signs being thrust up and down. When a few families turned at the picket line to go back home, a slender woman stepped in front of them. "¡*No se vaya todavía!* Don't leave yet!" She gripped the hands of her own two small children and, with them running to keep up, stomped up the sidewalk and deposited them at the door. Then she turned and motioned with both hands for others to come. Mentayer squealed and broke away from Frank. She grabbed Markus's hand, and the two of them skipped up the sidewalk with looks on their faces like they were conquering the world. Other students followed, some running, others more cautious, all of them smiling.

One hundred twenty students came to school that first day. By the end of the week, there were over six hundred in attendance. More substitute teachers, recruited by Dr. Alexander, showed up every day. And every day the picket line grew exponentially, both in size and volatility. Their chanting grew louder and more sustained. The number of tense interactions increased and threatened to erupt into violence at any moment. At the end of each day, when Frank picked me up in the parking lot behind the school, dozens of picketers accosted me. Sometimes they surrounded the van to block our exit.

The most volatile picketers started to invade my dreams at night. They appeared at the assassinations of Martin Luther King Jr. and Robert Kennedy. At the police riots outside the Democratic National Convention in Chicago. At anti—Vietnam War protests. More and more often I was waking up in the morning with an impending sense of doom. The whole world had turned violent.

I started getting hang-up calls at home on the weekends. Each time I heard a click on the other end of the line, I kicked myself for answering. We decided we'd take the receiver off the hook, but Mentayer objected.

"What if they call about Grandma?" she said. "What if Markus needs me?"

We agreed to leave the phone on until bedtime and then take the receiver off the hook until the next morning. Every Saturday and Sunday afternoon, Mentayer called Markus. The conversations were one-sided and always the same. "Don't you be sassing me, Markus. You do what Uncle Bert says even if the others don't. He didn't have to take you in, you know. You need to listen to him and not make any trouble, you hear? And you better be waiting outside tomorrow morning when Uncle Frank and I pick you up for school. No dawdling, okay? When I call Grandma, I'll tell her you love her. You know I will."

On Sundays at five o'clock, Mentayer called the hospital, and the nurse would hold the phone to Grandma's ear. Mentayer chattered away about what she and Markus were learning in school and kept telling her that everything was fine. After she hung up, we took the phone off the hook until Monday morning. One night we forgot, and when the phone rang, I made the mistake of answering it.

It was Frascatore. "What you're doing is destroying all unions, Sylvia." He didn't even say hello. "Maybe you don't care about your own rights, but think about the coal miners and other working people who had to fight so hard for theirs in the nineteen twenties and thirties. Think about the struggles of the teachers before our time. Do you want their suffering to have been for nothing?"

"Of course I don't," I said.

"Then you need to think about what you're doing." He spit the words out, a millisecond between them, each one a threat.

"It's not my intention to fight the union, any union," I shot back. "But the union is pitting teachers against children and parents. You've forced us to choose one or the other and that's wrong. Just plain wrong."

"No, Sylvia, *you* are the one who is wrong," he said. "You're sacrificing the entire union movement to give the parents of a bunch of kids who can't learn anyway a few days of free babysitting."

I slammed the phone down. My insides were vibrating. Why had I even bothered to talk to him? Why had I answered the phone in the first place? I closed my eyes and slowed my breathing. The phone rang again. I knew I shouldn't answer it. But I was still rattled and not thinking straight, and I assumed it was Frascatore calling back. He couldn't stand it that I hung up on him. Well, I was ready to give him a piece of my mind.

"Don't call anymore," I shouted into the phone, without waiting for him to say anything. "There's no point in us talking about this or anything else."

A man's voice came on the line, a deep, menacing, growl-like voice that I didn't recognize. "Stop what you're doing or you'll be sorry. You're treading in dangerous waters, lady."

Click. He hung up.

I started shaking. Then it occurred to me that the man on the phone could have been Frascatore, so angry at me for hanging up on him that he called back right away and disguised his voice. He was trying to scare me. His way of blowing off steam. I decided not to tell Frank about the call and spare him the worry.

It was a decision I regretted the next morning. If I'd told Frank about the threatening phone call, he wouldn't have left with Pastor Paul to go to a meeting in Connecticut. He would have insisted on taking me to school instead of me driving myself, and he would have been with me when it happened. When I put the key in the lock and it wouldn't go all the way in. When I tried other keys and none of them worked. When I walked around the building and couldn't unlock the other doors. When the key turned with a familiar click in the last lock I tried, but then the door wouldn't budge when I tried to pull it open. When, alone and scared, I ran back to the parking lot and locked myself in the van.

My left foot wobbled as I pressed it down on the clutch. My right hand shook as I fumbled to put the key in the ignition. I managed to shift the van into neutral gear and turn the engine on, but then the blast of the radio about shot me through the roof. I screamed and bolted forward to turn the volume down. Then I laid my head back on the seat and tried to catch my breath.

"Good morning, folks," the radio newscaster said. "Well, there's more trouble for our city's public schools today. Union janitors are demonstrating their sympathy with the striking teachers by blockading doors, changing or gluing locks, and even barricading themselves inside their schools. Windows have been smashed and locks broken at several schools. Arrests are being made. New York City School Superintendent Donovan has ordered all schools locked down for the day. Parents are being told to keep their children at home."

I shifted into first gear, pressed my foot on the gas, and peeled out of the parking lot. The tires squealed. At the corner stop sign, I glanced in the rear-view mirror at the school entrance. No picketers were there yet. Maybe the striking teachers had been notified in advance about the janitors' planned actions. Maybe they'd decided to take the day off since we couldn't get in the building anyway. But what if the picketers did come? One way to spare P.S. 457 the violent confrontations afflicting other schools would be to keep the substitute teachers and parents away from the building today.

That was it. I knew what needed to be done. I turned the van around and parked in front of the main entrance. I pulled a piece of paper from my backpack. I wrote *NO SCHOOL TODAY* in black marker and taped the sign on the front door. Then I ran back to the van and sped home to set the school telephone tree in motion.

Within an hour, the message had reached all our substitute teachers and volunteers and as many parents as possible: They should stay home today and wait for further instructions. I assured them that the school would reopen but didn't tell them when or how. That was something I still didn't know.

ELEVEN

April 2006

The day after our visit to Clarke Craine, J. B. and I linger over our breakfast coffee, each of us with a different section of the *New York Times*. In the international news section, I skim an article about Iran's successful enrichment of uranium and then put the paper down. I stare out the basement window at the colors and types of shoes passing by on the sidewalk outside, hypnotized by the rhythmic clip of people's steps. Then J. B. lets out a whoop and I turn my attention to him.

"There it is!" He waves a section of the paper in the air, a look of exultation akin to rapture on his face. "Two short paragraphs," he says, pointing to an article in the local section of the paper. "I almost missed it."

I lean forward and crane my neck to read the words. "Come on, J. B., hold still. Did they release more information about the body? Is that it?" I reach out for the paper but he pulls it back. He pushes his coffee cup and empty plate to the side, then flattens the paper on the table. He reads it to me, his voice rising in pitch with each phrase.

"'Additional details have been released... about the skeleton found in February of this year in the rubble of P.S. 457 in the Bronx. The medical examiner's office has said that the body is most likely that of an African American boy... between seven and nine years of age who, based on the state of decomposition, died between thirty and forty years ago. Cause of death could be an injury to the skull from an accidental fall or a blow to the head... A finger on the boy's left hand had been broken... suggesting a defensive injury.'"

He stops reading and looks up at me with his mouth open in a big *O*.

"That's the same information Dr. Goldmann gave us yesterday," I say.

"Exactly."

"What else does it say?" I scoot to the edge of my seat but am driven back by J. B.'s frown. "Not good? What?" He tips his head as if to say he's sorry. Then he reads the rest of the article.

"'According to a Police Department spokesman, identity and cause of death are unknown, and due to the difficulties of investigating a death that happened decades ago, it is expected that the case will be closed.'"

"That's all. That's it." He slides the newspaper over to me.

"No way," I say, the words shooting out of my mouth like a hurricane. "No way are we going to let them make Markus disappear again. They can't make it go away. What the hell are they thinking? That they can stop you from writing an article about it by publishing tidbits of information in an obscure part of the paper where no one will see it? Well, if they think this will be the end of it, they have another think coming." I stop and catch my breath. I expect J. B. to agree with me. If I were him, I'd be insulted by their feeble attempt to manipulate me.

"But don't you see what this means, Sylvia?" J. B.'s face is glowing. There's a glimmer in his eyes. "Think about it. Clarke Craine got the NYPD commissioner's gag order lifted. He got a couple paragraphs in the paper in less than twenty-four hours. That's how much influence he and the CSCH Corporation have in this town."

"So that makes you happy? They're still stonewalling us. The article says the police are going to close the case. Nobody cares what happened to that dead boy, whether it's Markus or someone else."

"But it helps to know who the stakeholders are. Know your enemy, you know what I mean?" He smiles, then adds, "And now we know there's more to this than meets the eye. For some reason, people in power don't want you digging around, no pun unintended."

"So what's next," I ask.

"I don't know. Maybe if we go and see CSCH's construction site for ourselves, it'll become clear."

"Let's do it," I agree. I'd thought it would take longer for Craine to take the bait and so we'd have today off, and I'd already planned to spend the day in the Bronx. "I want to see what the neighborhood is like now."

We take the number 2 subway at Christopher Street in the Village. It goes all the way up to the closest stop to where Frank and I used to live. The station is as dingy as ever, its railings rusty, its stairs steep, the stench of urine still overpowering to the senses. At the bottom of the stairs, we walk around a homeless man asleep with his hand wrapped around a bottle in a brown paper bag.

I slip into a reflective silence as we walk away from the station into the streets. With each step comes a new memory fragment. Smells of steamy dog poop and stale urine. Sounds of squealing children, the whoosh of an open hydrant, the super's good-morning grunt. Heat from the sidewalk sizzling through the soles of my cheap sandals. Mothers with tired faces waiting by their mailboxes on the first of the month. Heroin-addicted men nodding off on stoops. Pastor Paul walking the neighborhood all night after Martin Luther King Jr. was assassinated.

"How much farther?" J. B. asks.

I stop and look around. "Oh my, we're already at the building where Frank and I lived." I point up to the second floor. "That was our kitchen window. Across the street is the church where Frank did his internship."

According to the marquee sign, it's now a Baptist Bible Church. Hundreds of holes still dot the round stained glass window above the entrance. There are two posters on the front door, one about a weekly support group for parents of murdered children and the other about a free lunch program at noon Monday through Friday. Several dark-skinned men lean against the side of the church smoking cigarettes. A few others half sit, half lie on the church steps with their eyes closed. I glance at my watch. It's almost noon. Lunchtime.

I point to a new complex of apartment buildings, parks, and play areas on the other side of the church. "That redevelopment project wasn't there. You should have seen, when they tore down the first old building to make way for it, the long line of roaches crossing that street." I chuckle. "Sometimes, when I was in the kitchen, a roach would stop and wave to me like, 'Hey, it's me, coming by to get a snack is all.' To make matters worse, an elderly lady on our floor moved her furniture out in the hall once a month to spray her apartment, and an army of roaches marched right across the hall to our place. I swear it's true."

J. B. and I both laugh.

I look around and take in all the changes on the block. An attractive steel scrollwork entrance to our old apartment building is locked. No one can get in now to piss in the corner of the foyer or on the stairs. A metal fence with a locked gate closes off the space between the buildings. Now the lids stay on the garbage cans. There's a Laundromat where the super's apartment once was.

"It seems better now," I say. "Cleaner. Safer."

"Still stinks though." J. B. sniffs, wrinkles his nose.

I laugh. "That's the zoo. Sometimes when the breeze was right, the smell got so strong we had to keep our windows closed."

I act as a tour guide as we continue up the street. "More than two thousand people lived on this one block. That's twice the size of the town I grew up in. Most people were on welfare when we lived here. It was almost a perfect fifty-fifty, black and Puerto Rican, but the Puerto Ricans had already started moving out, like the Jewish people did before them."

As we near P.S. 457, the blocks become more crammed with drab, high-density buildings. There's more debris on the sidewalks and in the gutters—drug paraphernalia, signs of rats and other urban vermin. There's a chain-link fence around the empty lot on which the school once stood. The rubble's been cleared. A corner of the foundation still stands. I cling to the wire mesh to keep a rush of vivid images from flattening me to the ground.

"I didn't realize the school was so huge," J. B. says. "It covered a full block?"

"Part of it was a parking lot," I say. "There was a playground space, too, but that was filled with mobile classrooms. Funny, I don't remember thinking about how big it was."

He studies me for a few seconds, his eyes curious. "If you could travel back in time, knowing what you know now, what would you say to the young you?" he asks.

"That's easy. I'd say, 'Sylvia, you think you know the truth, but the truth is, you know nothing. You don't even know what you don't know. So what the hell makes you think you can be acting principal of a school this size... or any size?'"

"Would you listen to yourself?"

I laugh. "Of course not. I was twenty-five and clueless. I hadn't come into consciousness yet."

"Can't fault yourself for that," J. B. says with a grin.

"It was a turbulent time to be coming of age, in the sixties," I say. "I let the civil rights and anti—Vietnam War movements take me and shape me.

There was so much rage back then, and I had more than my share of it. But I was also infected with a sense of hope." I shake my head. "I can't believe now how unaware I was of the powerful interests being created to undermine the changes so many of us were working for."

My cell phone rings, and I dig into my purse and pull it out. The caller ID shows it's Mentayer. Before I can say hello, she starts talking.

"Did you see the paper today? Are you still in town?" Her voice sounds shaky, not at all what I expected.

"Where are you?" I ask. "Are you at work?"

"I'm at home."

"I'll come see you," I say. "Give me your address." J. B. hands me his pen and the little pad he's been using to take notes whenever we're out and about and he doesn't have a need for his briefcase. Mentayer doesn't say anything for a few seconds, but then, in a hesitant voice, she gives me her address. My jaw drops when I realize she still lives in the neighborhood.

"Really?" I say without thinking.

"Really what?" The chill is back in her voice.

"I'm surprised, that's all," I say. "Look, I'm standing right now at the school. I mean, where the school used to be. I can get to your place in a few minutes."

I drop the phone in my purse with a shake of my head. "Mentayer's apartment is a block from where she lived when she was in third grade," I tell J. B. "I don't understand. You can see for yourself why most people would want to leave this neighborhood. With all of her education, Mentayer could live on the Upper East Side of Manhattan if she wanted to. So why does she still live here?"

"And why did she call?" J. B. adds.

"I think something about the article scared her," I say, shaking my head. "Like she knows something." The expression on his face implies that one thing leads to another. No need to say it out loud.

As we walk, I point to where Mentayer and Markus used to live. The building is so deteriorated that I can almost hear the sound of it sagging into decay. "When I first met their grandmother," I say, "she was in the back, scooping up pigeon poop from a tiny little patch of dirt." The memory is bittersweet.

Mentayer's apartment is a block away in another building that has seen better days. The butterflies in my stomach multiply with each step up the four flights of stairs, flapping about, making me unsteady on my feet. I hang onto the railing for support. In front of apartment number 402, I lean over with my hands on my knees to catch my breath and give my nerves time to unrattle.

J. B. stands off to the side, and I ring the bell. The door opens to a sight so unexpected it takes my breath away: a hallway with white-on-white wallpaper and an eight-foot-long dark cream rug carved with a beige scrollwork and vine pattern. Then Mentayer steps out from behind the door.

She'd grown tall, her linen-clad legs long and slim but not gangly. Her slender arms blend with the tan of her short-sleeved silk blouse. The small gap between her two front teeth enhances her loveliness and gives her beauty an alluring uniqueness. I breathe in her essence. I long to hug her, but I freeze. I can't even reach out to shake her hand.

"Thank you for coming," she says, in a dignified voice that is betrayed by the downturned corners of her mouth.

I struggle for the right thing to say. Running through my head is an interior stream of phrases—*You look fantastic. It's good to see you after almost forty years. I've missed you.*—each as awkward and wrong as if speaking a foreign language and blurting out words that mean the opposite of what was intended. So I stand there mute, a tender smile on my face, basking in the memory of the child I so adored and marveling at the generous beauty of her as an adult. But she's a stranger to me now. It would be presumptuous and inappropriate of me to think or act otherwise.

Mentayer sees J. B. and gives him a long, appraising look, then tips her chin up, her assessment of him complete. I introduce him as an old friend, and he trips over the words "Nice to meet you." She turns away from him and leads us into her apartment.

The living room is bright and sunny, high-ceilinged and yet warm and cozy at the same time, with walls a blended palette, three of them in different shades of green and the fourth a brilliant yellow. The bright colors and bold pattern of a large, beautifully crafted area rug on the polished wood floor and the neutral fabric of the couch and chairs, offset by a collection of multicolored pillows, combine to elevate the room and set it apart from the neighborhood in which it resides. It's as if Mentayer has taken all the brilliance and love of life that have been held captive by the unacknowledged loss of her brother and exported it in high resolution onto her surroundings.

As I study her room, she studies me. I wonder what she sees. The too skinny, too white, too young, too earnest woman in a miniskirt who was her third-grade teacher? Someone who is a manifestation of life's losses? Or do I appear to her as a stranger? Is the soft gray bun of my hair grandmotherly and reassuring to her? Or is the intensity in my blue-gray eyes a threat to her, a warning to be cautious?

"Your place is beautiful," I say.

"I've done a lot of work on it," she says. "It started when I first moved in and had the kitchen torn out and remodeled. Please, have a seat."

J. B. bumps into the glass coffee table, an awkward move for him. He sits down on the couch and starts rubbing his shin. I sit next to him. There's an eight-by-ten black-and-white family photo on the end table next to me. Grandma's mouth is open and she's laughing, her hands slapping her knees. Markus leans into one shoulder, Mentayer into the other. Both of them are smiling. My eyes, like a camera zooming in on the room's main feature, are drawn to an overstuffed chair in the corner. Its arms are frayed where Grandma's hands once rested, its cushions still shaped to the form of her ample body.

"It still smells like her," Mentayer says with her lips turned up in a sad smile. "I can't let go of it."

"Is that why you still live here? To be close to your grandma?"

She looks down at her hands like she's trying to decide whether to tell me the truth or not. "I decided to stay here," she says with a sigh, "so Markus would always know where to find me."

The defensiveness in her voice is betrayed by the deep sadness in her eyes. It unleashes a force of long-sealed memories inside me of the innocent child she once was, the child who was unwavering in her belief that Markus was okay, in spite of all evidence to the contrary. I was careful not to tread on her childlike hope then and I won't tread on her hope now. A tear trickles down her cheek as she sits down in a chair across from me. She swipes at it.

"Grandma told me I was responsible for my brother." She looks at her grandmother's chair as she speaks, as if she were sitting there right now, talking to her. "I tried to put Markus in the back of my mind, but whenever I did, I'd hear her voice telling me to never give up. But now… " She takes in a deep breath. She squeezes her eyes tight for a few seconds, then opens them and blurts out the words. "Markus broke his finger once. He said he broke it playing baseball but... " Her eyes plead with me to finish the sentence.

"But now," I say, "his broken finger makes it more likely that the dead boy could be Markus."

Tears fill her eyes. She tries to stop them. She breathes in through her nose and out through her mouth. She crinkles up her face. But she's unable to keep the spigot from opening. The tears are slow at first but soon they fall faster and harder. Soon they are unstoppable. She drops her head into her hands and leans forward with her face on her knees as the pain of her illusions drain away. Her tears are drowning the room little by little, bringing the truth out and up to the surface, floating around Grandma's chair and quenching the lies, the years of denial.

I reach in my purse for a packet of tissues. I bring it to her, but she shakes her head, refuses my help. I sit back down and grip my knees, rock back and forth. She sobs out a choke and I rock in time with it. She coughs and I hold my breath. A tsunami of grief washes away her denial, making room for her to find a way to live in a world without her brother. It would be wrong for me to intervene. It would not be helpful for me to dissolve into her pain. All I can do is be with her and wait for her tears to stop.

And then they do. She blows her nose. "Lots of little boys break their fingers," she says. "Well, they do, don't they?" Her voice is strained with anger. I wonder if she's trying to squeeze out whatever shred of hope might still be there.

All of a sudden, she jumps up and walks over to the window. She opens it and a gust of fresh air blows into the room. I wipe my eyes with the back of my hands. I sit up and fold my hands on my lap. She turns and looks at me. It's done. She knows Markus is dead. It's over.

"You should get your DNA tested," J. B. says.

Mentayer flinches like she's startled to see him, like she'd forgotten he was here. She knits her brow.

"It's the next logical thing to do," he says. She looks at him as if this were the first time she's considered the idea, as if her grief has devoured the rational part of her that would, under normal circumstances, know that. She walks back to her chair and sits down, her face cloudy, maybe a bit puzzled.

"It's the only way to be sure," J. B. says.

I shake my head, annoyed by the edge of impatience in his voice. "No need to rush into it," I say. "You can do it when you're ready."

Mentayer averts her gaze and sighs, a long sigh. "Okay, then, I'll go to the police."

"I don't think they'll help you," J. B. says. His eyes are glued to Mentayer.

"I thought you said... " Her voice sizzles like a lit match and then sputters out.

"The medical examiner's office does the DNA testing," he says. "The person you should see is Dr. Goldmann."

Mentayer shoots him a withering look. "I'm sorry, but who are you anyway?" she says. "Why is this any of your business? Why are you even here?"

"I'm sorry," I say. "I should have told you J. B. was coming with me."

"Maybe I should have told you more about myself," he says in a voice that sounds uncertain and out of character for him. "I'm an investigative reporter. I came to New York with Sylvia to do some research for a story I'm working on."

"What? A story about Markus?" Mentayer's tone is sharp. Her eyes flash anger and suspicion.

"No, no, not about your brother," J. B. says. "I'm doing a series on charter schools."

"Sometimes," I rush in to say, "it helps to have an investigative reporter around. It was a direct result of J. B.'s interview yesterday with a CSCH Corporation investor that the information was released in the paper today."

Mentayer's shoulders twitch. Her body bristles.

"There's nothing to worry about," J. B. says. "My research is separate from your brother's case, Mentayer. The same goes for Sylvia. She was fighting to stop the CSCH Corporation from taking over our Monrow City schools long before the body was discovered. She didn't even know CSCH was building a school there until you told her." I've never seen J. B. speak this fast or with such a sense of urgency before.

Mentayer's eyebrows form an angry groove in the middle of her forehead. She presses her palms against the sides of her head. She takes in a deep breath, then lets it out through her lips. An image flashes through my head of her in third grade. She's sitting at her desk, hands clasped, revving up for an outburst. She has the same look on her face now that she did as a child. I brace myself.

"I shouldn't have called you," she says. "I knew you couldn't be trusted."

Before I can think of what to say, she flies out of her chair and hovers over J. B. on the couch. He leans back with a look of alarm.

"Nice try," she shouts in J. B.'s face. He leans back farther. "But I get it now. You used my brother as a ploy to get into my house so you could get information out of me about CSCH. Well, I have news for you, Mr. Hotshot Reporter. That's unethical. It's despicable. You're despicable."

"Mentayer, no." I plead. "You don't understand."

She straightens up, twists her body back toward me. "And you, you're as bad as he is. Ushering him in like this. Coming back into my life so you can use me. And to do what? To fight CSCH? You, the teacher who always put kids first? Huh! Not anymore. I don't even know who you are."

"Please, Mentayer, you've got it wrong."

"I don't suffer fools," she spits out through pursed lips. "I want you to leave. Get out. Both of you. Now."

TWELVE

April 2006

This is what I know: Mentayer has faced the possibility that Markus is dead. This is what I don't know: Why she kicked us out of her apartment. So here I am in bed at ten o'clock, once again unable to sleep.

I try to figure out what happened. It was a misunderstanding. She doesn't trust J. B. and his motives. Her grief was so deep that she misdirected her anger. Worse yet, she doesn't trust me. I consider calling her. I rehearse what to say. In case she calls, I sleep with my cell phone by my side. But she's much too stubborn, much too well defended. She doesn't want my help.

I'm on the verge of falling asleep when the phone rings. The caller ID says it's her. I sit up and take a deep breath before answering. She still needs to find out what happened to her brother. Maybe she still wants my help.

"Mentayer, I'm so glad you called," I say. "I was going to call you, too. There's been some terrible misunderstanding."

"I went to see Dr. Goldmann like your friend suggested." Her voice cracks. She sounds defeated. "My DNA was a match."

A lump fills my throat, a river of tears, my eyes. I'm sorry, I'm sorry, I'm so sorry. The words catch in my throat, won't come out. I'm having trouble breathing. Now that it's confirmed that the boy is Markus, I don't want to hear it. I'm not ready.

"I should have stopped him. I should have done more." The words escape in a whisper. It sounds like Mentayer might be crying. It was the wrong thing to say.

"I called the police right away and told them they needed to investigate." She pauses before continuing. "They think his death was gang-related."

"No," I shout. "No." I'm going under, drowning. What if it's true? What if Markus was trying to tell me something about a gang? I should have listened better. I should have protected him. This didn't have to happen.

"The police don't believe me." I hear the anger in her voice. "I told them my brother wouldn't have anything to do with a gang. They say breaking fingers was part of a gang initiation. I told them he broke his finger playing baseball. They think he was dealing drugs, too. I told them none of that was true. I told them it wasn't possible. I screamed at them, Sylvia. I told them Markus was a good boy. I told them how honest he was. I begged them to investigate and prove me wrong if they're so sure, and they say it's too late for that, and that 'given the circumstances,' gangs and drugs were quite likely involved. What if they put in the newspaper that my brother was an eight-year-old gang member who was dealing drugs and that's why he was killed?"

She goes silent for a few seconds. "I will *not* let people think that. Not about my brother. Markus was too smart to get messed up with gangs or drugs." She pauses. I hear her take a breath. "I'm not saying he couldn't have been killed by a gang," she says in a calmer voice. "But if he was, it was because he refused to have anything to do with them. I have to get the police to listen to me. I have to stop them from closing the case."

"We'll have to find evidence that they can't ignore, so they have to investigate," I say. "We'll disprove their theory. Because that's all they've got, Mentayer, a theory. They're just guessing."

I hear her expel her breath.

"J. B. will help."

She responds with a sharp intake of breath.

"He has influence," I say. "He knows people. He knows how to dig up the truth. We've been friends for a long time. I trust him." Mentayer doesn't say anything. I hear a whooshing sound, like she's blowing air into the phone. "Tell you what. Meet us for lunch tomorrow. Give us a chance to clear things up. If you still don't want to work with J. B., then fine. But at least give him a chance. Give me a chance. You don't have to do this alone."

We agree to meet at eleven thirty at a popular waffle restaurant in Harlem. Right after I hang up, I call to tell J. B. Then I lie down and stare out the window by my bed. It's raining, hard, the thunderstorm that had been forecast earlier. Raindrops splash against the window and turn silver against the dark sky. Puddles of water gather on the sills. I reach for the remote control and turn the television on to the weather channel. Rain is falling over the whole Northeast; roads are blocked, in some places flooded. I imagine it raining on the maple trees, the lakes, the fields outside the city, the drops dissolving on ocean waves. I imagine it raining in the Bronx, filling the hole where P.S. 457 once stood and covering the place that had held Markus's small body, the concrete that had become his cemetery. Did his soul cry out whenever the rain descended on him? Did he pray that someone would discover him? His spirit cries out to me now. He's begging me to find the truth about what happened.

"We will, Markus," I whisper. "I promise we will."

THIRTEEN

Fall 1968

Despite the janitors gluing the school locks in a show of sympathy with the striking teachers, I was determined to get back in. Within twenty-four hours we were poised for action. When the alarm buzzed at three thirty the next morning, I poked Frank awake and leaped from the bed.

"Rise and shine, sweetie," I called out to Mentayer, still asleep on the living room couch. We have a school to open."

At four o'clock the three of us crept down the steps. Teresa, her husband, Steve, and their daughter, Allie, were already waiting for us in the foyer. With the stealth of criminals acting under the cover of darkness, we unfolded and pulled over our heads the cheap plastic ponchos Frank had bought yesterday at Sam's Hardware Store after he heard the weather report. We dashed across the street in the pouring rain and clambered into the van. A flash of lightning cut through the black sky. Mentayer and Teresa's family huddled together in the back seat, shivering. I sat in the front and held my breath as Frank turned the key in the ignition. The engine roared to life. We gave each other a high five, and he shifted into gear. We'd worried that the battery might be stolen, because we left it in the van last night.

Frank drove at a snail's pace, hunched over and peering through the narrow strip of window being cleared by flapping windshield wipers we hadn't had time to replace. I turned on the radio, the volume high enough for all of us to hear over the noise.

"Week three of the New York City teachers' strike, and things are heating up," the newscaster said. "Yesterday morning, several people were arrested for smashing windows and breaking locks during their attempts to re-enter schools that had been sealed by union janitors. Some people camped overnight on school grounds to prevent further lockouts. Arrests for trespassing are now in progress, and police are being seen as sympathetic to the striking teachers. More violence is expected."

"Not at *our* school," Teresa said.

"Thanks to Dr. Alexander's quick thinking," I said. I slipped my hand under my poncho and into the pocket of my raincoat, my fingers tingling when I touched the letter the district superintendent had messengered to me last night. As Frank parked behind the school, the tingling in my fingers moved, like a rush of adrenaline, up my arm and into my shoulder, my chest. I'd never done anything this nervy or sneaky before. I felt like we were breaking the law, but we weren't. Dr. Alexander assured me it was legal.

Within seconds a truck with a logo on the door saying Ace Locksmith Company arrived. It pulled up next to our van. We all scrambled out, moving with a silence made all the deeper by the absence of Mentayer and Allie's usual nonstop chatter. Frank held an umbrella over my head while I shook hands with the driver through the truck's open window.

"This is from our district superintendent," I said as I handed him the letter. I kept my voice low but above a whisper. "It authorizes you to change the locks on all the doors and guarantees payment."

"Name's Pete," the locksmith said with a nod. He got out of the truck and reached into the back for his equipment, his matter-of-fact, business-like demeanor devoid of politics. We agreed to start with the back door and make our way around the building. I wanted to save for last the door on the south side where I had instructed the substitute teachers to meet us at six o'clock.

Pete turned on his flashlight at the first door and handed it to Teresa, asked her to aim the beam of light at the lock. Then he crouched down and got to work. Steve motioned that he was going to patrol the perimeter of the building. He pointed to his pursed lips, letting us know he would whistle if he encountered anyone on the grounds. Mentayer and Allie, in an amazing feat of self-control, confined their curious energy to a widening of their eyes and bouncing on the heels of their feet. We were all shivering, both from the chill in the air and the significance of what we were doing. Frank put his arm around my shoulders. I leaned into him, still warmed by the conversation we'd had yesterday after Dr. Alexander called with instructions about how to reopen the school.

"She needs you." That's all Frank had said. No questions like "Do you think that's such a good idea?" No judgments like "Do you think you have to do whatever she asks you to do?" I had been ready to defend myself, to tell him that I wasn't a patsy following orders, that I was determined to reopen the school and had been prepared to figure it out myself, and that I was relieved and grateful to Dr. Alexander for giving me the name of the locksmith and his phone number.

"People think I'm doing this because of you," I said, joking. "Bonnie says they think I have to go in because I'm a preacher's wife."

I loved the way he curled his lips up in a teasing smile and said, "I guess they don't know you're not too good at it."

I took it as a compliment and chuckled. But I turned serious when I thought about what we were going to do. "There could be trouble," I said. "Frascatore seems to have a knack for finding out in advance what we're planning. The sneaky bastard knew before I did that the locks were glued. That's why the picketers never showed up."

"I know you'll do fine without me," Frank had said. "But I'm going with you. We're in this together."

I snuggled into him now. This must be what it meant when people said support was the backbone of marriage. It's not that I hadn't supported Frank and his desire to be a minister, as much as a nonbeliever could, or maybe skeptic was the more accurate word for what I was. After all, I'd agreed to move to the Bronx for his internship, and when he expressed a desire to finish his studies at Union Theological Seminary, I agreed to stay for another year. And it wasn't like Frank hadn't supported me, too. He'd considered my needs when choosing his internship, and he'd helped during the first week of the strike when Bonnie and I decided to teach our classes in the church. Still, our support of each other up until now had been limited. One of us was always in the foreground, with the other providing support in the background. We'd been like cheerleaders on the sidelines of each other's lives. But this was different. This morning we were both foreground. We were on the same team.

At five forty-five, dawn began brightening the sky. Under a quivering cluster of black umbrellas, the substitute teachers and volunteer parents stood at the south side door. I ran to them.

"Thank you for getting here early," I said, trying to catch my breath and speak at the same time. "All the other locks have been changed. This is the last one. If we're lucky, the picketers won't show up today, but if they do, we should be able to head off any trouble by getting inside before they know we're here."

"What about our students?" someone asked.

Teresa stepped forward to answer. "I activated the parent phone tree last night," she said. "Word travels fast around here. I'm sure most people have heard by now that school will reopen at eight-thirty today."

"Then the UFT knows it, too," an anxious voice said. Several people nodded and grumbled to each other.

"I don't think so," Teresa said. "Ms. Sylvia's the only regular teacher who lives here. Word doesn't often spread beyond the neighborhood."

"I think the picketers would be here by now if they'd heard about our plan," I said. "So far, so good."

Pete the locksmith put his tools away and stood up. He handed me a set of new keys. I was warmed by the rightness of the moment, felt a sense of being at one with the world.

"All right, folks," I said as I dangled the keys above my head and shook them. "Let's get inside and go to work."

Everyone cheered. They stepped off the muddy grass and moved en masse toward the door. I shook my head, thinking about how, with the janitors now on strike, we'd have to clean up all the tracked-in mud ourselves. Then I smiled. It was a small price to pay.

"You go, girl," Teresa said when I pulled on the door handle. It didn't budge. I pulled again, then tried a third time. I turned the key to be sure it was unlocked, then pulled one more time.

Frank gave it a try. Nothing. Steve joined him, and together they pulled, grunting. The door gave way a fraction of an inch then snapped shut again.

"It's a tug-of-war," Frank shouted. "Someone's pulling on the door from the other side."

My pulse quickened. Frascatore had learned of our plan after all. Maybe some picketers had camped out in the school all night to make sure we couldn't get in. A vein in my neck twitched. Or maybe someone else was inside. Maybe the man who made the threatening phone call. Maybe the police were inside guarding the building.

My paranoia was getting the best of me.

"One more time." Steve said. "Okay. One. Two. Three. Pull!"

The door flew open. Frank and Steve fell back and landed flat on their backs in the mud. The teachers surged toward the entrance. Then the door snapped shut again, and I threw my body against it. I raised my arms straight out from my sides and shouted, "Wait! Someone's inside!"

There was a cold wetness under my arms. Something terrible was about to happen. Whoever was inside was going to charge out the door and attack us with their fists, their bodies, maybe even with guns. Maybe I could bargain with them. *Go ahead and keep the door closed,* I could say. *Barricade it if you want, keep us out all day if you want, but please make sure no one gets hurt.* Frank and Steve pulled themselves up from the ground and started walking toward me.

"Don't provoke them," I warned.

They took a couple steps back. I held my breath, then dropped to my knees like I'd seen civil rights marchers do on TV. One by one, other teachers and parents followed suit. A few remained standing, frozen in place, looks of alarm and confusion etched into their faces. Nothing happened for what seemed like an eternity. I stood, pulled my shoulders back, and turned to face the door. Time to try to negotiate.

I reached for the handle and turned it. The door opened, and I caught sight of two figures inside. I ducked. I was about ready to fall to the ground and yell to others to do the same, but then I recognized them. They were our school janitors. I had a good relationship with them, although it had been strained since I became acting principal. I reached out my hand to them, hoping we might talk and reason together.

But that was not to be. The two men, their faces white with terror, plunged through the door while pulling on their coats, stuffing their arms in the sleeves. They pushed past me, their hands up in the air, their eyes pleading to be spared. Then they ran, leaving a wide swath between us as they made their escape.

It was a zany sight, a poignant illustration of the delirium and rising fear that had gripped the city. We watched until they were out of sight, laughing. I laughed, too, but I was worried. Things were getting out of control, and that meant anything could happen. Next time we might not be so lucky.

Later that morning, I sat in the principal's office thinking about the strange early-morning turn of events, the terrified looks on the faces of the janitors so unreal it felt like watching a movie.

All of sudden, Frascatore charged through the door. He lunged toward me, his arms slicing the air. I ducked, covered the back of my head with my hands.

"How dare you," he shouted, skidding to a halt at the edge of my desk.

I reached for the phone, my pulse racing.

"You broke in. You fucking broke in." He hurled his upper body across the desk, jutted his clenched jaw within inches of my face, and glowered down at me. He looked like a wild animal, ready to snap.

"No laws were broken," I said in as calm a voice as I could muster.

He straightened to an upright position and sucked in his breath through his teeth. "The union's going to sue your ass off," he said as he pivoted toward the door. Then he turned back, shaking his fist. "You tell that Alexander bitch," he screamed, "she can kiss that big district superintendent job good-bye. We all know why she got that job in the first place."

He turned on his heels and dashed for the door, still shouting in words laced with expletives, most of which were too garbled for me to understand. He bumped into Frank on his way out.

"You all right, hon?"

"I'm shaky, but okay," I said. I went to the window and stood behind him. His body shielded me from the scorn outside, the makeshift signs that proclaimed me a traitor and a criminal, pictures of me behind bars.

"They're in shock," I said. "They didn't expect us to be inside."

Frank took a step closer to the window. "Is that Teresa? What's she doing out there? Over there, at the back of the picket line, I think she's trying to break up a fight."

I crossed my arms over my chest and watched in horror as Teresa grabbed the hands of two children, pulled them from the middle of a crowd of picketers, dragged them to the front entrance and deposited them in the door. With long, angry strides, she went back and threw her body between one of the picketers and the mother of the children. As I listened to the picketers' vile language and watched the ugly scene unfold, a seismic shift took place inside me. Any residual ambivalence I had about the union drained away and was replaced by a combative defiance that infused every fiber of my being. The union had crossed a line. It had proven itself unworthy of its association with the union movement. Something had to be done. The violence had to be stopped.

Hours later, Teresa announced that it was time to call the community together to talk about how to reduce hostilities on the picket line. That night, in our apartment, she convened a meeting of twenty parents and neighborhood leaders, a richness of colors and shades, a melody of accents, the quick turnout a testimony to her influence in the community. They all introduced themselves, and then we talked about the violence breaking out across the city. Broken windows. Burglaries. Spray-painted threats on school buildings. Break-ins and trashing of mobile classrooms. Death threats. The muscles in my stomach clenched as I listened. I was worried about the power of fear to distort, distend, and, in the end, explode.

"We need to reach out to the teachers," said Enrique Velasquez, the pastor of Iglesia Santa Maria. "We need to be positive."

"*Sí, pastor,*" a mother agreed. "Maybe we could make signs that say we love our teachers."

A black woman named Rachel frowned at her. "Shouldn't they say we love our children?"

"The important thing," Reverend Velasquez said, "is to let the teachers know we're not against them."

"It's not about them," a short, heavyset woman said. "It's about our kids. They need to be in school."

"That's right," another woman said, nodding at her pastor. "It's okay to let the teachers know we respect their rights, but let's not forget that our first job is to protect the rights of our *hijos.*"

At that point a woman named Kelly threw her hands up in the air. I leaned forward, curious about what the woman with the impressive Afro and bright yellow and black dashiki had to say.

"Look," she said with an impatient sigh. "I'm out there every day. I hear what they're saying on the line, and I'm telling you, it's not pretty. The teachers care about themselves, no one else. Arguing with them or telling them they should think about your kids isn't going to help. It will make things worse."

"But we need to let them know they're not the enemy," a woman who had introduced herself as Lupita said.

"Except they are," Kelly shot back. "Trust me. They are."

"Only love can counter violence," Reverend Velasquez said. "Forgiveness is the only way."

"Get real," Kelly said with a snort. "I've been doing organizing for East Tremont Housing for a while now, so I know what works and what doesn't." She shot Teresa a conspiratorial look.

"Kelly's right, folks," Teresa chimed in, speaking for the first time. "Our goal is to keep our kids safe, not suck up to the teachers."

In the silence that followed, I held my breath, not wanting the dissent within the group to erupt into useless debate. The mothers who had supported their pastor looked from Kelly and Teresa to him and back again, their faces showing ambivalence, mixed loyalties.

"Here's a compromise," Teresa said. "Some mothers could meet the picketers in the morning with signs that say 'Please, don't target our kids' or something like that. Some of you might prefer to take other actions to protect your children."

That seemed to do it. A torrent of ideas followed.

"How about 'Leave our kids alone'?"

"'Stop the violence.'"

"'Our children are your children. Please keep them safe.'"

"We could form brigades to escort groups of children to school."

"Now we're cooking," said a man from the Federation of Puerto Rican Volunteers on 186th Street.

"Let's get started," Teresa said as she placed heavy paper and black markers on the floor. One by one people responded to her prodding and started to make posters. No wonder the welfare centers held her in such high regard. I could see why most of the mothers who had her as their advocate won their cases.

The woman named Kelly exerted her own influence in the group as she started talking about ways to protect the children. Who was this Kelly, I wondered? And what was she doing on the picket line? She never said she was a teacher, or a parent for that matter, so what was she doing on the picket line every day?

All of a sudden, the light dawned. I slapped my forehead. Of course! She was planted on the picket line as a spy. But by whom? The district superintendent? Teresa? Then it occurred to me how easy it would be for the union to put a spy inside the school. Recruiting enough substitute teachers was already like reaching into the water, grabbing any hand you could find, and pulling it into the boat. Anyone could be caught in the net.

A knock on our apartment door interrupted my suspicious musings. I went to the door and opened it. Three black men stood next to each other, all wearing berets tilted to the side of the head in the same way and black leather jackets, under which were black T-shirts with something in red written on them. The tallest, the one in the middle, spoke first.

"Is this the meeting about P.S. 457?"

"It is," I said. "I'm Sylvia. I live here."

"My name's Derek," he said as he extended his hand to me. His handshake was warm, as was his smile. "And this is Bob. This is George." I shook hands with each of them.

"We're members of the Black Panther Party," the one named Bob said. "We're here to help."

"Please come in." More outside forces at work, I thought, as I stood to the side of the door to make way for them.

They stepped around the women scattered about on the floor making signs and squeezed next to each other on the couch. Teresa perched on the frayed arm of the couch with her hand on Derek's shoulder. I thought about the poster hanging in Teresa's apartment. Derek resembled the man in the picture, a father teaching his kindergarten-age son how to use an AK-47. I had been both thrilled and frightened by the image the first time I saw it.

Kelly smiled at Teresa, then plopped down on the other arm of the couch next to the man named Bob. Why hadn't Teresa ever mentioned Kelly to me before? I wondered. It was clear that they were friends.

"They're going to greet the picketers in the morning with these signs," Kelly explained with a sweep of her hand over the room. "They're worried about the kids getting hurt in this mess."

The three men observed the sign-making with indulgent smiles. Their faces showed no visible judgment or criticism about the futility of the mothers' desire to appeal to the picketers, but their eyes cut to the core of the parents' innocent assumptions.

"We haven't had any vandalism or break-ins like other schools are having," Teresa said. "But things are heating up."

"We can guard the building at night," Derek said.

Teresa clapped her hands together as if this was the first she'd heard of the idea. She looked at me, her eyebrows raised.

"I do worry about the school when I leave every night," I said. "And I dread what I might find when I come back every morning."

And so it was settled. We had a three-part plan. Two or three Black Panther members moved into my office at the end of each day and patrolled the building during the night with their German shepherd guard dog. In the morning they greeted me with smiling reports that there had been no trouble, left a box of donuts for the teachers and volunteers, went down to the cafeteria to prepare breakfast for the students, and then went home to get some sleep. A group of mothers greeted the picketers each morning with their goodwill and homemade signs; the mothers and teachers each claimed a separate space on the sidewalk, and there were no verbal or physical interactions. Parent brigades accompanied groups of children to school for their protection. There were no serious incidents, and the number of children coming to school increased.

While P.S. 457 remained calm most of the time, divisive chaos erupted across other parts of the city. UFT president Albert Shanker was branded a racist and burned in effigy. The union was charged with being Jewish-dominated, and Shanker and some Jewish groups countered with their own charges of anti-Semitism. A UFT pamphlet accused the Ocean Hill—Brownsville schools of preaching violence and black separatism. Another pamphlet said the idea behind community control was beautiful but that the greedy people in the black community had taken it over for the money. Bonnie's fears had come to fruition. Racial tensions were at an all-time high in the city. There were no signs that the strike would end soon.

Still, at our school, we managed to maintain an uneasy yet peaceful truce. Until the day when, outside my office, I found Mentayer's brother, Markus, jumpy and with his eyes darting from side to side. And after that, everything changed.

FOURTEEN

Fall 1968

The day I found Markus shaking with fear outside my office, he disappeared. Six days ago now. Frank and I were the last to see him, when we dropped him off at his uncle's apartment. No one had seen or heard anything about him since. I was beside myself with worry. We all were.

We searched everywhere. Asked everyone we could think of if they'd seen him, if they might have any ideas about where he might have gone. Knocked on every door in his uncle's building, the buildings on both sides, and across the street, but no one had seen or heard anything. Notified the police the day he went missing, then called and stopped by the precinct every day, but they didn't care, even acted evasive. Posted and distributed his picture. Dug for any possible clue. All to no avail.

I kept playing my last conversation with Markus over and over in my head. Whether I was awake or asleep, it haunted me.

What is it, Markus? Did something happen? Maybe we should tell the police?
No, no, not the cops. It's okay, Ms. Sylvia. I'm fine now. We'll talk more later.
Why did I let it go? Why didn't I follow up?
Did something happen, Markus? What is it?
It's okay. I'm fine now. No, no cops.
Why, I kept asking myself, did he get even more scared when I mentioned the police?

"It's not your fault," Frank kept repeating.

But I knew it was. Even when he reminded me that we'd watched Markus go into the building when we brought him home from school the day he went missing. Even when he argued that it wouldn't have made any difference if I'd gone inside with him. Even when he assured me that I'd done my best to listen to him, that I'd tried as hard as I could to find out why he was frightened, that anyone would have believed him, like I had, when he said he was fine. No matter what he said, no matter what anyone said, the image of Markus's fear-filled face was and always would be etched in my mind. His eyes would always tell me that I was responsible for whatever happened to him. It was my fault.

"He was fine when we left him," Frank said.

"You don't know that. How could you know that? He was afraid of something. I should have done more. I should have warned his uncle." *It's okay, Ms. Sylvia. I'm fine now.* I shouldn't have believed him. He wasn't fine. He said he was so I wouldn't call the cops. It was my fault. There was no getting around it.

Frank kept trying. "Markus wouldn't have told his uncle any more than he told you."

"You don't know that."

"The police will find him."

"They're not even looking."

"What you need is a drink."

"Why aren't the police looking? What are they afraid of?"

"A drink will relax you."

"I don't want a drink."

He handed me a glass of bourbon, and I drank it. It tasted foul and gave me a headache, but after downing another one, the conversation stopped playing in my head. And that made it possible for me to attend to Mentayer.

She remained stubborn in her optimism as her glorious mind spun tale after tale that kept her brother safe. He was hiding under a railroad bridge, scrounging for food in garbage cans. Riding the rails. Living the life of a hobo. He hitchhiked to New Jersey. To Connecticut. He stowed away on the Staten Island Ferry. He was hiding in a storage room at the Museum of Modern Art, behind the door he'd opened by mistake when we were there last summer. He slept in the stacks of the downtown library; no one would think to look for him there. Every day she created a new scenario that showed how smart he was. Smarter than her by a long shot. He knew how to survive. He was having an adventure, and when he decided to come home, she was going to kill him.

"You told me never to leave school without him," she said. "I should have made him come with me."

"It isn't your fault," I said. "He said he'd wait for me, and he did."

"The police think he ran away." Frank said.

"He did," Mentayer said, crossing her arms over her chest and jutting out her chin. "Cuz that boy never did think right. If something was bothering him, he could have told me."

"He tried to tell me," I said.

"Neither of you is to blame," Frank said. He paused, then added, "You heard what the police said. Sometimes kids go to a friend's house after school and stay too long, and then they're afraid to go home and face the music."

I stared at him. "You can't believe that. The police are hiding something."

"Good thing Grandma doesn't know," Mentayer said. "It would kill her for sure. And that's what I'm going to do to Markus when we find him. He'll never do this again. Not when I finish with him."

And so it went. As time crept by with no sign of her brother, the number of Mentayer's creative explanations diminished, but her belief that he was okay intensified. So did her anger.

"That boy is gonna be so sorry" was the first thing she said every morning, "I can't wait to get my hands on him" the last thing she said each night.

I wanted, more than anything, to believe, like Mentayer, that Markus was okay. But I couldn't shake the withering dread that followed me around every day and invaded each sleepless night. *What is it, Markus? Did something happen? What has you so frightened?* Markus would not have run away. Someone hurt him. *No, no, not the cops.* Did the cops hurt him? Is that why he was so afraid of them? *You sure you're okay? Want me to walk you in?*

I'm fine. Thank you.

Whatever happened was my fault. Someone hurt Markus because I reopened the school. It was an act of revenge. A warning for me to stop. Or maybe it was a random act related to the violence that was spreading across the city. Zealots were prowling the schools at night. Breaking windows. Defecating at entrances. Carving obscenities into buildings and on sidewalks. Random and unpredictable violence was firing frightening and unexpected neurons in the brains of even some of the city's most upstanding citizens. Maybe it was a cop. Maybe someone went crazy.

The hang-up calls started again, then death threats. It got so bad that we started leaving the phone off the hook at night again. But that meant if someone found Markus, we wouldn't get the call. And then the rumors started. I had kidnapped a boy. A child was missing because I kept the school open. The rumors and lies confirmed for me that whatever happened to Markus was my fault. His disappearance had something to do with me. Doomsday dreams at night bolted me upright in bed, screaming out for Markus. Frank would hold me and tell me it wasn't my fault. He'd bring me a glass of bourbon so I could sleep, or at least get a few hours of rest. One night he brought me a glass before we went to bed, saying, "Here, hon, this will help you get to sleep," and I fell asleep and slept through the night.

After that I started having a drink every night before going to bed. After a while, it took two or three drinks to do the trick. I developed a taste for bourbon. I started to look forward to the evening ritual of drinking with Frank.

With my head pounding, each morning I faced the onslaught of incendiary language that had invaded the picket line. *Kidnapper. Child molester. Lock her up.* Fear-filled parents started keeping their children at home. The Black Panthers started ushering students in and out of the building. Additional parent brigades were organized to escort children to and from school. Yet the number of students coming to school dwindled a bit more with each news report about another incident, with each day that passed with no word about Markus.

I became hyper-attentive at school. I was in a constant state of anxiety, afraid there could be a flare-up at any moment. I bit my nails down to the quick. Sometimes they bled. And then one day I stepped into my office and heard a crunching sound underfoot. Something sharp bit into the bottom of my shoe and I screamed.

Shards of glass covered the floor and the top of my desk. There was a jagged hole in the window, its audacity made all the bolder by the sun's rays. The villain, a rock the size of a tennis ball, lay on the floor. A piece of paper was wrapped around it, fastened with masking tape. I went to the window and, hiding from view, peeked out to see who'd thrown it. But the sidewalk was empty. I pressed my back against the wall. Where was everyone? Had all the picketers run away after someone threw the rock? Then I remembered. There was a union meeting today. All the striking teachers were downtown. Someone must have taken advantage of the picketers' absence. Some young hooligan broke the window for the hell of it. Things like that were happening all over the city.

I bent down and picked up the rock. I pulled the tape off, careful to leave the paper intact, not an easy task with my fingers shaking like they were. I placed the rock on my desk and unfolded the piece of paper. A note was written in large, childlike print. I thought it must be the action of some disgruntled juvenile delinquent. But then I read the message.

We know where you live and who lives with you.

I felt a pain as sharp as a six-inch spike in my stomach. I doubled over. The note dropped from my hand onto the floor. This was not some infantile harassment. This was a serious threat. They were going after Mentayer now. First Markus, and now his sister. I could no longer keep the school open. I had to quit. I had no choice. It was over. Right then and there, in the middle of the day, I walked out of the principal's office and went home.

I was on my third drink when Bonnie called. "I heard what happened, Sylvia." Her voice was so soft it was almost inaudible. "You need to stop now. Before anyone else gets hurt."

I hung up on her. I dropped my head down into my hands. *I know, I know, I know.* All of a sudden, I felt a hand on my shoulder, and I looked up to see Teresa.

"How'd you get in here?" I asked.

"You didn't lock the door." She sat down next to me at the kitchen table.

"I can't do this anymore," I said.

"Mentayer is safe, Sylvia." Teresa's voice was firm, filled with confidence. "She will be okay. We'll make sure she is."

I stared at her and shook my head. "It's too risky."

She stood up and took the drink out of my hand. She walked over to the sink and poured it down the drain. Then she pulled her chair close to mine, sat down, and took my hand. "We'll take care of Mentayer. You take care of the other students." She paused and wrapped her hands around both of mine. "It's for the students' sake, Sylvia, but it's for your sake, too. If you quit, you lose hope. And if you lose hope... " She glanced, with a tip of her head, at the bottle of bourbon on the table. "I have to get to a meeting right now, but I'll come back later. Get some rest now, okay?" Then she left, taking the bottle with her.

Could she be right? Could we protect Mentayer and keep the school open? I laid my head down on the table and fell asleep with the sound of Teresa's mellow voice slipping through my fears like scissors through silk.

When I woke up, Frank was home. When I told him about the rock, the attached message, Bonnie's warning, and Teresa's reassurance, he looked both angry and afraid. He didn't say anything for a long time. Then he leaned forward with his arms stretched out on the table, his fingers not quite touching me.

"So how does Teresa think they can keep Mentayer safe," he said. He snorted. "Does that mean the Black Panthers will guard her twenty-four hours a day? How will they do that? Move in with us? No, Sylvia, this is crazy. We should give the note to the police."

I rolled my eyes. "Are you crazy, Frank? Do you think they'll provide protection? No, we have to hide her ourselves."

"Whoever wrote that note knows where we live. All anyone has to do is follow her home from school to find out where she is."

"Maybe we should move."

It was his turn to roll his eyes.

And so it went, late into the night, back and forth. I suggested ways to keep Mentayer safe; he told me why they wouldn't work. I said Mentayer could stay for a while with old Mrs. Nelson, a member of the church who lived in Westchester; he said it would be too much of a burden for someone her age. I said Mentayer could stay with different members of the congregation, move around every few days, both to avoid detection and so it wouldn't be a burden on any one person; he said that was asking too much of people, and it would be too hard on Mentayer. I said she could move upstairs with Teresa and Allie; he said that would be too obvious. One by one he poked holes in all my ideas. They were too complicated. They wouldn't be fair to Mentayer. They would put others at risk. They didn't feel right.

"I've got it," I said with a snap of my finger. "It's so obvious I don't know why I didn't think of it before. The parsonage! She can move in with the Winstons. We'll keep her out of school so no one can follow her. I'll prepare lesson plans, and the Winston boys can teach her at home. They'd love it. You know they adore her. And she worships them. It will be fun for everyone. They'll make it an adventure. It's perfect. And no one will ever suspect that she's right across the street."

Frank crossed his arms. "I won't ask the Winstons to do it," he said. "She can stay with us. You can teach her here. Let someone else run the school."

"There isn't anyone else."

"Then let the school close. You've done enough."

Teresa's words rang in my ears. *If you lose hope, Sylvia, then...*

I finished her sentence in my head: *Without hope, I will die.* Without hope, life would have no meaning.

"Bonnie's right, Sylvia," Frank said. "You need to quit before anyone else gets hurt."

"I'll ask Pastor Paul and Linnea myself," I said. "First thing tomorrow morning."

That was it. He opened his mouth to talk me out of it, and I raised both hands in the air to stop him. End of discussion. We went to bed in silence and lay each on our side, facing opposite walls, both of us exhausted, neither of us able to fall asleep. A few minutes later, my plan went up in smoke.

The sirens sounded far away at first. It was a familiar sound in the city. But then they started getting closer, louder, became as deafening as if they were on top of us. The sirens stopped, faded away. Red lights flashed across our ceiling. We jumped out of bed and stumbled over to the window. Watched the furious flames reaching skyward. Heard the firemen shouting, water shooting through hoses. Felt the smoke burning our noses and throats. It was the church. It was on fire. Everything had changed.

FIFTEEN

April 2006

It's one of those perfect New York spring days, the air cool and windless. A few clouds smear the blue sky and intermittently cover the sun. Tissue-paper pink blossoms litter the sidewalk from blooming fruit trees.

J. B. and I arrive at the Harlem diner in time to grab the last available patio table. I duck inside the restaurant to see if Mentayer's there, then come back outside and sit down at our table. I look for her among the white, youthful faces, women sporting colorful scarves at their necks, here and there a few black folks who look like they might still live in this quickly gentrifying neighborhood. A waitress, dark-skinned and middle-aged, hands us each a menu. Without asking, she pours coffee in the white mugs on our table as if she's been doing it all her life, and then leaves.

"Popular place," J. B. says with a wave of his hand.

The sun warms my skin, and the long-ago memory of taking Mentayer here fills my soul. "Close to Columbia," I say.

"College for the indulged and fussed over," J. B. jokes. He sounds relaxed, but he looks wary.

"Mentayer got her doctorate there," I say. "I'm sure *she* was not indulged or fussed over."

He starts to say something, and then seems to change his mind. After a brief pause, he tries again. "I'm not knocking Columbia. Some of the world's best journalists went there. Daniel Leacham, for one. Speaking of whom, I tried reaching him earlier to feel him out about maybe getting together later today with Mentayer. If she's interested, that is." He pulls out his smartphone and tries again. "Hmm. Still no answer." He slips it back in his pocket, then glances at his watch. "I don't think Mentayer's coming," he says.

So that's what he's worried about. It makes sense, after what happened at her apartment, that he might be wary of what Mentayer thinks of him. He doesn't know if she'll talk to him at all.

"It's not like her to be late like this, but she'll be here," I say. "I still don't know what she was so angry about. And last night, when she called, she was so upset about her brother being identified that I didn't want to ask."

"She's afraid I'm going to ask her about CSCH."

"See, I don't get that. J. B. Mentayer doesn't know anything about CSCH. I mean, other than the new school they're building."

"I'm sure she knows quite a bit more than that." He pauses. "Since she works there," he adds, setting his coffee mug down on the red and white checkered tablecloth.

"What? Where did you get that idea?"

"Her name is on CSCH's staff roster. She's a public relations manager."

I fall back in the plastic chair and stare at him. "And you waited until now to tell me?"

"Don't look at me that way, Sylvia. I didn't go looking for the information."

"No wonder Mentayer got so angry," I say with a shake of my head. "She must have assumed that we knew she worked at CSCH. And no wonder she thought you were using her brother as an excuse to get some inside information out of her. And why she attacked me when you told her I didn't want CSCH in Monrow City. It all makes sense now." I stop to catch my breath. "It makes sense why you've had that tense look on your face all morning, too, by the way."

He leans closer, his tone conspiratorial. "I didn't want to say this, Sylvia, because I know how you feel about Mentayer. But I suspect she knows something about CSCH. I think that's why she was so upset to hear about my work."

"You can't know that, J. B. She was upset because she thought you were using her position in a dishonest way to elicit information. That's why she called you unethical."

"And despicable. Remember?" He looks sad.

He starts to say more, but then falls silent and stares, spellbound, at Mentayer, who is standing on the sidewalk in front of the restaurant. She's a vision of loveliness in an understated but expensive black sheath, short sleeves and short skirt next to brown arms and brown legs, a touch of white at the neck. Chiffon, flowing. An ensemble not fancy but as striking as if it were. She sees us and blinks. I watch J. B. watch her walk toward us with long, determined strides.

"Glad you came," he says with a big smile.

She doesn't return his smile. Instead, she tips her head to one side, then another, in a gesture that says, *What made you think I wouldn't?* She sits down, pulls her white scarf to the side, and tugs at the hem of her skirt.

"I didn't know you worked at CSCH," I say. "Honest." She turns to me, her appraising eyes studying my face. "J. B. told me a few minutes ago," I say. "It's the truth."

Her eyes darken in a flash, and she turns toward J. B. He stumbles over his words as he explains to her that he came across her name in CSCH documents when he was investigating some fraud allegations that had been made against the corporation. When he takes a breath, he seems to regain his composure. "Yes, I'm investigating some fraud charges, Mentayer. None of them are formal or legal at this point, but you should know I plan to follow up on them. Sylvia asked me to help you find out what happened to your brother, but if my other work is a problem for you, then... "

"What allegations?" Mentayer asks.

"Things like financial irregularities, tax improprieties, misrepresentation of student success outcomes, possible altering of standardized test scores." J. B. locks his eyes on Mentayer and then continues. "I *am* after information about your employer," he says, "but not from you. I don't know what, if anything, you know, and I will not ask you to tell me anything. You have my word."

Mentayer nods but says nothing, which I find strange. I can't tell if she's satisfied with what J. B. said and now thinks she can trust him or if she's being dismissive. But before I can ask, she turns and looks me straight in the eye.

"I am committed to CSCH's vision, Sylvia. I believe in charter schools. That's why I promote them. I lost all faith in the public school system a long time ago. I'm sorry that you, of all people, don't seem to know that charter schools are better than public schools for poor kids. Black kids. Kids I thought you cared about."

"I do care," I say, "but I don't think charter schools are the answer when someone's making a profit on the backs of the poorest kids. But, Mentayer, all I care about right now is getting justice for Markus. That's why I came to New York. It's true that J. B. came to learn more about CSCH for his series, but he's willing to help us, too."

Several seconds of silence pass. Then Mentayer nods at me. I nod back. I don't know if we'll be able to navigate the complications. The number of connections between our investigation about what happened to Markus and the CSCH Corporation seem to be growing by the day: the building site where Markus's body was found, Daniel Leacham's intense and angry interest in CSCH, CSCH investor Clarke Craine's friendship with Frascatore, Craine's influence with the NYPD, Mentayer's job as one of CSCH's public relations managers... It seems like a field of land mines to me, but for J. B. it probably seems like a gold mine of leads.

"I'm sorry about your brother," he says to Mentayer.

She looks down at her hands resting on the table. "Sylvia says you're the best," she says.

I let out an audible sigh of relief. "So let's get started," I say. "I have a million questions in my head."

"The first one," Mentayer says, "is how can we make sure none of that stuff about Markus being involved with drugs and gangs is made public. Is there some way to keep Markus's name out of the paper for now? J. B., do you have any contacts in the NYPD? Maybe you can find out if they're going to do a press release now that the body's been identified? How about media contacts? Can you find out if anyone's planning to do a follow-up story? Do you know anyone else who can help us?"

"Daniel Leacham," J. B. says. "He's the reporter who first broke the story when your brother's body was discovered. I've been trying to reach him. Maybe he can answer some questions for us. He seems interested in CSCH and, since you work there, I think we can convince him to help us. I've left a couple messages for him, but let me try again. I'll see if he can meet with us today."

J. B. reaches into his pocket for his smartphone. Mentayer puts her hand on his to stop him. There's an expression of horror on her face.

"What is it? What's wrong? Do you know Leacham?"

"Daniel Leacham is dead," she says. "I heard it on the news on the way over here. He killed himself."

SIXTEEN

April 2006

Mother African Methodist Episcopal Zion Church, the oldest black church in New York State, is popular on the tourist circuit for sheltering runaway slave Frederick Douglass. The moment J. B. and I walk through its scarlet red doors to attend Daniel Leacham's funeral, the church captures my soul.

Viewed from our seats in the front row of the balcony, Mother Zion's sanctuary is as much magic as it is beauty. Rows of dark wood pews, their backs straight and shining with polish, are imbued with the spirits of people like Harriet Tubman, Sojourner Truth, the Reverend Martin Luther King Jr., and labor leader A. Philip Randolph, who all once worshipped in this place. Nine carved chairs, ornate and proud, stand behind the pulpit, the tallest one in the middle now occupied by the current pastor, Reverend Gregory Robeson Smith, whose uncle, all-American athlete and civil rights activist Paul Robeson, once preached and sang here.

The souls of past dignitaries gather now alongside the notables of today. Hundreds of heads below, some hat-covered, hair in shades of gray, a range of other colors and textures, faces forward, silent, stiff, and attentive, waiting. Eyes absorb the gold cross, the Bible between two lit candles, the polished coffin that cradles the body of Daniel Leacham. The sweet floral scent of death—emanating from the elegant arrangements and wreaths of white roses, lilies, snapdragons, mums, and carnations—competes with the smells of lemon furniture polish and the heavy cologne of the mourners.

A stream of light from the multipaneled stained glass window behind us casts a soft glow over the ruby red carpet on which Mrs. Leacham now walks. Dressed in black, a veil covering her face, she makes her way to the front of the sanctuary, hand in hand with two children, a boy about ten and a girl younger by a few years. There's a noble air to her stunned grief. She holds her head high, a testimony to what I imagine to be her silent words: *No, my husband did not kill himself. He would not do that to his family.* She tightens her grip on her children. *His* children. The children he would never have left by choice. She sits in the front pew with an arm around each of them, pulls them close. They lay their heads on her breast and weep. The red-robed choir in the balcony behind the pulpit sings with voices sweet, soft, respectful.

J. B. leans toward me and whispers in my ear. "I have to talk to his wife. She knows he didn't commit suicide."

Pastor Smith rises, steps up to the pulpit, arms outstretched under his black robe like an eagle taking flight. As he begins to pray, his voice recedes into the background. The humming of the choir stops. There's no coughing or sniffling, no shuffling of feet. In the strange silence of my mind, I'm back in the Harlem diner of several days ago.

"There is no way," J. B. said, right after Mentayer broke the news of Leacham's death to us, "no way that man killed himself."

"And, if he was an alcoholic," I add, "and I'm not saying he was, but if he was, he wouldn't get drunk on his ass first and then inject himself with heroin. It doesn't work that way."

"Besides, Leacham was angry," J. B. said. "People who are angry don't kill themselves."

"They do if they want to get revenge," I said, "but then he would leave a note. If his death were an expression of anger, he'd want people to know."

"And didn't he tell us he was working on something else now," J. B. said, "that he was interested in something new? Does that sound like someone about to do himself in?"

Mentayer looked up at the sky and let out a long sigh. "Why is it so hard for you to believe he killed himself? Maybe he got tired. People do sometimes, you know. They get tired."

"Not Leacham," J. B. said with a shake of his head. "He had too much going for him. Mark my words, someone wanted him dead."

A shadow of irritation crossed Mentayer's face. "No one knows what's going on inside anyone else's head. No one knows what's happening in other people's personal lives."

"Someone killed him," J. B. said, with a sharpness that was not to be argued with. "It was made to look like a suicide. He was investigating something. He knew something."

A cloud of tension came over Mentayer's eyes. "What are you trying to do, scare me now?" she said.

I didn't add to her fear by telling her that Daniel Leacham had been investigating her employer. Something about CSCH had made him angry. Did it have to do with fraud? Was it something about Frascatore? And why had he suggested that J. B. talk to Clarke Craine first? It seemed to me that Leacham knew something that he hadn't told us.

Pastor Smith's deep, thunderous voice startles me out of my reflections and brings me back to Mother Zion church.

"When I was a boy," he says in a booming voice from the sanctuary below, "I spent countless Sundays in the front row of this church listening to my grandfather, the Reverend Benjamin Robeson, preach. I grew up here. This is home." He pauses. He stretches out his arms, palms open in the direction of the body in the casket. "When Daniel Leacham was a boy, he sat in this sanctuary every Sunday. This was his home, too. I was older than Daniel, off to college and seminary by the time he was coming up, so I didn't know him back then. But over the years, I've had several opportunities to meet with Mr. Leacham. We are proud to call him one of our own. And today we gather here to honor him, to thank him, to say good-bye."

Pastor Smith turns to walk back to the tallest chair. His steps are heavy. The choir sings, their voices soaring upward, echoing downward, bringing sniffles, handkerchiefs from pockets. When the music stops, the man who had been sitting in the chair next to the pastor steps up to the pulpit. His thick white hair and white stubble form a halo around his walnut-brown face.

"My name is Lewis Blair," he says. "I'm the founder and director of the Center for Boys in the Bronx. Daniel Leacham was my friend. I knew him well." He pauses, tugs at the red bow tie at his neck, the one touch of formality to his otherwise casual attire: a brown sport coat, roomy beige trousers, and thick-soled white sneakers.

"When I was coming up, I went to school in Ocean Hill—Brownsville. In my twenties I became active with the Black Panther Party. Some of you are old enough to remember that time, all that turmoil over community control of our schools that resulted in the longest teachers' strike in the history of our city. I got to know some of the kids back then, and that influenced me to start my program for at-risk kids in 1970."

I move to the edge of the seat and lean on the railing. Lewis Blair and I were in the Bronx at the same time? Was it possible that he knew Markus and Dion Brown, or at least heard about what happened to them? Did he know about Frascatore? I squeeze J. B.'s upper arm and whisper, "Another lead." He nods and whispers back that he'll try to catch Mr. Blair after the service and make arrangements to meet with him.

"When he was ten"—Lewis Blair's voice resonates through the sanctuary—"Daniel Leacham started coming to the Center for Boys. Everyone called him Leech back then. He was a scared little thing at first, afraid of his own shadow. It took a while for us to turn him around. But he found his courage, and God bless him, he turned into one of the most persistent boys I've ever known. I have not been at all surprised by his many successes, as a prize-winning journalist, a good husband and loving father, and above all, as one of the most decent human beings that ever lived."

He pauses, wipes a tear from his cheek.

"Daniel Leacham loved life," Lewis Blair says, his voice now raised in both volume and triumph. "He became one of the Center's most generous supporters, and for that we will be forever grateful. He wanted to give back, and he did so with a generosity of spirit that was nothing short of rapturous."

Silence descends on the sanctuary. Then Mr. Blair takes a deep breath and focuses his eyes on Mrs. Leacham in the front row. "Now, folks, I know many of you are asking, if Daniel loved life so much, then why is he gone? I must admit that question troubles me, too. I suspect something was consuming Daniel Leacham, something that drove him to do what he did." He pauses. "And what he didn't do."

He tugs on his bow tie. I glance at J. B. from the corner of my eye. We both raise our eyebrows.

"Our boys at the Center often ask why." Lewis Blair says. "About lots of things. Why do I have to go to school? Why does my dad drink so much when we don't even have enough money for food? Why, why, why? Sometimes I have an answer, but sometimes all I can tell them is that I don't know why. Well, folks, maybe this is one of those times. Why did Daniel Leacham leave us so soon? We don't know. Not yet. But the question demands an answer."

His eyes roam over the sanctuary and up to the balcony. It's like he's making a promise to Mother Zion to find that answer.

"But while we may never understand why he's gone," he says with a sigh, "we do know why we'll miss him. And we do know why the world will forever be diminished by his absence. That we do know."

He chokes up, looks down at the coffin.

"And now, it is with a heavy spirit that we must say good-bye to you, dear friend. Thank you for making the world a better place. Your spirit lives on in other boys who will carry on the work. As it does in all of us."

With footsteps heavy with grief, he returns to sit in the chair next to Pastor Smith. J. B. and I nod to each other, a signal that we agree. No words are necessary. Lewis Blair doesn't think that Daniel Leacham committed suicide either.

SEVENTEEN

Winter 1968

The night of the church fire, the four Winstons huddled in front of the parsonage, arms around each other. They stared at the flames with their eyes watering and covered their noses and mouths with tissues and pajama sleeves.

I knew right away it was arson. I didn't have to wait for it to be made official. I knew who did it, too. I told the police about the rock thrown through my office window that day and showed them the note—*We know where you live and we know who lives with you.* I told them I was sure Frascatore had a hand in it. But all they did was shrug. Five hundred fires a month in the Bronx, they said, nothing different about this one. A sloppy job, the fire department captain said, a fire set by kids for kicks, happens all the time.

The fire did more than damage the church. Our idea of hiding Mentayer in the parsonage drained down the gutter along with the water from the hydrant. The fire extinguished our hope that we could keep the school open and protect her at the same time. It also propelled everything that happened next. Mentayer's Uncle Bert called the next day to say that Grandma's condition had deteriorated, and we told him about the threatening note and the church fire. After that, decisions were made in rapid succession, decisions that would shape Mentayer's future in ways no one could have anticipated.

"We can't take any more chances," her Uncle Bert said in a panic. "Not after Markus. We have to get Mentayer out of the city. I'm calling child welfare."

"There has to be some other way," I said.

"There isn't."

"But... "

He cut me off. "It's what her Grandma would want... if she could tell us what she wanted."

What could I say? Grandma was his mother. He knew her wishes and I didn't. He was Mentayer's family and I wasn't. It was their decision, not mine. And I had nothing better to offer.

Everything happened with astonishing, and unstoppable, speed. Uncle Bert knew someone in the Bureau of Child Welfare, so within hours a social worker named Betty Levy called. Mentayer was to be placed on a temporary basis in a foster home certified as a safe house in upstate New York. The worker would drive her there.

Early the next morning, an agonizing love caught in my throat as I watched Mentayer asleep on the couch, curled into herself with her hand tucked under her cheek. When I tried to walk over to her, I couldn't move. My feet were stuck in a grief as impervious as concrete.

"Ms. Sylvia." She jumped up, smiling, arms open for her morning hug.

I forced my feet to move, to take me to her. "Good morning, sweetie." I wrapped my arms around her like I'd done every morning since she'd come to stay with us. But this time I held on tighter, longer, tried to hide the tears filling my eyes.

"I'll be okay, Ms. Sylvia. I won't be gone long."

"I still get to miss you," I said. I planted a kiss on her forehead and tried to smile.

"Me, too." Mentayer giggled.

"Up and at it, then," I said with forced enthusiasm. "Miss Betty will be here before we know it."

I ached to speak but my mouth wouldn't form the words. *Everything is going to be okay. Grandma will get better and she'll be home soon. Markus is okay and we're going to find him. The foster parents are nice. They have a daughter your age. You're going on a fun adventure.*

Mentayer gobbled up her cereal with slices of banana on top and chattered away like she was going on another field trip.

"Do you think they have a dog or a cat?"

"You can ask Miss Betty."

"If they have a puppy, maybe he'll sleep with me. Do you think I'll have my own room?"

"So many things to find out."

"I bet they'll have horses."

"I kinda doubt that."

"But wouldn't it be great if they did and I could go riding?"

"You'll get to go to a new school, you know."

Mentayer picked up her cereal bowl and slurped down the remaining milk. "I know," she said as she wiped her mouth with her sleeve.

"Use your napkin, sweetie."

"And when the strike ends, I'll be back here in regular school."

"Right. It won't be long now."

"And we'll write every day. Both of us, right? Promise?"

"I'll write every day, sweetie. I promise."

A knock on the door set things in motion, and after that everything was a blur. Mentayer pushing back her chair and skipping down the hall; sounds of the door opening, pleasant voices, indistinguishable words; Frank coming out of the bathroom, drying his hands on a towel, shaking hands with a nondescript woman in a gray raincoat that matched her hair; my lips stretching out in a smile that wasn't my own.

The child welfare worker, what was her name again? Betty something. Oh yes, Levy. Betty Levy. *Nice to meet you, Betty Levy.* Words tumbling from my mouth in a voice that wasn't mine. Frank leaning down and picking up the suitcase packed with Mentayer's clothes, enough for a week. That would be enough. Mentayer's arms around my waist. *Good-bye, Ms. Sylvia. See you soon. You bet, sweetie. Have a good time. I'll miss you. You, too. Take good care of her now. Of course.* The door closing. Sounds moving away. Mentayer chattering, jumping from step to step going down, mumbling sounds getting more distant. Then silence, the look of grief on Frank's face stripping the skin from my body.

The wound was made fresh every morning when the alarm went off. My first thought, to wake Mentayer, was followed by an ache where a hole had been left in me. Before getting out of bed, I said a prayer for Mentayer and Markus. *Please let them be okay. Please bring them back.* Next I took a deep breath in and blew it out to release my grief and anxiety. Then I vacuumed up all the responsibility inside me and got up, got dressed, and went to school. More and more often, I brought a hangover with me.

Day after day, the union defied the new Taylor Law that prohibited teachers from striking. Day after day, a loyal cadre of substitute teachers and parent volunteers kept P.S. 457 open. As the weeks dragged on, more and more parents sent their kids back to school. Dr. Alexander struggled to find enough teachers to meet the growing demand; some days she succeeded, some days she didn't. I had no more nails left to bite. I chewed the skin around them until they were bloody. Frank begged me to quit by trying to make me aware of all the flaws in my thinking and actions. "Your quest to perfect the world is futile," he'd say. "It's time to quit." What he didn't understand was that my existence depended on *not* quitting.

After two and a half months of struggle, everyone was tired—the picketers, the substitute teachers, the parents, even the children. It seemed that no one would ever give up the fight. We were all going to keep pushing our disparate boulders up the hill even if they rolled back down and destroyed us. But then, all of a sudden, we stopped. The strike ended on November 17, 1968, twelve days after Richard Nixon was elected president of the United States. The community control experiment was over: Ocean Hill—Brownsville lost direct control over its schools, and other districts never gained control over theirs. A million New York City children had been denied an education for almost one-third of the school year.

On my first day back in the classroom, Miss Huskings summoned me to her office.

"Please sit down," she said. I sat, resigned to the inevitable. I was about to be fired.

"I want to thank you, Mrs. Waters."

I let out the breath I'd been holding in and stared at her.

"Except for the broken window that you had replaced, P.S. 457 wasn't damaged or vandalized during the strike," she said. "I'm grateful to you for that. I know you were responsible."

My mouth fell open. I hadn't seen that one coming, wouldn't have guessed it in a million years. I laughed. "The Black Panthers get the credit for that," I said. "They stayed in your office every night and guarded the building."

The look of shock on Miss Huskings's face was gratifying, but my triumph was short-lived. It ended as soon as I walked into the teachers' lounge. Several teachers were huddled together in deep conversation, which stopped when they saw me. Some of them jumped up and left the room. When I sat down to eat, the ones sitting near me picked up their lunches and moved to the other end of the table, as far away from me as they could get. Even Bonnie wouldn't look at me. I pretended not to notice.

My isolation at school was now complete, but I was okay as long as I could anticipate Mentayer's imminent return. I called her uncle to make arrangements for her to come back to stay with Frank and me now that the strike was over.

"Child welfare is recommending that she stay in the foster home for the rest of the school year," he said. "She's doing well there. She's happy."

I held back my tears. "I guess that explains why she hasn't answered any of my letters," I said.

"You know how kids are," he said with a laugh. "They live in the moment."

"If Mentayer's having a good time," I said, "then of course she should finish fourth grade there." I made my voice sound good-natured, but inside I was crying.

Frank withdrew into himself at the news. We didn't talk about it. I put on a happy face at school and put one foot in front of the other. My third-graders needed me to focus my passion and energy on them. But my classroom was haunted by Markus's absence, his empty desk a daily reminder of his mysterious disappearance. I tried to forge on, but it became more and more difficult for me to act enthusiastic with my students.

What made things worse was that Frascatore was still teaching in the classroom across the hall. I saw the guilt in his eyes, the puffy black circles under them, his face pasty and wasted. He was disheveled and his clothes hung loose on his diminishing frame. I knew his conscience was eating him alive. He knew what happened to Markus. I became convinced he was responsible. Finally, I contacted the police to demand an investigation, and they sent someone to talk with me in Miss Huskings's office. An hour before the scheduled meeting, I walked to the bar where Frank and I had started going for drinks after school. I was too nervous to eat so I fortified myself with several glasses of white zinfandel wine and a handful of peanuts.

"Are you old enough to do this?" I joked to the young, still wet-behind-the-ears cop waiting in Miss Huskings's office for me. He screwed up his face like he was tired of comments about his youthful appearance and then ran his hand through his short butch haircut like a teenager.

"I'm here to take your statement, Mrs. Waters," he said with a huff. He placed a pad of paper on his lap. In his left hand was a pen. He pointed it at me with a stern look on his face.

"Markus LeMeur," I said, "has been missing since last fall. As I'm sure you know. And so far, no one has questioned Mr. Anthony Frascatore about his disappearance. Now, you see, that's a problem because he is without a doubt the prime subject. I mean, suspect. As I'm sure you also know, Mr. Anthony Frascatore was suspended last year pending an investigation into the death of a student named Dion Brown."

The young cop put his pen down and studied me.

"Mrs. Waters," the principal said, "you know that Mr. Frascatore was cleared in that case."

"I'm here to take your statement about a boy named Markus LeMeur," the cop said.

I hit my thighs with my hands. "Do you have a name, Mr. Little Boy?"

"Mrs. Waters," Miss Huskings said, "if you can't be respectful, I will terminate this interview. It seems you might be a bit under the influence? I thought your concern was about Markus, not Dion."

"Wrong," I said. "Mr. Frascatore gave Dion a concussion. I saw him do it. And the medical examination, the medical examiner, his report says Dion died from a concussion. I gave my statement then. You can read it for yourself."

"One more time, Mrs. Waters," the principal chided. "This gentleman is here to take your statement about Markus LeMeur, not Dion Brown." She turned to the young cop with an apologetic look.

The cop nodded his gratitude to Miss Huskings. I still didn't know his name. "So, tell me, Mrs. Waters," he said, "what do you think happened to Markus LeMeur, and why do you think Mr. Frascatore is responsible for whatever you think happened to him?"

"I don't know what happened to Markus," I said. "But I know it's your job to find out. And one way to find out is to ask people questions, right? So why haven't you asked Mr. Frascatore any questions? He should be brought in for questioning, don't you think? He abuses students. Everyone here knows it. You can ask anyone here in the school. They'll tell you. I've seen him do it with my own eyes. There were others besides Dion Brown. I know what he's capable of."

I started crying and swiped away my angry tears. Miss Huskings shot me a warning look, not at all sympathetic. It felt like I'd been punched in the stomach.

"What if Markus is still alive?" I said. "What if Mr. Frascatore knows where he is? What if Markus is dead and Mr. Frascatore killed him? What if Mr. Frascatore knows how he died? Why isn't anyone doing anything? Do the police have something to hide? Markus was afraid of you. Why? Why?" I covered my face and sobbed into my hands. No one would listen to me. I started shaking. Was I going crazy? Did I even exist?

"Mrs. Waters," the principal said, shaking her head. "I think it's time for you to go home and sober up."

The nameless cop put his pen down and closed his notebook. He stared at me like I was a madwoman. I stumbled out of the office, ran home, and drank until I passed out.

That was the end of it. Nothing more was done. There was no investigation. I saw Miss Huskings one more time at the end of the school year when she called me into her office to tell me that my services would no longer be needed at P.S. 457 when school resumed in the fall. She said she was sorry.

Then came the final blow. Mentayer's Uncle Bert called. "I have bad news," he said. "Grandma has passed. The foster parents will be adopting Mentayer."

I fell to the floor with the phone still in my hand. Mentayer wouldn't be coming back. Ever. Neither would Markus. The price for keeping the school open had been too high. Markus was dead. I'd lost Mentayer, and her life had been forever changed. Frank and I, unable to talk about our grief, were further apart than ever. Community control was defeated. Unity among teachers was destroyed. Frascatore was still teaching. So what had it all been about?

Despair plunged deep into the pit of my stomach, sickening as a sudden drop in turbulence on an airplane. I'd come to the Bronx filled with hope. It had given me an expression to my passion and a purpose more fulfilling than anything in my life before or since. And, in the end, it had gutted me.

"We've done our part here," Frank said. "It's time to move on."

He'd decided that maybe the ministry wasn't for him after all and that he wanted to go back to the Midwest. Our next adventure, as he called it, would be to live in the country, in a cabin on a lake, where we might find like-minded people to live with us, like a commune. We'd grow our own food, heat with wood, make candles, and macramé curtains. We'd get part-time jobs, make enough money to get by, me as a substitute teacher, him as a manual laborer. We'd live off the grid and resist the Vietnam War by refusing to pay federal income tax.

It never occurred to me to venture out on my own or to remain in the Bronx without Frank. Our relationship was in shambles but we were still bound up with each other like tangled hair, and I was in too much pain to try unraveling the knots. And the truth was, there was nothing left for me in New York.

The one thing that kept me from going under was writing to Mentayer. If she ever needed me, I wanted her to know I would be there for her. If her teenage years were hard, she could call me instead of running away or getting in trouble. If she needed a reference letter as an adult, a shoulder to cry on, if she needed anything, I would make sure she knew where I was and that I'd always be there for her.

When we packed up our apartment, I sent her a box filled with some of her favorite things: the plush orange and lime-green pillow on our couch, the blue and white striped throw blanket crocheted by my grandmother, the stuffed puppy that had been mine as a child, her favorite drinking glass, an empty honey jar with a picture of a teddy bear on it. Inside the package, I wrote a note with my new address. I told her I would always let her know where I was. She would always know where to find me.

We left the Bronx in the same van that brought us there two years earlier. Frank left with a seminary degree, a sense of satisfaction, and a new dream. I left with a drinking problem and a hope that Mentayer wouldn't be lost to me forever if I just kept writing to her. As we drove away, I turned for one last look, with the guilt I always carried inside weighing heavier on me than ever, still demanding everything of me and offering nothing in return.

EIGHTEEN

April 2006

"I wish Mentayer was coming with us," I say to J. B. I glance at my shadowy reflection in the train window. My thoughts are split between Lewis Blair's provocative comments at Daniel Leacham's funeral yesterday and Mentayer's decision not to come with us to see him today. What could be more important to her than getting information from Mr. Blair that might shed light on how Markus died? "I wonder if she's afraid of finding out that her brother's death was gang-related," I say. My stomach hurts when I consider the possibility that we might not have known Markus as well as we thought we did.

"Or maybe she's hiding something," J. B. says.

I give him a withering look. "It isn't like you to jump to conclusions."

"I'm wondering, that's all," he says. "Let's think about this. She doesn't tell us she works for CSCH. She agrees to meet with us, then shows up late. She's upset when she tells us Daniel Leacham's dead, but then doesn't go with us to his funeral. And now, all of a sudden, something at work is more important than coming with us today to see Lewis Blair."

"I hate when you do that," I say with a shake of my head. I'm referring to when J. B. and I first met. An American Indian boy had died in a foster home and everyone but J. B. assumed it was an accident. He had used a list to push me into helping him investigate. I was uncomfortable then because there was no trust between us. But J. B. and I are collaborators now; this time I'm uncomfortable because I want to trust Mentayer.

"I'm brainstorming," he says with a grin. He pulls out his smartphone. "Before we get to Mr. Blair's office, I need to return some calls."

I decide that, while he's on the phone, I'll go into the corner market and get us a snack. But at the entrance, my stomach goes into spasms. The stench of what passed for our neighborhood supermarket in the Bronx comes back to me, the smell of apples grown soft, bananas black, potatoes rotten. Lee's Grocery jacked up their prices on the first of the month when the welfare checks came. But what were mothers to do when their babies were crying and they were out of milk or it had gone sour?

I take a deep breath, square my shoulders, and forge my way through the door. Once inside, I discover, much to my relief, that this market is nothing like Lee's Grocery. It's a quick in-and-out store for cigarettes and lotto tickets, its narrow aisles stacked with processed foods, snacks, and candy. In the back are foods to go—dried-up hot dogs, packaged lunches, sandwiches, fake crab salads—and a fruit and vegetable section with decent-looking produce and prepared fruit salads in small plastic containers. No swarming roaches or buzzing flies. There's a cooler with a few rows of juices, sodas, and bottled water. The rest of the shelves are stocked with a million different kinds of beer. I reach in and snatch two cans of Diet Coke and, on my way to the checkout counter, grab two Snickers candy bars.

"How are you today, ma'am?" The cashier's voice and smile are pleasant. From his frayed white T-shirt and wrinkle-free brown skin, I might assume him to be in his early thirties at most, but the graying hair at his temples suggests middle age.

"I'm fine," I say. "How about you?"

"Can't complain." He rings up my items, puts them in a small paper bag. "Will that be all, ma'am?"

I nod and hand him a twenty-dollar bill. He hands me my change, and I notice that the index finger on his left hand is curved off to the side in the middle. He sees me looking at it and pulls his hand back.

"I broke it as a kid," he says. "It's been like this ever since."

"I didn't mean to stare." I bite my lower lip. I don't want to seem intrusive, but my insides are screaming at me to follow my instincts. "Did you hear about the boy's body they found in the rubble of P.S. 457?" I say at last. "Maybe you saw it in the paper."

He nods.

"The dead boy was a student of mine back in the sixties," I say. "His name was Markus LeMeur. His index finger was broken, too. The police think it was part of a gang initiation ritual."

The man hesitates for a few seconds, then shrugs. "When I was coming up, the cops thought we were all gang members. Still do. But the real problem back then wasn't us, it was those white boys coming up to the Bronx, using us poor kids to make a few bucks, acting all tough."

"Markus was a good kid."

"Maybe why he got his finger broke, then."

"By who?"

His face turns more serious, his eyes nervous. He turns away and glances out the window.

"You think someone broke his finger because he was good?"

He shrugs and keeps looking out the window.

"Markus disappeared in 1968," I say. "I knew he was scared of something, but he wouldn't tell me. Wouldn't tell his sister either. When I told him maybe he should tell the police, he freaked out and wouldn't talk anymore. And then he went missing. It was during the teachers' strike. No one knows to this day what happened to him. The body they found was identified the other day. His sister is taking it real hard. She's desperate to know how he died."

The whole time I'm talking, he keeps busy. He straightens the stack of cigarette cartons behind him. He reaches into the money drawer and starts straightening up a stack of one-dollar bills.

"I can't imagine how she feels, can you?" I say. "I mean, what if it was your brother? What if being good got him killed?"

"Look, ma'am," he says, "so I made an offhanded remark. You know, like the song *Only the Good Die Young*. I never knew anyone named Markus LeMeur. Sorry."

"The person who killed him," I say, "might still be walking around hurting other good little boys. So, if you know anything... "

But his eyes have gone cold. I take the receipt he gave me and write my name and cell phone number on the back. "Please," I say as I hand it to him. "If you think of anything, call me. Anything at all. Please."

He crumbles up the receipt and drops it into the garbage can under the cash register.

Outside, J. B. leans against the side of the building, his arms crossed as he observes two men arguing at the curb. I hand him a candy bar and a can of soda. As we walk away from the market, I give him a play-by-play account of my conversation with the cashier.

"He knows something," I say. "Everything was fine until I started asking questions. Then he clammed up, wouldn't say another word. I swear, something spooked the man. Like something spooked Markus."

"Another broken finger, huh?" J. B. peels down the paper on the sides of his candy bar and takes a bite. "It'll be interesting to see what Lewis Blair has to say about that."

J. B. finishes eating his candy bar and tosses the wrapper in a garbage can next to a building we pass. "I talked on the phone to someone I thought might have a lead for me, while you were in the market," he says. "But he can't find anyone at CSCH willing to talk about the fraud allegations. It's like they've been forewarned... by someone." He scrunches his eyebrows together in a scowl.

His accusation lands like a punch to my gut. I stop walking. "What are you suggesting?" I shout. A woman passing by jumps. I lower my voice. "Mentayer would *not* do anything like that. Maybe the reason you can't find anything is because there isn't anything to find."

He shrugs. I simmer in silence for the next two blocks.

Lewis Blair's office is on the first floor of an unimposing, dullish-gray building. His name isn't on the engraved sign on the door that says "Administrative Office, The Center for Boys: A Place for Winners since 1970." We knock and he opens the door himself, dressed in the same clothes he wore yesterday at the funeral. His humble appearance is a sharp contrast to the dazzling array of trophies, awards, team photos, certificates of accomplishment, and newspaper articles in his office.

"Your office, Mr. Blair," I say with my voice filled with awe, "elevates optimism and confidence to an art form."

"After thirty years, the victories add up," he says with a smile. He strokes the stubble on his chin as if drawing from it each word. "Their victories. Not mine. Please, folks, make yourselves comfortable."

We sit down on two worn brown leather chairs facing his desk. He sits behind it in a tattered chair that looks like a Salvation Army reject. There's a Langston Hughes quote hanging on the wall behind his head. I read it out loud. "*Hold fast to dreams, for if dreams die, life is a broken winged bird that cannot fly.*"

Lewis Blair nods and taps his fingers on the desk in time with the poem's cadence. "It's harder to coax boys off the ledge when they're already on it," he then says. "Best to get them young."

"That's why I liked teaching third grade," I say.

"The best age," he says. He points to a photograph hanging on the wall, a black-and-white picture of a boy holding a basketball. "That's Leech. Daniel Leacham. He was about that age when he first started coming to the center. See that frightened face? I've never seen anyone that scared, always looking over his shoulder. He hung out at the center all the time. It was where he felt safe.

"See that larger picture there, the one in color? That's him a few years ago. He was the keynote speaker at our annual fundraising dinner. He's our biggest success story." He pauses, looks back and forth between the two pictures. "No way Leech killed himself," he says in a deep, trumpeting voice. "No way."

"I agree," J. B. says. "The question is how to prove it."

"He was a fine man, fine as they come. A generous man. On the first of each month, without fail, he had a substantial amount of money deposited into our account. He's been doing that for years." He takes a deep breath and lets it out. "Until now."

J. B. trains his detective-sharp eyes on Mr. Blair. "Do you have a record of those deposits, with information about what bank they came from, the dates, amounts, things like that?"

"Certainly, Mr. Harrell, but what do you think that has to do with how he died?"

"Maybe nothing. But you know what they say: never leave a single stone unturned. You never know what you might find."

"I'll get copies of everything to you."

J. B. thanks him and leans forward. "Mr. Blair, do you have any idea why Daniel Leacham was so angry at the CSCH Corporation?"

Lewis Blair shakes his head. "Afraid I can't help you there." He pauses and strokes his stubble. Then an "aha" expression crosses his face. "I do recall him making a disparaging remark about CSCH's schools once. He suggested that we start a charter school here at the Center for Boys, but I told him I couldn't in good conscience siphon money out of the public schools and put it into a charter school. He pushed back a bit, said I should think about all the boys who would benefit. I told him it would leave more boys behind than it would help, and they'd be stuck in public schools that were even more depleted and disadvantaged than before because of us. But now, you know, I'm rethinking the idea. I could set it up with private money. I think it might be a good way to honor Daniel."

"Do you recall anything more specific that Daniel said about CSCH?" J. B. asks.

"He didn't go into any details," Mr. Blair says, "but I do recall him saying something about CSCH ripping off poor kids."

I tip my head toward the picture of Leacham as a boy. "What do you think Daniel was so scared of when he first started coming to the center?"

He gazes at the picture along with me as he answers. "Can't say for sure. Poor boy didn't talk much. The streets weren't safe, we all knew that. Then there were the gangs. I do recall Leech being afraid of a teacher before his family moved and transferred him to a different school."

I lean forward. The blood is pumping in the veins of my neck. "Was the teacher's name Anthony Frascatore, by any chance? Did Leech go to P.S. 457?"

Mr. Blair tugs at his bow tie. I hold my breath and wait as he considers the question. "Hmm. Leech did go to that school for a while. And that name does ring a bell. I recall thinking it sounded Italian, and now that you mention it, yes, I think Frascatore sounds about right."

"Did Leech tell you why he was afraid of him?"

"No, like I said, Leech didn't say much. But I know other boys were terrified of that teacher, too. There were whisperings about him. How he got out of control, how he'd fly off the handle and start acting weird, knock students around. The boys seemed to be as scared of him as they were of the gangs trying to recruit them to run drugs for them. Almost like he was involved in the business, or maybe even on drugs himself. I got the idea he was unpredictable. Maybe that's why they were scared of him."

"Frascatore's classroom was right across the hall from mine," I say. "A boy named Dion Brown died of a brain injury after Frascatore slammed his head into the wall. The boys were right to be afraid of him, even more so when he got away with killing Dion." I try to still my pounding heart. "And you know about the body they found when the school was torn down? Well, I think Frascatore may have killed that boy, too."

Lewis Blair shakes his head. "Broke my heart to hear about that boy. First thing I wondered was whether I knew him, if he was someone who'd come to the Center."

"The body's been identified," I say. "His name was Markus LeMeur."

"Name doesn't ring a bell, I'm afraid."

"The police think his death was drug- or gang-related, but it's not true. I knew Markus. He was in my class. The LeMeur family was solid, thanks to the grandmother. Markus did whatever she and his sister, Mentayer, told him to do. He would never have gotten involved with gangs or drugs. Never. He disappeared in 1968, and no one ever knew what happened to him. Do you remember hearing about him?"

"Oh my, yes," Mr. Blair says. "I do recall hearing about a boy that went missing. There were all kinds of rumors about what happened. Some people thought it had something to do with the long teachers' strike going on at the time. Course, there was all kinds of gossip back then, what with all the violence and vandalism, crazy stuff—accusations of racism and anti-Semitism flying back and forth, no one trusting anyone. Nasty, nasty business, all those black teachers crossing the picket line. And a few white ones. I knew of one white teacher who was acting principal. There was talk about her kidnapping the boy, but we all knew that wasn't true. What was her name again? I can't seem to pull it up."

J. B. breaks out in a smile. "Her name was Sylvia Waters," he says.

"That's right. Mrs. Waters. I recall, though, that everyone called her Ms. Sylvia."

J. B. points at me and laughs. "*This* is Ms. Sylvia. One and the same."

Lewis Blair slaps his hands on his desk. "Well, I'll be. But I thought you said your name was Jensen."

"Waters was my married name," I say with a smile.

He knits his eyes together and studies me for what seems like a long time. Then he claps his hands together. "Yes, indeed. I do believe I can see it now. Two cream-filled donuts with chocolate frosting. Are they still your favorite?"

"What?" I place the tips of my fingers on my parted lips. "How do you... "

"I worked security detail for the Panthers at your school a few times," he says. "It was my job to buy the donuts in the mornings."

"I... I'm sorry. I should remember you, but I don't."

"I'd be surprised if you did," he says with a wave of his hand. "I was a backup, not a regular. I left the donuts on the counter outside your office before you got to school. Then I'd go down to the cafeteria to help fix breakfast for the kids."

Memories start racing through me with the force of a pickup truck at top speed. Images of black berets and black leather jackets; fleeting exchanges of *Good morning* and *Have a good day*; the tantalizing aroma of pastries, sweet taste of sugar, bitterness of coffee; acrimonious sounds from the picket line.

"So *you're* Ms. Sylvia." Lewis Blair slaps his hands on both knees. His chuckle soon becomes a full-throated chortle. I frown, wonder what's so funny. He senses my confusion and stops laughing. "I recall a Panther meeting when a man named Steve talked about you being acting principal of P.S. 457. He said 'That skinny little white woman'—well, he may have said 'bitch'—'is tough as nails, that one. Shit, man, she even broke into the school. I know. I was there.'"

He leans back in his chair. His eyes crinkle with delight as he starts laughing again. J. B. laughs along with him. Warmth creeps up my neck and onto my cheeks. "Steve was my upstairs neighbor," I say. "I didn't know he was with the Black Panthers."

"His wife Teresa's the one who started the New York City chapter."

"I didn't know that," I say. "I knew she maneuvered things behind the scenes during the strike, though. And I was pretty sure she was the one who recruited the Black Panthers to do security." I wonder now why I never asked her about it. I must have figured if she wanted me to know more, she would have told me. But why didn't she? Was it because she didn't trust me? Maybe we weren't as good friends as I thought we were.

"You must have heard what happened," Mr. Blair says. "The cops hauled twenty-one of our leaders in on trumped-up conspiracy charges."

"I did hear about that," I say.

"In the end, of course, they were all cleared," he continues. "But it took a long time and a lot of money. It set us back bad. That's what the FBI wanted. They never got Steve and Teresa, but after it was all over, they got out of New York, just in case."

"I never knew what happened to Teresa and Steve," I say.

"No one knows where they went," he says. "Cuba maybe. I think about them every time I look at that rug of theirs."

I look down at the worn patchwork rug under my feet. That explains the feelings that were stirred up in me when I first sat down. It was a nostalgia as warm as the sweet aroma of Teresa's coffee and her cinnamon rolls fresh from the oven. I breathe it in now and savor her presence in the room.

"Oh my, oh my, oh my," Lewis Blair says after a few seconds of silence. "How Teresa would go on and on about what a courageous young woman you were."

"Thanks to the chutzpah of youth," I say with a chuckle. "Trouble was staring me right in the face and I never knew it. Not until... until Markus." I bite my bottom lip. "I thought Frascatore had something to do with his disappearance. I was afraid he'd come after Markus's sister next if I didn't quit as acting principal. But now... "

"Now you're not sure?"

"I know Frascatore hated that I was keeping the school open. And I know he killed Dion Brown, I don't care what anyone says. But after talking to the cashier in a store a few blocks from here, I'm thinking maybe something else was going on. The cashier's left index finger was broken when he was a boy. Markus's left index finger was broken, too. The cashier knows something, but wouldn't tell me what. So, even though I always thought it was Frascatore who Markus was afraid of, well, now I'm wondering if it was someone else. He tried to tell me but... " My voice trails off. *But I didn't listen. I was too stupid to understand.*

Lewis Blair strokes the stubble on his chin. "I do seem to recall some whisperings about someone else the boys were afraid of," he says. "But they never dared tell me anything, not even his name. I always assumed it had something to do with drugs. Everything seemed to have something to do with drugs, but... " His voice trails off like he's trying to figure something out, or pull up another memory.

"What are you thinking?"

"Let's say Frascatore was a scared-straight disciplinarian who knocked the boys around to make them act right. That was what some people said about him, so let's go with that. And let's say there was someone else, some two-bit drug dealer who scared boys into working for him. So maybe, when

Frascatore suspected boys like Dion of working for this dealer, he roughed them up to get them to stop, you know. To protect them."

I shake my head. "Uh-uh-uh. Frascatore didn't hurt kids to help them." I can hear my voice rising with each word. "What he did had nothing to do with discipline."

"Okay, so let's say instead that Frascatore was doing drugs himself. That could explain his out-of-control behavior. So then the question is, where did he get his drugs? So let's say he got them from this two-bit dealer. Maybe Dion and Markus delivered the drugs to Frascatore."

"Markus would never do anything like that," I say. "I don't know anything about Dion."

"Okay, so let's say Dion delivered drugs to Frascatore," Lewis Blair says, "but then Dion dies, so the dealer needs a new delivery boy. He breaks Markus's finger to force him to take Dion's place."

"Markus would say no," I say.

"So maybe that's what got him killed." Lewis Blair shakes his head, slips into silence.

"The cashier," I say, "suggested Markus could have been killed because he was a good kid. So maybe Frascatore didn't kill Markus. Maybe some drug dealer did." I pause, think about that some more before continuing. "It's easy for me to imagine Frascatore hitting Markus hard enough to kill him, like he did with Dion. But it's not as easy to imagine him killing on purpose and then going to all the trouble of hiding the dead body. It's even harder for me to imagine him hiding Markus's body in the school basement. Unless, I suppose, he killed him in the school. But that doesn't make sense, because Frascatore was out on strike and not in the building. And there were a lot of people around. Someone would have noticed."

I glance at J. B. sitting next to me. I'm about to ask him what he thinks when his phone rings. He pulls it from his pocket and looks at the caller ID.

"Excuse me," he says, "It's Dr. Goldmann."

I wonder why the medical examiner is calling J. B. If she had some new evidence or had determined the cause of death, wouldn't she call Mentayer?

"That's what I thought," J. B. says into the phone. "There's never only one... or even two. You have been most helpful... Yes, yes, I will. Thank you again."

"What? What did she say?" As soon as I heard the words "there's never only one," I knew Dr. Goldmann had told J. B. something important. Those were the same words he'd said last year when he learned that another child had been injured in the foster home we were investigating.

"I had a hunch," he says, "that there might be a connection between Markus and Dion. So I asked Dr. Goldmann if she could review the medical reports on Dion Brown and let me know if he had a broken finger, too."

My hand flies up, covers my mouth.

He nods. "Yup. Index finger. Left hand."

I don't move. I sit up straight and try to process the information. Three broken fingers, same ones, same hands. Markus. Dion. The cashier. I flinch. I can no longer rule out the possibility that Markus's death might be related to drugs or gangs. I know he would have said no to both. But I've learned from J. B. that evidence is evidence. A lead is a lead. We have to follow it.

"Dr. Goldmann also said the cause of Markus's death was a blow to his head that was inflicted by someone of average height, not a tall person."

"Frascatore wasn't tall," I say. "I always thought he suffered from short man syndrome."

J. B. tucks his upper lip under his lower lip and nods. "I think it's time to pay him a visit, don't you?"

"Tomorrow morning," I agree.

Lewis Blair stands up and extends his hand. "I am most pleased to know you," he says. "I can see that you folks are on the right path to the truth about what happened to both Markus LeMeur and Daniel Leacham."

"You've been a big help," J. B. says as the two of them shake hands.

We promise to keep each other informed and walk toward the door. But when we get there, I stop, don't want to leave. Mr. Blair senses my hesitation. He places his hand on my shoulder and leans to whisper in my ear. "Whatever it takes, I know you'll do it, Ms. Sylvia. Whatever it takes."

At nine o'clock that night, when I go to bed, his words ring in my ears. What could I have done to get that cashier to talk, I wonder? What did I say that made him clam up? Should I go back and try again? *Whatever it takes,* comes the answer. *Whatever it takes.*

I reach for my cell phone and call J. B., but he doesn't answer. I leave a message. "J. B., I'm going back to that little market. If you get this message in the next five minutes and want to go with me, give me a call."

I get out of bed and put on the same pullover top and slacks I was wearing before and head out the door. If I hurry, the cashier might still be at work. If I take him by surprise, maybe he'll talk.

A cab is idling outside the hotel entrance. I slide into the back seat and tell the driver where I want to go. He shakes his head, not after dark, he says, too dangerous there for cabbies, he'll take me as far as the 125th Street station on the green line, it's not far from there to where I want to go. *Whatever it takes,* I tell myself and accept his offer.

Once I'm on the train headed for the Bronx, I second-guess my decision. The cab driver was so worried about his safety that he wouldn't take me all the way. Maybe I should worry as much about my own safety. I look around at the tired faces of people going home after grueling sixteen- or eighteen-hour workdays, the closed eyes of some, the eyes of others staring off into space, others with eyelids drooping, heads nodding off then jerking up. Three young, sinister-looking men with slicked-back hair get on the train. They gape at everyone, jostle each other. They leer at a young woman cradling a sleeping baby on her lap. One of them says something to her, they all hoot.

One of them spots me and pokes the others. They gawk at me, the sole white-faced older woman in the car, a curiosity or an easy target. I pull the strap of my purse over my head and lay it across my chest, cover the purse with both arms. Maybe going back to the market isn't such a good idea after all. It's not too late to get off at the next stop and take the southbound train back to Manhattan. The cashier must be off work by now anyway. And even if he is there, even if he gives me key information, it's still too late to save Markus and Dion. The past can't be changed for them.

But what about the thousands of children across the country who are being subjected right now to abuse based on Frascatore's brand of "no excuses" discipline in CSCH's charter schools? And what about the two-bit drug dealer Lewis Blair mentioned? What if he's still around, recruiting boys, doing damage, issuing orders from the top of the drug chain, and fueling the drug epidemic? I look out the window and catch glimpses inside apartments as the train flies by. I wonder about the people who live there, what their lives are like, where their children go to school. No, what I'm doing is about more the past. It's about more than getting justice for Markus. It's about those people, too, whether I know them or not.

We approach my stop, and I reach in my purse for my cell phone. A message from J. B. gives me pause. "What the hell are you thinking, Sylvia? Don't go back there tonight. We can go together tomorrow." The train stops and I get off. It's not too late to go back. A southbound train approaches from the other direction. I stand on the platform as it comes to a stop. The doors open. I watch them close, then head for the stairs. How can I turn back now when I've come this far?

It's several blocks to the market, and the sidewalks are dimly lit. In my twenties, when I used to walk alone on dark streets like this, I was unaware of their hidden dangers. But now, forty years later, I have the heightened awareness and suspicious caution of a vulnerable older woman who hears in every sound and sees in every shadow a threat, either real or imagined. I take long strides, arch my back to look confident. But my eyes dart back and forth. Anyone could be lurking, ready to jump out from the black spaces between buildings.

I cross paths with an elderly black woman. I can see she's struggling to carry her two bags of groceries. She says hello, and I give her a sympathetic smile. I'd offer to help but I'm afraid of going in the opposite direction with her, perhaps down an even darker street, and I'd have to walk back alone.

A group of teenagers stands on the corner, cans of beer in their hands. Their eyes follow me as I pass. They laugh. I clutch my purse tighter to my chest. I break out in a sweat. Lewis Blair's words—*Whatever it takes*—are drowned out by J. B.'s warning. *What are you thinking, Sylvia?* I walk faster, berating myself with every fear-filled step. *You fool, you fool, you fool. Why are you so driven? Don't you know when to stop? Do you have no brakes?* I search for something familiar, but everything looks different in the dark. I grip my cell phone in one hand, ready to call for help that I know will be too slow in coming.

I hear a rustling sound to my right. A shadow moves in the darkness, between two buildings ripe for ambush. Something small darts in front of me and I scream. I screech to a halt on my toes. It's a cat. I let out my breath. I massage my neck until I can start walking again.

The market's neon sign appears in the distance and I pick up my pace. But then I trip on the curb and stumble a few steps forward. I break the fall with the palms of my hands and land on my knees. I pull myself up and brush off the dirt. Then I race toward the sign. I tear into the store. It's bright inside, warm, welcoming. Safe. I rest my back against the wall and my legs collapse like cooked noodles.

The cashier is still standing at the cash counter. "Ma'am? Ma'am? Are you okay, ma'am?"

He walks over to help me. When he puts his arms around my waist I can feel the moisture under my arms. My cheeks flush with embarrassment. He leads me to the counter and pulls out a stool. I sit down and wipe drips of sweat from my brow with the back of my hand.

The cashier places a box of Kleenex on the counter in front of me. "Did someone mess with you out there? Are you hurt?"

I pull out a tissue and pat my cheeks, the back of my neck. I put my hand to my temple where strands of fuzzy gray hairs curl in the sweat. "I'm okay. I'll be fine as soon as I catch my breath."

"I'll be right back," he says. "It's ten o'clock, closing time." He walks over to the window. His eyes search up and down the sidewalk for trouble, and then he turns the open sign around to the closed side. He switches off the neon light.

I'm a fool. What was I thinking to come back here like this? This man made it clear to me that he didn't want to talk. So what do I do instead of respecting his wishes? I rush up here and make a fool of myself.

"Why are you here?" he asks as he walks back from window. Then he reaches under the counter for a bottle of water and opens it, sets it in front of me.

"I came back to talk to you more about Markus LeMeur," I say. "But you told me when I was here earlier today that you had nothing to say, and now you're being so kind, and I'm sorry I didn't listen to you. I'll be on my way now."

He smiles and runs his fingers through his thick hair. "Where did you come from? And don't tell me you live around here, because I know that is not true. How did you get here?"

"I'm staying at a hotel in Greenwich Village. I took the train."

He gapes at me, shaking his head. "Okay... shoot." He pulls out another stool from behind the counter and sits down, facing me.

"Thank you," I say, taking a deep breath. "After talking to you earlier, I heard about a man who may have been dealing drugs at the time Markus went missing. Do you know anything about that?"

He rests his hands, fingers splayed, on the counter. "Drake," he says. "I don't know if that was his real name or not. He recruited young, innocent boys to deliver drugs for him. He scared the shit out of them to make 'em do it."

"Markus would have refused."

"And that could have been what got him killed." His voice is soft and his eyes look sad.

I glance down at the crooked index finger on his left hand. "Did Drake break your finger?"

He nods. "I was seven. After that I done whatever I was told. That's why I'm still here, why I didn't end up dead." He shifts his weight on the stool. "I worked for him until I was twelve. Then I guess I wasn't of any use to him anymore. After that all I had to do to stay alive was keep my mouth shut."

"But you're telling me now. Does that mean you're not afraid of this Drake guy anymore?"

He shakes his head. "Naw, he's been long gone. Least that's what I hear. And the world's a better place for it. Can't think of anyone more deserving to die. I'm guessing he died. Don't know for sure. Maybe he's retired and living in luxury off his spoils on some island. I'm glad he's gone from here."

"Markus didn't deserve to die," I say.

He shakes his head. "I'm sorry."

"Did you ever hear anything about a teacher at P.S. 457 named Anthony Frascatore?"

"Sure. Everyone did. He was one scary dude. Pretty messed up." He pauses and crosses his arms over his chest. "That's it. That's all I know to tell you. I didn't know Markus. I don't know how he died. It's too late to know if Drake killed him, but I'd put bets on him having something to do with whatever happened. I wouldn't rule out the cops either. There were some bad dudes back then."

"You've given me one more piece of the puzzle," I say. "I'm grateful."

"My name's Hank," he says with a smile.

"I guess you already know I'm Sylvia," I say, even though I know he threw my note away earlier without looking at my name.

He reaches into a drawer for a piece of paper and scribbles something on it. "Here. My phone number. In case other questions come up. I hope you find out what happened to Markus."

"Thank you, Hank." I stand up and head toward the door, then turn back to face him. "I'm curious," I say. "Why did you decide to talk to me?"

He grins and gives a shrug. "I had time to think about it after you left, and then you came all the way from Greenwich Village by yourself to give me another chance." He smiles and walks over to me. "Come on. I'll walk you to the train."

From the train, I call J. B. and tell him about my trip to the market. "So now we have confirmation that there was a drug dealer named Drake," I say. "He broke Hank's finger to force him to deliver drugs for him. It sure seems to me he broke Markus's and Dion's fingers, too, don't you agree?"

"Good grief, Sylvia." J. B. says. "Good grief."

"Maybe this Drake guy killed Markus," I say. "Maybe Dion, too. Maybe it wasn't Frascatore after all? I've never doubted his guilt until now. It'll be interesting to see if he says anything about Drake tomorrow."

We both agree that anything is possible, and before hanging up, J. B. tells me to call him when I get to the hotel so he knows I'm safe. I sit back, close my eyes, and smile.

NINETEEN

April 2006

The next morning we drop in at Anthony Frascatore's CSCH office unannounced. Maybe the element of surprise will rattle him. As might J. B.'s debonair appearance, his expensive briefcase, his designer pen. It won't be easy to get him to slip up, much less talk at all, with me, his old nemesis, in the room. I promise J. B. I'll keep my mouth shut, even if it kills me. It just might.

I sit across the table from Frascatore, not daring to move a limb, not even so much as my little finger. Frozen in place, the accuser facing the accused. I shift my attention away from him for a second. There's nothing to see in his office, no decorations or personal items, a few standard issue prints on otherwise bare walls. Frascatore hasn't looked at me once since we got here.

But when J. B. says we've come to talk about Markus LeMeur, he blinks.

"I suppose his sister sent you," he says with a jerk of his head toward me.

J. B. answers. "Mentayer has no idea we're here, Mr. Frascatore."

"I find that interesting, Mr. Harrell, given your avid interest in CSCH these days."

I wonder how much he knows about J. B.'s investigation. It's hard to tell how much information he might have access to. I suspect he has little influence in the corporation. The location of his office, tucked away in a back corner with no secretary or other gatekeeper, suggests a fabricated job consisting of little or nothing to do.

J. B. smiles. "You can rest assured, Mr. Frascatore, that the series I'm doing on charter schools has nothing to do with Mentayer or her brother." His voice is calm, patient.

"Well, no matter any longer," Frascatore says with a smirk and a wave of his hand. It seems to me that he wants us to think he knows something but is not going to tell us what it is.

"Like I said, we're here about Markus. He was one of Sylvia's students, as I'm sure you know."

Frascatore's face twitches but he refuses to look in my direction. Then he laughs. "Ah yes, Ms. Sylvia, not Mrs. Sylvia, not Miss Sylvia, but *Ms.* Sylvia, aka the bleeding heart out to save the world."

I pull my shoulder blades back and lift up my chin. I will retain my dignity. I will not let myself get hooked. I will not jump down his pink throat even though every fiber of my being wants to.

"You should have seen how naive she was, Mr. Harrell. She threw all her eggs in that community control basket like that was the solution to every problem our public schools ever had. And that black power shit? Man, she fell for that, hook, line, and sinker. Our own little Jane Fonda, she was, would have joined the Panther party herself if they'd let her in. She even put those terrorists in charge of the school at night so they could do drugs and have sex and who knows what else right there in the principal's office. All that work she did, poor thing, and nothing but failure to show for it."

His upper lip curls into a sneer. Same way it did in the meeting with Miss Huskings decades ago when he set me up to keep me from telling what I'd seen.

I clench my jaw. I shove his taunts back down his throat with my eyes. But then he snickers, and my self-control fades. J. B. clears his throat and rests his forefinger against the side of his nose. That's the signal we'd agreed on, a warning to me if used by him, and a cry for help if used by me. I use my fingers to seal my lips.

"We've been talking to witnesses about what happened to Markus," J. B. says, "and your name keeps popping up."

Frascatore reaches for a plastic Starbucks glass of iced coffee. He brings it to his lips and takes a sip.

"Seems like you instilled fear in your students?" J. B.'s voice, to my ears, is devoid of blame.

"I had to scare the shit out of them," Frascatore says, "to keep them from ending up dead or in jail. Best they could hope for their future was joining the military. I taught them how to take orders. At least in the army they'd get structure, three meals a day, and a paycheck. I knew what they needed long before anyone came up with those Scared Straight programs that are all the rage nowadays. You can bet those boys were scared of me. But they knew I cared. Everyone did."

He scoots to the edge of his chair and straightens his back. I clench my fists. Hearing him tout himself as the big savior is like eating glass with my mouth shut. Knowing it's an image that even Lewis Blair seemed to consider viable leaves me screaming inside. *Liar! Bully!* I'm on the verge of either crumbling into myself or attacking, but J. B. remains erect and focused. He looks at me with his eyebrows raised. I nod, hanging on to my trust in him like a rope, gripping it so tight that a pain shoots through my neck and starts to move into my shoulders.

I step back and turn myself back into a social worker, with Frascatore as my client. I'm conducting an assessment. The first thing I notice is his schlubby physical appearance. His gray suit pulls and bunches when he lifts his arms. The wide diagonal red, dark green, and gray stripes on his tie don't quite match his dull green shirt. His greasy black hair is dyed, and there are funny little bumps above his upper lip, no longer hidden by a handlebar mustache, his little square teeth yellowed with age. Beneath his bombastic and arrogant image is one of a self-employed consultant with no clients. An even deeper level of assessment suggests a man with an unsettled past to which he is bound and cannot escape.

"Clarke Craine spoke about your views on discipline," J. B. says. "I can see why he thought you'd be a good addition to the CSCH team."

Frascatore's chest puffs up. "Here's the thing, Mr. Harrell: public schools have no idea what kids need. Their parents let them run wild, no discipline, no attention, no help with their homework. Bring back the eugenics movement, is what I say. But look, I'm a realist. That's not going to happen. So we do what we can. Nothing wrong with a good swat to the back of the head once in a while to get a kid's attention, hey, Ms. Sylvia? Hell, that's the best thing my dad ever did for me."

He leans toward me. Winks. His aftershave is a strange combination of citrus and talcum powder. *Blow to the back of the head? Is that the best thing you ever did for Dion and Markus?*

J. B. rests his finger alongside his nose again. I take a deep breath and then another.

"What can you tell us about a man named Drake," J. B. says with a glimmer in his eyes.

"Who?" Frascatore says with a blank look on his face. I turn away to hide my disgust.

"You know, the drug dealer who forced boys to work for him."

"What does that have to do with Markus?"

"I was hoping you might answer that question. This guy Drake interests me. Considering how much you cared about the boys, I thought you might have heard something about him. Maybe you know something that could help us understand what happened to Markus."

"Was his finger broken?" Frascatore glances down at his own fingers.

J. B. nods.

"Well, maybe that's your answer."

"So you think Drake broke Markus's finger to make him deliver drugs for him?"

"I have no idea."

"So why do you think the police never arrested this Drake guy? They must have known about him."

Frascatore shrugs. He takes a last gulp of iced coffee and tosses the cup in a trash can in the corner. "The cops were useless, could have even been getting a cut of the drug money, who knows. Maybe they were in on it." He shakes his head and lets out a self-sacrificing sigh. "I tried to protect the boys. That was all I could do." He clears his throat and turns to stare at me. I squirm and hold my breath. It's like his eyes are roaming around in my brain. He turns back to J. B., and I let my breath out.

"*She* knows," Frascatore says, "I didn't have anything to do with what happened to Dion Brown. That poor boy died from a subdural hematoma caused by an earlier injury."

"Caused by whom?" J. B. asks.

"Who knows? I heard a rumor that the police roughed him up. I don't know why. All I know is that he was one of the boys I wasn't able to save."

Dion's presence fills the room. His ghost shakes his head in protest. Frascatore reaches into his pocket, pulls out a piece of Dentyne gum and pops it into his mouth. The smell brings me back to P.S. 457's funky school auditorium, pieces of chewed bubble gum stuck under the seats, Frascatore reaching for one of my students, me scowling at him, his hand withdrawing. I press my back against the chair and try to calm myself.

"Do you think Dion worked for that Drake guy?" J. B. asks. His voice is soothing. I'm able to breathe again.

"Maybe so," Frascatore says. "Depends on if his left index finger was broken, I suppose."

"As a matter of fact, it was."

"Then I rest my case." Frascatore holds out his hands palms up.

"So if it could have been the cops or Drake who killed Dion, maybe one of them killed Markus, too."

"No way of knowing."

"Whoever killed Markus managed to hide his body in the school," J. B. says. "What are your thoughts about that?"

"Could have been an accident."

"But if it was, and Markus died in the basement, why was he down there?"

"I don't know. Maybe he could have been killed there, then."

"By who? And without anyone seeing or hearing anything?" J. B. says.

Frascatore snorts and shoots me an accusing look. "*She* knows who was in that school every night. She knows who was still there after everyone else went home. They could have gotten away with *anything* and nobody would ever know. Even murder."

My neck and shoulders stiffen. I want J. B. to confront him. *You see what he's doing, don't you? He's guilty as hell. See how he's trying to put the blame on the Panthers? Did you notice how his voice changed?* But J. B. doesn't say anything more. Instead, he stands up and pushes his chair back with an abruptness that baffles me. He reaches down for my hand. Confused, I give it to him and let him help me up. He cups my elbow with his hand and steers me toward the door.

"Thank you for all your help, Mr. Frascatore," he says. "Your candor is much appreciated."

"Any time," Frascatore says with a tip of his head.

When we reach the door, J. B. turns around. "About the charter school story I'm working on," he says. "I'd like to talk to you about that some time."

Frascatore shrugs, matter-of-fact-like. "I thought you might," he says with a smile.

When we're outside on the sidewalk, the venom I'd held inside starts oozing out of my pores, leaves me raw and exposed. I lash out at J. B.

"What do you mean, 'your candor is much appreciated'? He was lying through his teeth. What do you mean, 'thank you for all your help'? What help?"

"He was a big help," J. B. says with a grin. "Daniel Leacham was right. The man's got loose lips."

"Enlighten me, please. Because all I saw was a minnow darting back and forth. He dodged all your questions. He was *lying*."

"Of course he was. But he slipped up. Did you notice how he denied knowing much about Drake, but then knew which of the boys' fingers were broken? Think about it. I never told him it was the left index finger. That information wasn't in the paper either. So how did he know?"

I slap my forehead with the palm of my hand. "Because *he's* the one who broke them."

TWENTY

April 2006

Right away I call Mentayer to tell her the news. She doesn't answer, so I leave a message that we're on our way to her apartment. We should be there by the time she gets home from work.

"I'll have to meet you there later," J. B. says as he slips his phone into his pocket. "I got a message from Mrs. Leacham that she can meet with me now."

We wish each other well and go on our separate quests, he to prove Daniel Leacham didn't commit suicide, and me to tell Mentayer that we are close to getting justice for her brother. There's an extra spring to my step that propels me from CSCH's corporate headquarters to the subway in less than ten minutes' time, a record. I grab the last vacant seat on the northbound green line train as it pulls away from the station. The chanting in my head does rhythmic victory laps in time with the rattling of the train. *It was Frascatore. I knew it all along.*

My eagerness to see Mentayer increases along with the growing number of people packing themselves into the train at each stop. Bodies press against each other, rock from side to side, and lurch forward as one at sudden stops. Stacks of hands grip the poles, people jostle their way off the train and new arrivals slip into their emptied spaces, the trade-offs made without rancor or incident.

The train screeches to a halt at my stop, and a teenager, full of bluster, swaggers off in front of me. I walk at a fast clip the several blocks to Mentayer's building, then rush toward the staircase in the foyer. My foot slips on the bottom step where the marble is chipped and I grab the bannister to right myself. At her apartment, I stop to catch my breath and then knock. I rock back and forth from the balls of my feet to my toes and wait for her to come to the door. When there's no response I knock again. I look at my watch. She should be home from work any minute. I sit down on the floor to wait. But when I rest the back of my head against the door, I hear sounds inside the apartment. I jump to my feet and knock again. I hear footsteps, a cough.

"Mentayer," I call out. "It's me."

No response.

"Are you there?"

I press my ear to the door. Silence. I knock louder.

"Go away."

"What's wrong, Mentayer?"

"I'm not doing this anymore. I'm done."

"What happened?"

"Just leave."

"I can't do that."

"Why not? You left me before. You sure as hell can do it again."

Her anger stuns me into silence. I press my back against the wall and squeeze my eyes shut. So here it is. The history I feared would catch up with us. But why did she wait until now to unleash whatever unresolved pains and regrets she has about the past?

"We need to talk, Mentayer," I say. "But not like this. Not through a closed door."

An unrelenting silence follows. Why did she accuse me of leaving her? What about all the letters I wrote? All the packages I sent? Why did she wait so long to tell me how she feels? Why not tell me when I first called her?

"I did a lot of things I regret," I say, "but leaving you was the one thing I did not do, and I will not do it now. I'm not going anywhere."

"It doesn't matter if you do. I'm a grown-up. I can take it."

"Open the door, please. We have to talk."

"It's water under the bridge. I was a kid. I'm over it."

"I never left you, Mentayer. That's why I kept writing to you even when you never wrote back. The one thing I never did was leave you."

I press my forehead against the door. I strain to hear a sound, any sound. The silence is deafening. I don't know what to say, how to get her to change her mind, to open the door so we can at least talk, at least see each other's faces. I hear a shuffling sound inside the apartment and straighten up, drop my arms to my sides. The door creaks open, an inch at a time.

We search each other's faces. It's so quiet you could have heard a pin drop. Mentayer looks terrible. Her anguished face is without makeup, her hair uncombed, her neck strained against the pleats of an inky silk robe, her wrists vulnerable against its silky cuffs. She grips the robe's wide shawl collar with one hand and with the other slips a wad of wet tissues into its pocket.

"You wrote to me?" she says, her voice raised. "You expect me to believe that?"

I reach out, touch her cheek with my fingertips. She doesn't pull away. "Oh, Mentayer, Mentayer, I wrote to you every day like I said I would. I kept my promise."

"Then maybe you can explain why I didn't get any of your letters."

"I thought you did. I never left you, Mentayer."

She rests the side of her face against the doorframe. She looks both confused and suspicious.

"Please, may I come in?"

Reluctantly she stands to the side. I walk in and follow her down the hall. I hear a click as the door closes on its own behind me. In the living room, a worn, homemade quilt is thrown over the back of her grandmother's old overstuffed brown chair. Next to the chair sits an ancient metal TV tray with a chipped white mug on it. All the windows are closed and it's warm and stuffy. I stand in the middle of the room, confused. I don't know what to say. Why didn't she get my letters? How can I explain something I don't understand? Why should she believe me?

Mentayer wraps the quilt tight around her body and then sits in her grandmother's chair in the corner. She reaches for the mug on the metal tray. She brings it up to her face and inhales the aroma of coffee inside as if it were life-saving oxygen, but doesn't drink any. She doesn't look at me. I pick up a lightweight leather and wood footstool, place it a few feet in front of her chair, and sit down.

"At the foster home, there was a mailbox at the end of the driveway." She looks at me sideways. "I checked it every day at first, but after a while I gave up." She grips the mug with both hands and stares off into space. "My foster mom told me you didn't write because you were afraid it would make me too sad. So I wrote to you and promised I wouldn't be sad if you wrote back." Her voice tightens. "But you never did. You disappeared... same as Markus."

Tears cloud my eyes and stream down my cheeks. "You wrote to me?" I say. "Even when you didn't get any letters from me? You kept writing? You kept hoping I'd answer? Oh, poor baby, poor baby." I get up from the footstool, bend down, and put my arms around her. I lay my cheek against her cheek. She brings her arms out from under the quilt and lays her hands on the back of my head.

"I wrote every day," she whispers.

"So did I," I whisper back. "We both kept our promise."

After several minutes we pull away from each other. A questioning expression takes over her face.

"I don't understand what happened," she says. "Why didn't we get each other's letters?"

"I think I know," I say. I bite my bottom lip, clench and unclench my fists. "I was instructed to send all correspondence to you through the child welfare office. It's obvious they never passed my letters on to you."

Mentayer's eyes flash with anger, and she sputters, "How dare they? And why?"

"I worked in the foster care system for many years," I say with a sigh. "So I can venture a guess. It could be that child welfare thought it was in your best interests to cut off all contact with me."

She lets out a snort. "How does that make any sense? How could they possibly think that could be good for a child?"

I shake my head. "Maybe they believed your attachment to me would make it hard for you to adjust to the foster home."

"But it was supposed to be a temporary placement. I didn't have to adjust."

I shake my head again and ball my fists tighter. "I've seen my share of misguided child welfare policies over the years. Usually based on the latest theory about what's in the best interests of children."

"Well, what they did to us was wrong. No, more like dishonest. Downright sinister. They let me think you didn't care."

"They should have told us," I say. "They lied." My anger erupts from inside and swirls around my head, dive-bombing me. I swat it away. *Sue for damages*, it shouts at me. *Sue for harm done.* All of a sudden it occurs to me that if child welfare lied about the letters, they may have lied about other things, too. I turn to Mentayer and look deep in her eyes.

"They told me you were happy in the foster home, that it was the perfect place for you," I say. "You were happy, weren't you? That wasn't a lie, too, was it?"

"No, that wasn't a lie. My adoptive parents love me. They gave me a good life. I wouldn't be who I am or where I am today if it weren't for them. Or for Grandma." She pulls the quilt off her and lays it on the arm of the chair. "Or for you, Ms. Sylvia."

She reaches for my hands. The invisible cord that held us together in the past holds us together still. I believe the truth has set both of us free. I can now understand my time in the Bronx—a persistent past with frustrating and irritating feelings that refused to vanish and shaped my future—as more than a series of steps and missteps on a journey to some larger destination, but as a statement of the truth of who I am at my core. It taught me that nothing more can be expected of us as human beings than to do the best we can. It is arrogance to believe otherwise of myself.

After a while, Mentayer pulls her hands away and suggests we move to the couch.

"I always wanted you to know that I would be there for you if you ever needed anything," I say as we sit next to each other. "That's why I called you about Markus. That's why I came to New York.

"I didn't trust you," she says, "but I needed your help to find out what happened to my brother."

"And we're getting close," I say. "That's what I came to tell you. I think we can prove Markus's death was not an accident."

She leans back on the couch and stares into space for a few seconds with a worried look on her face.

"What is it? I thought you'd be happy about the news. Is something else bothering you?"

She sits up straight, turns toward me, and pats my arm. "I'm sorry," she says. "Something happened that set me off, and it's bothering me. But first, tell me, what did you find out about Markus?"

"Well," I say with a return of my earlier excitement. "It's all coming together. As you know, J. B. and I met with Lewis Blair. He told us about a drug dealer named Drake. He also talked about how Daniel Leacham and other boys were afraid of Frascatore. He said it made him wonder if Frascatore might have been in the drug business or maybe doing drugs himself. A cashier at a market near Mr. Blair's office confirmed the existence of a drug dealer named Drake who forced kids to work for him. It's a long story, but the short version is that there were three boys, Markus, Dion, and Hank, who all had their left index fingers broken. So this morning, J. B. and I went to see what we could get Frascatore to tell us."

Mentayer's eyes widen. A stunned look crosses her face. "You went to CSCH headquarters?"

I nod. "I came here directly from Frascatore's office. Why?"

"No matter now," she says with a sharp shake of her head. "So, do you think this Drake guy killed Markus?"

"That's what Frascatore *wanted* us to believe," I say. "He kept giving us the runaround like he was being clever, but then he slipped up without even realizing it. He insisted he didn't know much about Drake, but he knew it was the boys' left index fingers that were broken. We never told him which fingers had been broken, and that information wasn't in the paper either. So how did he know about Markus's finger? Because he was the one who broke it. So now we have what we need to go to the police."

Mentayer lets out a long, drawn-out sigh. She shakes her head. "That's not going to convince the police to do anything, Sylvia. Frascatore could have heard about which finger it was from anyone—the boys, even Drake himself."

"Maybe so, but we have more to go on than that. Maybe one piece of information won't do it, but we have several pieces of the puzzle, and when you put them together they look like Frascatore."

Mentayer's shoulders slump and she falls back on the couch. "Not going to happen," she says. "Not going to happen." She holds her head in her hands. "God, I should have known this was all going to get complicated and cause trouble."

"What trouble? What happened?"

She clasps her hands in her lap, looks down at them. "What happened," she says through gritted teeth, "was I got fired yesterday."

My mouth drops open. She was fired? Lost her job? But for what reason? And why didn't Frascatore gloat about it when we saw him? Was it that he didn't know? All of a sudden I realize that of course he knew! That's why, at the mention of Mentayer's name, he'd smirked and said, "Well, no matter now," or "No matter any longer." Something like that. It seemed like a strange comment at the time, but now it makes sense. He said it didn't matter anymore because he knew she was gone.

I take Mentayer's hand in mine. "Oh dear, I'm afraid it's our fault," I say. "Do you think you were fired because someone at CSCH discovered that you know J. B.? Maybe they suspected you of colluding with his fraud investigation."

"No, that's on me, not J. B.," she says. "I got myself fired. I wanted to prove the allegations against CSCH were false, so I did some digging on my own. I should have left things alone. They said they fired me for embezzling funds, falsifying my travel expenditures, things like that. But I know the real reason. They fired me because I was asking too many questions." All of a sudden she stops talking. Her eyes widen as if she's just considered something for the first time.

"What is it, Mentayer?"

"I don't want to end up like my brother." She places her hands over her eyes and bursts into tears. I put my arm around her and pull her close. Her terror flows into and through me.

"How bad is it?" I ask in a whisper.

She takes a deep breath, and blows it out. Then she sits up and starts talking, fast, like she's in a race for her life. "They falsified some standardized test scores. They lied on tax returns. Some money is missing and unaccounted for. Someone *is* embezzling funds, but it's not me. I have all the evidence right here. Thank goodness I had the sense to make copies before they let me go."

She looks at a stack of papers on the coffee table. I gape at the evidence as she rattles off in more detail some of the fraudulent practices she uncovered. A terror in the pit of my stomach keeps me from tracking what she's saying.

"Does anyone else know?"

She shakes her head no.

"Are you sure?"

She nods.

"No one suspects?"

"I don't think so. No one asked me anything."

"Okay, good. The first thing we have to do is get this evidence far away from you, somewhere secure."

I lean forward on the couch and reach for the papers. My fingers touch them and Mentayer snatches them away. She presses the evidence against her chest and sits back on the couch.

"I won't let them get away with this, Sylvia."

I clutch at my throat. It feels clammy. "We don't know what they're capable of, Mentayer. We don't know everything that's involved here. But you can't have this evidence in your possession or anywhere near you."

"I believed in CSCH," she says. "It was more than a job for me."

"I know, Mentayer, I know." My eyes dart around the living room. I check the windows to make sure they're still closed. "The most important thing right now is your safety. I think you should leave New York for a while. Take a long trip, say you're going on vacation. Say you're going some place to figure out what to do next with your career."

She shakes her head, grips the stack of papers even tighter.

"You got the evidence, and that's good, Mentayer. But no one can know you have it. How about giving it to J. B.? He'll hold CSCH accountable. He can make sure nothing is traced back to you."

I hold out my hands for the documents, raise my eyebrows. "J. B. can say he uncovered the evidence himself during his investigation. No one needs to know you had anything to do with it."

She loosens her grip on the papers, but there's an ambivalent expression on her face.

"We'll make them pay. I promise. Please, Mentayer."

She lowers the papers onto her lap. I stare at them, sitting there like dynamite threatening to destroy her.

"I'm on your side, Mentayer."

Time stops until finally she picks up the papers from her lap and hands over the proof of CSCH's fraud. I look at her and nod. She nods back. Neither of us has to say a word. We both know. We're in this together. Outside, a soft rain starts falling. A pigeon perches on the window ledge.

A jarring knock on the door shatters the silence. We both jump up from the couch at the same time. We glance at each other and turn away when we glimpse the reflection of our own panic and terror in each other's eyes. The papers burn my hands like hot embers. I lift up a couch cushion and shove them under it. In a flash I lower the cushion and plop down on top of it. Mentayer sits next to me. Her hand is over her mouth. Her eyes are huge saucers. Neither of us dares make a sound.

TWENTY-ONE

April 2006

There's another knock on the door. We grab each other's hands. They've found out. They already know. It's too late.

"Mentayer? Sylvia? It's me, J. B."

We trip over each other as we race down the hall. Mentayer opens the door. Then she and I stand shoulder to shoulder with our backs flat against the wall as J. B. flies past us.

"I got here as fast as I could." He snatches a piece of paper from his briefcase and waves it in the air. "You'll never believe what Daniel Leacham just said."

Mentayer and I look at each other, then at him. "Daniel Leacham's dead," we say in unison.

"He may be dead," he says, out of breath. "But he's still talking."

All of a sudden J. B. stops. He blinks, sees Mentayer in her robe, her face without makeup, her hair uncombed. Then he looks at me, still standing with my back against the wall. "What's going on? You two look like you've seen a ghost. What happened?"

What happened? Answers swirl around in my mind but no words come out. What can I say? It's been a day of surprises, not all good but not all bad either, a day of hope crashed by despair, of unfinished pain and healing, of worry and fear, of a threat so big I can't wrap my head around it? Should I tell him that all I want to do is huddle with Mentayer in a closet, make her invisible so she'll be safe? That history is repeating itself, that my need to protect Mentayer must take precedence over anything and everything else, and that now, on top of all that, he was talking about Daniel Leacham as if he were still alive and maybe, maybe it's all too much right now for me to think about? There's a piece of paper dangling at J. B.'s side, but in my mind's eye all I can see is the stack of papers in the living room, peeking out from under the couch cushion, waiting to be discovered, waiting to destroy Mentayer.

"We'll be okay," I hear Mentayer say. "Come into the living room and sit down."

I stumble behind the two of them and sit down. In the background I hear Mentayer telling J. B. she was fired and filling him in on the details. By the time she tells him she found evidence of CSCH's fraud, I have enough presence of mind to reach down and pull out the stack of papers from under the couch cushion. J. B. snatches it from my hands and stuffs it in his briefcase.

"You're aware of the danger this puts you in, are you not?" he says.

"Yes." Mentayer tucks her hand under mine.

"You, too, Sylvia," he says.

"Me? Why? From whom?"

"Frascatore. Because of this." He picks up the piece of paper he'd pulled from his briefcase earlier and reads: "'In the event of my untimely death, I, Daniel Leacham, being of sound mind and body, declare the following to be true.'"

J. B. lowers the paper. "It was a fluke that we found this," he says. "I was checking Leacham's bank account deposits and withdrawals so I could match them with the record Lewis Blair gave me of the monthly contributions received by the Center for Boys. In the process, I discovered that Leacham used a safety deposit box in a bank he and his wife don't do business with. I told Mrs. Leacham about it, and when she went there, she found *this*." He waves the paper in the air again. "It's all here. Everything."

"What's all there?" Mentayer asks.

"Read it, for God's sake," I say.

"'When I was in elementary school, a teacher named Anthony Frascatore slapped me around until I agreed to bring drugs to him from a man named Drake.'"

I lean forward and Mentayer removes her hand from mine, places it in her lap.

"'I brought Mr. Frascatore drugs a couple of times and then I told him I didn't want to do it anymore. He got angry and threatened to hurt my family if I quit. So I kept doing what he asked. Then one day he stopped asking and left me alone. About the same time a boy named Dion Brown died after Mr. Frascatore slammed his head against the wall at school.'"

I cover my mouth with both hands. More proof of Frascatore's guilt.

"The next part is about Markus." J. B. raises his eyebrows at Mentayer. She takes in a deep breath and gives him the go-ahead with a dip of her chin.

"'After Dion Brown died, another boy named Markus LeMeur told me about something he saw.'" J. B. pauses. Mentayer sucks in her breath. "'Markus was a few years younger than me and lived in the same neighborhood. He said he saw Dion handing something over to Mr. Frascatore. He was frightened. I knew that what he'd witnessed was a drug exchange, but I didn't say anything.'"

Mentayer looks up at the ceiling. A tear runs down her left cheek. She wipes it away.

"'After that, Markus disappeared. I told my parents I was scared something bad happened to him because maybe he saw or knew something. They asked me what it was, and I lied and said I didn't know. We moved away after that and my parents transferred me to a different school. I never told anyone what I knew about Mr. Frascatore.'"

"That's it," I say. "Now the police will do something."

Mentayer nods. J. B. continues reading.

"'I know that Mr. Frascatore used other little boys like he used me and Dion. It was a way for him to get his drugs delivered to him at school.'"

Mentayer slams the palms of her hands on the coffee table. "No, not Markus. He was not one of them. He would *never* allow himself to be used like that. He wouldn't. He was killed because he said no."

She starts weeping into her hands. She leans against me. Her arm is shaking.

"Markus knew what he saw. That's why he was so scared," I say. My eyes fill with tears. "He tried to tell me, but I didn't understand."

Mentayer moves away from me and sits up. "He should have told *me*," she says. "I would have understood."

"He was afraid Frascatore would hurt you if you knew," I say. "He was protecting you."

We both fall silent. J. B. picks up Leacham's statement again. "There's more," he says with a lift of his eyebrows. "May I?"

I nod. Mentayer wipes away the tears from both her cheeks with the backs of her hands.

"'I have proof of Mr. Frascatore's guilt. When I met with him to confront him, he admitted his involvement with drugs and confessed that he'd hurt a boy badly. A recording of that conversation is included with this statement.'"

I reach for Mentayer's hand and squeeze it. "There it is," I say. "*Now* we have all the proof we need."

"And now, for the grand finale," J. B. says. "Are you ready for it?" He smiles, then reads.

"'Dion and Markus might still be alive if I had said something. I have lived for years with the shame of not speaking up. To make amends, I've tried to save other boys from the fate that befell them, which leads me to this confession.'"

J. B. pauses to look at us. "Here comes the best part," he says. "'I have been blackmailing Mr. Frascatore, based on a presumption, which has proven to be correct, that throughout his life, he has lived in fear of being found out. I promised Mr. Frascatore that, in return for five million dollars, I will keep his secret about what he did to Markus LeMeur and others while in the throes of his own drug addiction. My motivation for blackmailing him is, I believe, a noble one. I pledged a contribution to the Center for Boys for the exact amount of money that Mr. Frascatore agreed to pay for my continued silence.'"

J. B. sees the stunned looks on our faces. "It gets even better," he says with a lopsided grin.

"'Included with this statement is a bank account record showing deposits of one hundred thousand dollars each month from an anonymous source and corresponding monthly payments in the same amount to the Center for Boys, in care of its director, Mr. Lewis Blair.'"

Another pregnant pause, and then he says, "Are you ready for this?"

"There's more?" I say.

Mentayer gives J. B. a knowing look, as if she already knows what he is going to read next.

"'I have reason to believe that Mr. Frascatore's payments to me came from CSCH funds, but so far I have been unable to substantiate my suspicion.'"

J. B. places the statement face up on the coffee table.

"So *that's* why Leacham was so interested in CSCH," I say.

"And why he wouldn't tell us what story he was working on," J. B. says. "It was going to be an expose of CSCH."

"We know something else, too," Mentayer says. "Take the evidence out of your briefcase, J. B., and I'll show you."

He hands the stack of papers to her, and she starts sorting through them. "Here they are," she says as she pulls several pages from the pile. She lays them side by side on the coffee table. "Copies of some of CSCH's monthly financial statements." She points to items highlighted in red on the expenses column of each. "See these expenditures? One hundred thousand dollars. Miscellaneous expenses. Every month. The same amount. Caught my eye right away, but I couldn't explain it." She sits back on the couch and crosses her arms. "Until now."

J. B. places Leacham's statement on the coffee table next to the other papers.

"So, Frascatore was addicted to drugs," I say as I stare at all the evidence. "He killed Markus because he wouldn't be his delivery boy and because he was afraid Markus would tell someone that he saw Dion Brown doing what he'd refused to do. Daniel Leacham, who had delivered drugs to Frascatore as a child, was blackmailing him in exchange for not telling anyone about his sordid past. At the time of Leacham's death, he was trying to prove that Frascatore was embezzling CSCH funds to make the blackmail payments. That's why Leacham was so angry about CSCH. He couldn't stomach the idea of Frascatore further victimizing poor children by stealing money from their education."

"Then Frascatore killed Leacham, or had him killed," J. B. says. "To keep him from finding out he was paying the blackmail with CSCH funds."

"And with Leacham out of the way," Mentayer adds, "he doesn't have any more payments."

"You're sure no one knows you have these?" J. B. says with a glance at the financial statements and other papers in front of us.

A chill comes over the room. Mentayer goes over to her grandmother's chair and wraps the old quilt around her shoulders. J. B. puts her evidence back in his briefcase along with Leacham's statement. He uses the combination lock to secure it. This is the first time I've ever seen him use it.

"Mentayer, we need to get you out of the city," he says. "And, Sylvia, you need to lie low, hide out in the hotel until Frascatore is in police custody."

I pull out my cell phone, dial the number for the Bronx NYPD precinct.

"Detective Gretchen Crannower, this is Sylvia Jensen... Good, I'm glad you remember me. We need to see you. It's urgent. Someone's life is in danger."

TWENTY-TWO

April 2006

Two days ago we turned all our evidence over to Detective Gretchen Crannower. And now we wait for it to go through forensics and for a warrant for Frascatore's arrest to be brought before a judge. J. B. keeps busy writing, and Mentayer is visiting her adoptive parents in upstate New York. As for me, after telling folks back home in Monrow City that they could expect an exposé of CSCH's fraudulent practices soon, I've been sitting in my hotel room watching old movies and trying not to worry. Mostly, I have not been successful.

Tonight, just like the last two nights, I can't sleep. I toss and turn, get out of bed, stare at the ancient black and white square tiles on the bathroom floor, and then go back to bed again. I wait for dawn to come by reviewing all the evidence: Daniel Leacham's statement, a direct witness account of what happened; his recording of Frascatore's confession, solid admissible evidence; CSCH's financial statements including documentation of Frascatore's payments to cover up what he did to Markus; written evidence of CSCH's other fraudulent practices; witnesses that can attest to Frascatore's violent past. But then I break those pieces down into the minutest of details and come to a depressing conclusion. It won't be over until it's over. Not until Frascatore is in custody. Not until he's tried and convicted. Not until Monrow City's mayor cancels the contract with the CSCH Corporation. Not until...

Then I move from the "not untils" to the "what ifs." What if there's a reason we haven't heard from Detective Crannower yet? What if something went wrong? So many things could. What if forensics determined the evidence was too weak? What if forensics didn't but a judge did? What if the police decided to use their limited resources to investigate Leacham's death first? What if they put Markus's cold case on hold? My mind races from one bleak scenario to another, each one replaced by an even more pessimistic one, each one converging down a dark tunnel that ends with my biggest fear. Frascatore could get away with it.

I stand up and pace from the bed to the window and back again. I need a drink. One is all. It'll settle me down. Just one, to stop my obsessing. Just one, to help me sleep. The hotel bar calls out to me, and I start getting dressed.

Whatever are you doing, Sylvia? Are you forgetting how cunning, baffling—powerful—alcohol is? Stop and think it through!

I sit down at the desk, turn on my computer, and open the Internet. I log in to the North American Indian Clean and Sober recovery website.

"Hehewuti," I type in the chat room. "Are you there?"

Hehewuti's instantaneous reply pops up on the screen. She's always online, no matter what time of day or night.

Hehewuti, a Hopi from Arizona, has been my online sponsor ever since I got sober in 2000. Even though the first thing I learned in recovery was that rigorous honesty was essential, I passed myself off to Hehewuti for years as an Ojibwe from Canada, thinking my lie was okay as long as I was scrupulously honest about everything else.

"Is this Numees, my little Indian wannabe?"

Just last year I confessed to Hehewuti my true identity as a white woman from the Midwest with no American Indian ancestry. She forgave me, but she still calls me Numees, the Algonquin name I'd chosen as my original screen name. She likes to tease me about it. I don't mind. It keeps me honest.

"I'm still Sylvia," I type, "but I'm in New York City right now."

"And what trouble have you gotten yourself into this time, Numees?"

I type a quick summary of what's been going on, without mentioning any real names or facts.

"So you're at it again," she says. She's referring to the last time something shook me to the core—and almost back to the bottle. It was last year, when J. B. and I stumbled on some disturbing evidence while we were investigating the death of an American Indian boy in a foster home.

"This time someone's out there who hurt people in the past, and I'm afraid he will hurt me next or, even worse, will hurt someone else, someone I care about, and it's my fault because I could have stopped him years ago and I didn't and now more lives are in danger." I stop and wiggle my fingers. They hurt from typing so fast.

"So what happens when you think you're the reason people get hurt, Numees?"

"It's hard to live with myself when I can't protect people I care about. It makes me crazy. I'm making myself crazy."

"So you want me to restore you to sanity now, Numees?"

"If only you could."

"Gonna have to do it yourself. So tell me."

"An old friend here is suffering because of me. And now she could get hurt or even killed. It's my fault."

"Is your friend safe right now, Numees?"

"Yes, but... "

"Is this an immediate emergency? Do you need to call 911?"

"No."

"Okay then. So, you're consumed by guilt, right? You're making yourself crazy by thinking all the things that have happened and could happen are your fault. Right?"

"It's what I do."

"Okay. Walk through each thing you feel is your fault. What is the one thing you can do to make it worse?"

"I can drink."

"Bingo! Want to?"

"My disease does."

"Okay, you know the drill. Go ahead and talk to it. In writing."

I take a deep breath and start typing.

"Why do you want to dangle a glass of wine in front of me now? When I'm reunited with two people who are as precious to me now as they were as little children? You want me to get drunk now that we're close to getting justice? Is that what you want, alcoholism? Well, too bad for you, disease. There's no way I'm going to do that. No way."

"Good job, Numees."

"Thank you," I type, and then I sign off.

The muscles in my neck and back are no longer in knots. The garbage is gone from my head. I go back to bed and start to drift off to sleep. And the room phone rings.

I jump up. My bones creak as my bare feet hit the floor. It's the front desk. "There's a detective in the lobby who would like to talk to you and Mr. Harrell."

My foot starts jittering on the floor. "Detective Crannower?" I say into the phone. "At this hour?" I hear voices in the background.

"Yes," the front desk clerk says. "It's Detective Crannower."

"I'll be right down," I say.

I throw on the last clean blouse left in my suitcase and a pair of soft tan twill slacks with an elastic waistband. I dab some rouge on my cheeks and brush my hair, pull it back into a bun. On my way down the hall, I make a quick call to J. B.

"I'm on my way down to the lobby," I say when he doesn't answer. "Frascatore must be in custody. Why else would Detective Crannower come to see us now? I bet she wants to tell us in person. I'm so excited. Be there in a minute."

On the elevator, I bounce up and down on my feet. The wait is over. We did it. We did it. I'm like a kid on a roller coaster. I've reached the crest of the steepest hill and am about to fly over the edge, hands up in the air, a conqueror plunging to hard-fought victory. It takes my breath away.

I step off the elevator and look around. The hotel clerk points to the bar. "In there," he says.

I rush to the bar and step inside. My senses are assaulted by the smell of liquor. But that's not all that gets to me. It's the allure of the seductive music, the dim lights, the laughter and loud voices and all the fun times that go along with it. Less than an hour ago, I'd almost come down here for a drink to alleviate my anxiety. Now the idea of celebrating Frascatore's arrest with a toast is appealing. I am in dangerous territory.

I stand in the doorway for a few minutes and brace myself. Neither J. B. nor Detective Crannower is sitting at the bar, so I go from booth to booth looking for them. When I reach the last one back in the corner, someone grabs me around the waist and thrusts something sharp, like a gun, into my side.

"Slide all the way in and don't make a sound," a man says in a low voice.

I hold my breath and do as I'm told. The man slides in next to me. He pushes the sharp object into my rib cage. I turn to see who it is. His features are distorted in the light of the tea candle on the table, but I know it's him. There's no doubt in my mind.

"You bastard," I say under my breath. "What the hell do you want?"

"No need to get upset," Frascatore says in a smooth, conciliatory voice that doesn't even sound like him. "I want to talk to you. That's all. I don't mean to scare you. I ordered you a glass of the house wine, but if you'd like something more substantial, no problem. I'm buying."

He slides a large glass of shimmering white wine in front of me. I push the glass away. He slides it back.

I force myself to look away. My eyes land on five shot glasses in front of Frascatore, three empty, two still with a brown liquor in them, the color of bourbon. My favorite.

"All I want is to talk, Sylvia. I want you to hear me out. I've been doing a lot of thinking and I need to talk. That's all." He moves the glass of wine a few inches closer to me.

"I don't drink," I mutter. "And I don't talk to anyone with a gun pointed at me."

"Oh, this?" He raises the side of his jacket. Something is pointing out of his pocket. He lowers it to his side. "I'm sorry, Sylvia. I didn't know how else to get your attention. Please, have a drink with me. Come on. It won't hurt you."

His tone is sugary and his speech slurry. I could jerk my elbow into his arm and scream. I could try to grab the gun, if that's what's in his pocket. But it's within inches of my hip, so I think it's best to play it safe.

Frascatore nudges the wineglass closer. I can smell the wine's sweetness. I lick my lips. I turn my head away. I look at him and try to mold my face into an interested expression.

"Okay, so what do you want to talk about? Why did you tell the clerk you were a detective?"

"That's the thing, Sylvia. I got a call from this detective. She starts asking me all kinds of questions. Some of the same questions you and Mr. Harrell asked when you came to see me. You know, about Markus LeMeur and a drug dealer named Drake. They're conducting an investigation. But you already know that." He downs a shot and slams the glass onto the table. "I don't blame Mentayer for wanting to know what happened to her brother. I think it's good of you to help her."

Sure you do, I say to him in my head. *Sure you do.* I look into his eyes and see fear. The muscles in my neck relax.

"Why are you telling me this?" I say. "Why me?"

"Because I know you're talking to the police and I need your help. I know I don't deserve it, the way I've treated you, Sylvia. But if you could find it in you to at least listen." He stops, gulps down the bourbon in the last shot glass. "I think the police suspect me of killing that boy, Sylvia. I need your help."

He stops talking and hangs his head down in a pathetic gesture.

"I know you killed Markus," I say. "And I think you were afraid Mentayer was going to find out. That's why you got her fired. So go ahead and shoot me if you want. But you won't get away with it, not with all these people here."

I brace myself. I cross my arms over my chest to ward off the blow. But he doesn't go into a rage. He doesn't even look at me. Instead, he moans and curls into himself as I stare, wide-eyed, at the best performance of a disappointed and defeated man I've ever seen.

At long last, he raises his head. His cheeks are wet with real tears. His eyes are desperate. What do I do with this dance I'm in, one minute distancing myself from him as if he's as toxic as diphtheria, the next minute sympathizing as if he's a fellow sufferer?

"I did a lot of things back then, Sylvia." He stops, chokes on a sob that almost sounds real. "I did a lot of things that were wrong and hurtful. I'm ashamed of myself for all of it. But, Sylvia, you have to understand. I was nothing but a pathetic drug addict. I lived with the humiliation of that every day. The drugs. The lying. Losing control. The... you have to believe me, Sylvia. Do you have any idea what it's like to be at the mercy of something you can't control?"

Oh yes, I do. I know. I stare at the glass of wine in front of me. Imagine reaching for it, pretending to tip the glass to my lips, a distraction, an avoidance of feeling, of empathy. But then I hear Hehewuti say my name. *Sylvia?*

I hurl the glass across the table. It smashes to bits. Frascatore doesn't flinch. His head hangs down so low his chin touches his chest, like a man whose shame has been laid bare, whose degradation is now complete. Against my better judgment and in spite of myself, I lift my hand and reach out to touch his shoulder. That's when all hell breaks loose. Cops are yelling. They storm the booth. They grab Frascatore by the collar.

"Hands up! Now! Okay, cuff him. Let's go. Get him out of here."

It all happens so fast. There's shouting and banging and then all of a sudden it's over and I'm still sitting in the booth, scrunched up against the wall, shaking, unable to move. Then J. B. is sitting next to me. His hand is on my arm.

"It's okay now, Sylvia. It's okay now. They got him. Good thing you called me or I never would have known."

I release the air in my lungs. An ocean of tears pushes me facedown onto the table. The wine wets my arms and hands, the shards of glass cut my skin. A tremor moves into my throat and flows out in tsunami waves of tears.

A wound is healing over, a scab forming then shed, a scar in honor of a small boy's life, taken unjustly, the man who took it himself wounded and now in custody.

"It's over," J. B. says as puts his arm around me and helps me sit up. He takes my hands and pulls me from the booth. My legs are shaky, but I manage to walk out of the bar. J. B. sees me to my room and asks me if I'm okay. I nod, and he leaves. I go into the bathroom and fill the sink with cold water. I take off my blouse and soak it in the water. I smell like a winery. I take a long, warm shower. Then I go to bed and fall into a deep sleep.

The next morning I wake to the ringing of my cell phone. I push myself up on my elbows, then flop back down, light-headed. The room is hot, muggy. My hair curls and mingles with the sweat on my cheeks. I grip the fabric of my cotton nightgown and dry myself. I bring the phone to my ear.

"Good morning," J. B. says. "I thought you might sleep in, so I waited to call."

I glance at the clock. It's one o'clock. "I must have slept like a log."

"No doubt," he says, laughing. "Quite the night you had."

"Tell me about it."

"I talked to Detective Crannower this morning," he says. "She called Mentayer this morning to tell her Frascatore's in custody. They haven't charged him yet. Have you eaten anything?"

"Are you kidding? You woke me up. I'm starving. Give me half an hour."

The hotel restaurant is almost empty, the breakfast crowd long gone, a handful of people still lingering over lunch.

"Well, aren't we bright and spiffy today," the waitress says as she approaches our table. I smile and hold out my striped multicolored cotton shawl for her to admire. "I missed you this morning," she says. "Breakfast is over, but for you two, I can always make an exception. Looks like you slept in today."

I order an omelet with the works: bacon, sausage, three kinds of cheese, onions, and broccoli. J. B. orders the usual continental breakfast with a smile as reserved as his conservative navy blue suit. I tell our waitress we're going to be leaving New York in a day or two. I gush to her about how much I've appreciated her friendliness every morning. Her eyes dance as she says she'll miss me.

"So what are we going to do to celebrate?" I say to J. B. I notice the look on his face and pause. "Why such a skeptical expression? We did it, J. B. We both got what we came here for. And I must say, this hotel is losing its charm for me after being cooped up all weekend. I'm ready to go home. No one in the coalition believed we could win this one. I want to celebrate with them, too."

J. B. raises one eyebrow. "It's not normal for things to fall into place like this," he says as he reaches into his jacket pocket for his smartphone.

I laugh and reach across the table to give him a playful tap on his arm. "Come on, J. B., this isn't the time for second-guessing. We did it. Now's the time to celebrate."

He ignores me and talks into his phone. "I'd like to speak with Clarke Craine, please. This is J. B. Harrell calling... I see, and when did you say you expect him?... No, no need to leave a message. I'll try again later. Thank you."

"Why are you calling Craine?"

"I thought maybe I could get a quote from him about Frascatore before any of this hits the news. I'd like to hear what he has to say about his old buddy Tony now."

I laugh. "I'll bet CSCH doesn't want to own him now," I say.

J. B. stares down at his phone. "Hmm. There's a message here from Mentayer. She must have called while I was trying to reach Craine."

He pushes the speaker button and places the phone in the middle of the table. I lean forward.

"I hope she's back in town," I say. "Maybe we can go out for a fancy dinner or something."

J. B. turns on the phone and we listen. "This is Mentayer speaking."

We look at each other, our expressions echoing the same thing. Something's not right.

"I am leaving now and will be gone for some time. I am calling to inform you that there is nothing to worry about."

Alarms are going off in my head. "That doesn't sound like her at all," I say. "Not the voice. Not the words. What does she mean, she's leaving? From where, her parents' house? And she'll be gone for some time? Gone, where? What does 'some time' mean? Play it again." I lean closer to the phone as we listen a second time.

"That's not her," J. B. says. "It's not her language."

"She sounds like a robot. She doesn't even say your name. It's like she's talking to an anonymous person. And she doesn't mention Frascatore or anything about what's happened. Didn't you say Detective Crannower called her?"

He plays the message a third time. I hold my breath as I listen.

"This is Mentayer speaking. I am leaving now and will be gone for some time. I am calling to inform you that there is nothing to worry about."

I jump up and push my chair back. J. B. stands at the same time. "She's speaking in code," he says.

"Let's go," I say. I'm already heading for the door.

We rush outside and flag down a cab by the curb. We throw ourselves into the back seat. Several seconds pass. I stare out the window. I press my foot down on the floor as if that will make the cab go faster.

"Maybe we're worrying for nothing," J. B. says at last.

"Right," I say. "After all, Frascatore's in custody."

We don't look at each other. We don't say anything. We both know it's a lie. There's plenty to worry about. Mentayer's message was clear. She's in trouble.

TWENTY-THREE
April 2006

We race up to Mentayer's apartment, with J. B.'s long legs leaping up three stairs at a time to my two. At the second-floor landing he makes a sudden stop and holds his arms straight out from his sides. I make a nosedive into his back. He tips his head to listen. We walk on our toes down the hall.

"Her door's open," he whispers.

I take in a sharp breath. The door is ajar.

With a sweep of his hand, J. B. covers my mouth. We press our backs against the wall and listen. He pushes the door in a few inches with his foot. We wait a few seconds. He pushes it open a bit more, then a bit more. No one is lying in wait on the other side of the door. We slip into the apartment. The door is closing behind us. I swing my leg back and catch it with my foot so it comes to rest against the doorframe. A muscle tightens in my leg.

We slide our backs along the wall and make our way inside, one side step at a time. A chair is on its side in the living room. Books and papers are scattered on the floor. I shudder and my neck vibrates. Someone was here. Might still be here. We're being stupid. We have to call the police.

I reach into my purse for my cell phone, but J. B. stops me with a sharp shake of his head. He purses his lips and presses his forefinger against them. He pokes his head around the corner from the dining room to the hall and motions that all is clear. Two more steps, and I hear a blood-curdling scream.

J. B. and I crash into each other as we fly down the hall. Our feet skid to a halt at the door to Mentayer's bedroom. Clarke Craine is standing behind Mentayer with one beefy hand around her throat and the other pressing a gun against her temple. His grayish-brown pompadour hairstyle is in disarray and his white shirt is unbuttoned. His suit jacket lies crumpled on the bed and his tie on the floor. Mentayer's tan silk blouse hangs out on one side and her matching linen slacks are askew. She grips Craine's hands at her neck and looks at us through eyes filled with both dread and fury.

"Come any closer and she's dead."

His voice is low and sinister and his face twisted. The upstanding entrepreneur who spoke in the library and the successful businessman J. B. interviewed are gone, replaced by someone unrecognizable.

I stand in the doorway with my eyes and mouth open. My legs and feet are stuck at awkward angles to each other. Even the act of breathing is unthinkable. I strain to keep my balance.

"Why are you here, Mr. Craine?" J. B.'s voice is calm, his words measured.

"To get what this bitch stole from CSCH." He squeezes his hands tighter around Mentayer's neck. She makes a gurgling sound. Her eyes widen.

"I left a message for you this morning," J. B. says in a conversational tone that is disarming. "I hoped to get a quote from you about the police taking Anthony Frascatore into custody. I mean, with the two of you being friends and you getting him that job at CSCH and everything. I imagine the news was quite a shock to you."

"Tony's a fucking idiot," Craine says.

"You think so?" J. B. shrugs his shoulders and raises his eyebrows in feigned surprise. "It seems to me it takes someone pretty clever to get away with what he's gotten away with for so long."

Craine snorts and rolls his eyes. "That fool was born with half a brain. I've been bailing him out ever since we were kids, always cleaning his messes up, cleaning *him* up."

"I met him, you know." J. B. flashes Craine a crooked grin. "He seemed pretty smart to me."

Clarke Craine cackles. "That's the funniest thing I've ever heard."

It's working. J. B.'s taunts are distracting him, taking his attention off Mentayer.

"I'm serious," J. B. says. "It takes brains to embezzle money from CSCH for such a long time without being detected."

"No way Tony did that. Shit, he couldn't even steal money from the teachers' union without screwing it up and landing in jail."

J. B. is getting Craine to talk. That must mean he expects us to get out of here alive and with more information, maybe even a confession. My legs are numb from holding them in one position for so long. But with J. B. as our lifeline, I find the courage to move my left foot. At a snail's pace, I align it with my right foot. I hold my breath and keep my eyes on Craine the whole time. The feeling starts coming back in my legs.

"Let me see if I understand you, Mr. Craine." J. B. says. "It sounds like you think Frascatore's not smart enough to steal CSCH funds. But the police think he was paying Daniel Leacham to keep his mouth shut about Markus LeMeur's murder. Are you saying they arrested him for nothing? Can I quote you?"

"Oh no, not for nothing. It's true that Tony's an idiot for going and getting himself in trouble for something he didn't do. But that doesn't mean he's been arrested for nothing. Oh no. His arrest serves my purpose. And, to be clear, Mr. Harrell, you won't be quoting me about any of this."

"So, Frascatore didn't kill Markus. *You* did. And now you're going to let your friend take the fall for it."

Craine strikes Mentayer on the side of her head with his gun. She cries out. I freeze. J. B. must have miscalculated. He went too far. He shouldn't have accused Craine of murder. I start praying. *Please, God, we need your help bad.* But why would God hear me now when the rest of the time I ignore him, or her, or it? I suck in my breath. God isn't going to save us. I have to do something myself.

"I know you didn't murder Markus," I say. "I know it was Frascatore."

Craine laughs and laughs. "Oh, Tony killed that kid all right."

I bite my bottom lip. "I always knew he did," I say. Then I quickly add, "I'm agreeing with you," so he won't think I'm being a smart aleck or showing off.

"Stupid bastard," Craine says with disdain. "I sent him to scare that kid, not kill him. I said, 'Tony, go take care of him.' So what does he do? What he always does. He screws it up. Okay, so maybe he misunderstood. Maybe he thinks I meant to kill him, but then he doesn't even have the sense to do it right. He kills that kid right where he lives. Geez. So now he's got a dead body on his hands and he doesn't know what to do with it, right, because he's got no brains. So what does he do? What he always does. He calls me. He's like a guy who squashes a spider with a concrete block, and when it lands on his own foot, he hobbles over to me, howling for help. That about sums up Tony's whole damn life."

I'm nauseous but I force myself to keep him talking. "So you helped Frascatore hide Markus's body in the basement of the school." I swallow the sour taste in my mouth.

"Helped him? Shit. I worked the whole thing out myself. Pretty smart, I'd say. You gotta admit I did a pretty damn good job of hiding it way in the back of a storage hole. If that school hadn't been torn down, that kid's body would never have been found. And I figured, even if it was discovered, you, Ms. Sylvia, would have been blamed. That's why I had Tony start a rumor that you kidnapped the kid. At least that's one thing he got right. That story spread like wildfire.

"Why are you looking so surprised? Hell, I knew you were Ms. Sylvia first time we met." He laughs and laughs. "And here's the best part. During that strike, you were bringing those Black Panthers into the school every night. Man, that was perfect. If anyone found that kid's body, they woulda gotten nailed for it in a minute, no question about it."

I'm on the verge of throwing up. "That kid had a name," I say through gritted teeth.

J. B. pokes me with his elbow. He brings his finger up to the side of his nose. I grasp my arms with my hands and purse my lips. I take in a short breath and let it out. *His name was Markus,* I say in my head. *He was a good little boy, an exceptional little boy.*

Craine opens his mouth and bares his teeth. He tightens his grip on Mentayer's neck but aims his gun at me. He sneers. "You know what, Ms. Sylvia, I should have sent Tony after you instead of after that kid. You were the real problem back then. You bring this one," he slides the barrel of the gun along Mentayer's cheek, "into your house to live with you like she was your goddamned daughter or something. What was I supposed to do? Sit back and let Markus rat us out to his sister? And then his sister tells you and you blab it all to the cops? Are you fucking kidding me?" He narrows his eyes and glares at me.

My shoulders tighten. "Blab what to the cops?" My voice is weak, unconvincing.

J. B. jumps back in. "About his drug business. He didn't want you blabbing to the cops about his drug business."

The corners of Craine's lips curl up in a creepy smile. "That's right, Mr. Harrell. I was in the drug business. And I was successful at it. You wouldn't believe how much money I was raking in. The last thing I needed was to have the cops shut it down because some goody-goody squealing bitch like Ms. Sylvia here couldn't keep her mouth shut."

He aims the gun at me. I'm his target now, as I was his target then. It's because of me that Markus is dead. It's my fault. My fault. My ears are ringing. Craine is going to pull the trigger now. He's going to shoot the right target this time.

"I have a question," J. B. says. Craine takes his eyes off me. I let out my breath.

"Aren't you the curious one, Mr. Harrell?"

J. B. smiles. "Did you work with a guy named Drake?"

Craine laughs. It's an ugly laugh, a laugh filled with contempt. "I guess you could say that, Mr. Harrell."

"Did Drake break Markus's finger? Or was it you?"

"Yes."

J. B. hesitates. He scrunches his eyebrows together.

"What do you mean, 'yes'?" I ask.

"'What do you mean, yes?'" His voice drips with sarcasm.

J. B. slaps his thigh. "So *you're* Drake."

Craine chuckles under his breath and puffs out his chest. "One and the same."

I stare at him. What did he say? I can't get my head around it. *Watch the gun. Watch the gun. Don't hyperventilate. Keep breathing. Keep breathing.*

"And you killed Daniel Leacham," J. B. says. "Or did you hire someone to do that for you?"

"Nah. That one I did myself. Piece of cake. Simple injection did it. He was so drunk he didn't even see me."

"So with Leacham out of the way, his blackmail scheme goes away."

"Bingo, Mr. Harrell! And so does his attempt to prove that the blackmail money was coming from CSCH funds."

"Oh my, yes," J. B. says in a matter-of-fact tone. "It would have been bad for you if Daniel Leacham had exposed your embezzlement scheme."

"Let me put it to you this way, Mr. Harrell. The smartest decision I ever made in my life was to get into the investment business."

J. B. nods. There's no need to prod Craine. He's a most willing, even eager, witness. He's sure he's going to get away scot-free, and he's lording it over us. He's letting us know there's nothing we can do about what he's telling us because he is going to kill us.

"I'm a legitimate businessman," he continues, "and, as you know, I am one of the best. I know a lot of people in this town. I make a lot of money. A lot. More than you can imagine. Now, do you think I'm going to let anyone spoil all that? Like Miss LeMeur here." He jabs the gun into Mentayer's cheek. She gasps. "Did you think you could walk away with CSCH documents and get away with it, sweetheart?"

I panic. My head's in a scramble. I blurt out the first thing I think of. "Frascatore killed Dion Brown, didn't he?" I hold my breath. Please, let him bite.

He laughs. Then he laughs some more. "Naw, Ms. Sylvia," he says at last. "Not that it couldn't have been Tony, but I guess that one's on me." He laughs harder. I hold my stomach. I can taste the vomit in my throat.

J. B. raises his finger. "I have another question, Mr. Craine. How do you know Frascatore isn't going to tell the cops everything you're telling us? Do you think he's going to go to prison for you without a fight?"

"My oh my, oh my, oh my, Mr. Harrell. Maybe you're not so bright after all. Let Tony talk all he wants. The police are not going to believe him."

"Maybe not. But they are going to believe Leacham. He put everything in writing."

"Ah, the Daniel Leacham statement." Craine chuckles. "So get this. Tony gets one phone call today, and who does he call? *Moi*, of course. The idiot wants me to bail him out, like I always do, and I can tell how scared he is, you know, because he goes on and on about Leacham's statement, and the more he tells me about what's in it, I'm going, 'Look, Tony, they can't prove anything from that, it's nothing but the speculations of a man with a guilty conscience who committed suicide. Nothing to worry about.'" He takes in a breath, then cracks his lips into an I-told-you-so smile.

"Nothing to worry about because the cops are in on it?" I say.

Craine burst out laughing. "As naive as ever, aren't you, Ms. Sylvia," he says in between laughing.

"Okay, then why was Markus so afraid of the police?" I scowl.

"Maybe because they beat people up whenever they wanted to?" he says. "But don't get me wrong, a few cops were willing to help us out every once in a while. For a few bucks."

"How did you do it?" J. B. says. "How did you manage to use CSCH's money to pay Leacham without getting caught?"

"You are aware, are you not, Mr. Harrell, that I am on the corporate board?"

"Yes, I am, but who did you get to handle the money?"

"Do you reveal your sources, Mr. Harrell?" He chortles, then all of a sudden turns dead serious. "But enough of this. It's been fun, folks, but now it's time to get back to what I came here for before the two of you crashed the party. So, Miss LeMeur, it's decision time. Do you want to give me the evidence you stole or do I have to kill one of your friends first? Which one? Mr. Harrell or Ms. Sylvia? Your choice."

"I don't have any evid—" He hits her on the side of her face with the butt of the gun. A splotch of red springs up, then rivulets of blood begin to trickle down her cheek. She doesn't wipe them away. She doesn't touch her face. She doesn't move at all.

"I have it," J. B. says. "I have what you're looking for."

"Well, well, Mr. Harrell. If what you say is true, then I might as well go ahead and get rid of this one." He waves the gun in front of Mentayer's face. "But if what you say isn't true, then I might as well shoot you now. I bet that will make her cooperate. So, you see, it's a matter of who I believe and who dies first. Oh, what to do, what to do." He waves the gun back and forth in a mocking motion. Then he points it at J. B. His finger is on the trigger. A chill runs through me.

"It's in my office across the hall," Mentayer says.

"Now we're getting somewhere." He shoves the gun into her ribs and pushes her toward the door. "You two first."

J. B. goes first and I stumble through the door behind him. My head is speeding a mile a minute. Craine is faking it. He doesn't know what evidence Mentayer has. He isn't even sure if she has any. That's why we're still alive.

He knows she was fired for asking a lot of questions. Maybe someone told him she took some papers with her, but he doesn't know what they were. He's here to find out if she has any solid evidence, and if she does, he plans to get rid of it. He doesn't know CSCH's monthly financial statements are already in the hands of the police. If he did, there would be no reason for him to keep us alive.

We're in Mentayer's office now. We're one step closer to Craine finding out there's nothing here, one step closer to death. But maybe there is something here. Maybe Mentayer kept other copies of the evidence that she didn't tell us about. Even so, as soon as Craine gets his hands on them, he's still going to kill us.

"Where is it?"

Mentayer hesitates. Craine grabs her around the neck. She's struggling to breathe. "Don't make me ask again," he says, releasing her.

"In the bottom drawer of my desk."

"Get it."

"The drawer's locked. The key's over there." She points to a cabinet along the opposite wall.

"Hands up. Go!"

Mentayer holds her hands high in the air. She lifts one foot up and places it in front of the other, then lifts the opposite foot, repeating each movement with caution as she makes her way toward the cabinet. Nearing the wall, she stubs her toe on the edge of an area rug. She pitches forward, and J. B. lunges at Craine from behind, pushes him face-first into the cabinet. Craine recovers in a flash. He twists his body around and punches J. B. in the jaw. I watch J. B. drop to the floor. Craine shoots the gun.

I leap onto Craine's back, my arms flailing and unable to get a grip on him. He shrugs me off like a mosquito and I land on the floor. He comes after me. The gun drops to the floor. I snatch it up. Craine lurches for it, and the gun goes off again.

He howls and grabs one leg. I hold the gun in both hands, my fingers shaking. I didn't mean to shoot him. The gun went off by accident. I've never held a gun before in my life.

Craine glares at me, still holding his leg but ready to pounce. Will I have to shoot? Can I pull the trigger? Will I kill him? Can I? I don't want to kill him. But if I don't kill him, he'll kill me. I have to shoot.

All of a sudden, he grabs the gun from my hands. *Run. Run.* I turn around, and he hits me with something on the back of my head, something hard. I crouch down, cover my head. Crushing blows to my shoulders, my back, my arms. He kicks me in the head, a fierce kick filled with rage. Personal.

His hands grip my shoulders and turn me onto my back. I look up at his bared teeth. Mentayer stands behind him. Her arms are raised. She holds something round in her hands. Then everything goes black.

TWENTY-FOUR

April 2006

I hear a voice. A woman's voice. Is she talking to me? Am I dreaming? I turn toward the sound and my ears ring. I'm going in and out of a thick fog. I try to wake up, but my body wants to sleep. A lead weight holds my eyelids down. I pry them up with my fingers. There's a globe of light in the middle of a flawless white ceiling above me. It's bright, much too bright. My eyes snap shut.

"Welcome back, Sylvia."

I open one eye halfway and try to push myself up on the bed with my elbows. A wave of nausea comes over me. My head hurts. Everything hurts. I cry out and fall back on the pillow.

"Don't try to get up."

Mentayer stands over me. She smiles as she tucks in the sheet around my neck. She pats my shoulder and it all comes back to me. Clarke Craine choking Mentayer at gunpoint, shooting J. B., punching him in the jaw, boasting about drug dealing and killing, telling us he's Drake. *Craine is Drake.* Drake broke Hank's finger so he'd deliver his drugs. Drake broke Dion Brown's finger and killed him. Drake broke Markus LeMeur's finger and threatened him. *Drake is Craine. Craine is Drake.*

Drake broke Daniel Leacham's finger as a boy, and Craine killed him as an adult. Craine tried to kill us. Drake the drug dealer, Craine the hedge fund manager, different points in time, one and the same person. The magnitude of it crushes me, like a swelling wave, the kind that hurls you up, pushes you down, then flings you onto the shore and leaves you battered but breathing and grateful to be alive.

"It's okay, Sylvia. Everything's okay now." Mentayer's hands are on my shoulders, holding me, keeping me safe.

"How long have I been in the hospital?"

"Two days."

"My head hurts. I hurt all over."

"I'm not surprised. You got a concussion, some broken ribs, a dislocated shoulder, and some ugly bruises. They kept you unconscious to make sure there isn't any bleeding in the brain. They did an MRI this morning."

I take in the room. My eyes are half-open, blinking against the glare. To the left, behind Mentayer, a chair cushioned in beige plastic; behind that, a picture window, a sunny, too-bright blue sky. To the right, hospital equipment, a cabinet, an open door to a toilet, a sink. I lift my head a few inches. At the foot of the bed, a table tray, a pitcher of water and a glass, a vase of daisies and daffodils, signs of spring. I press my head back into the pillow and close my eyes. There's a sharp sound out in the hall, a gunshot. I gasp and my eyes pop open, too wide; they burn.

"It's okay," Mentayer says in a calm, soothing voice. "Someone dropped something outside the door."

"Where's J. B.? Why isn't he here? Is everything okay?"

"He's gone, Sylvia. It's okay."

I bolt up in the bed, panic piercing my pain, slicing through my grogginess. "He's gone? *Gone?*" My eyes fill with tears. My throat closes and I can't breathe. I assumed he was okay because no one said otherwise. People don't always tell you right away. I grab Mentayer's hand and hold onto it for dear life.

"Oh no, no, no, no, no, Sylvia. J. B.'s fine." Her hand is cool on my forehead. I suck in some air. "Really, he's fine. What I meant was that he's gone to Monrow City. But he's coming back on the red-eye. He should be here soon."

"Craine shot him. I heard it. Didn't I?"

"Hah!" Mentayer says with a wry smile. "The idiot managed to pull the trigger, but he forgot to aim his gun. Left a nice bullet hole in my office wall."

I release her hand and take a full, deep breath. "And you're okay," I say as I let it out.

"I'm tender here and there, but mostly I'm pissed."

"I saw you standing behind Craine. What happened?"

"Grandma's old paperweight did a job on that monster. Knocked him right out. I don't know how long it took for him to come to, even if he ever did, and I don't care. I guess he's alive, though, because he's still in the hospital."

"He's *here*?"

"Under police guard," she assures me. "With an army of high-powered attorneys by his bedside, I'll bet. He's going to need them."

"If it weren't for you, we'd all be dead."

She laughs. "He underestimated the power of this woman. But it wasn't just me. We all took him down. It was a team effort."

"We did it. We did." I smile and close my eyes.

"You rest now, Ms. Sylvia," she says. Her hand covers mine. It's warm and soft.

The affection I hear in her voice opens a door inside to ten-year-old Mentayer, the child filled with the exuberance, unflinching honesty, and unrestrained curiosity that won my heart and sometimes challenged my patience.

"You were a handful," I mumble as I drift back into a Vicodin haze.

"You called me a precocious little imp," she says with a giggle. "I still remember everything about the time I stayed with you and Uncle Frank. Every day was like summer camp. I used to tell Mom stories about you, my adoptive mom. She called them the Ms. Sylvia adventure series."

I open my eyes. "For real?"

She scrunches her eyebrows together and puckers her lips, an expression of curiosity that reaches back across the decades to ask, *What do you mean, for real?*

It's a question I'm not sure I can answer, and may be best left unanswered. There are no words for the shift happening inside me; it's a change as big as the realignment of the stars. Can I, should I, tell Mentayer that in the narrative I'd created of her life, my role had been temporary, one that for her was no more than a minor childhood memory, if a memory at all? To tell her that I had minimized my significance to her in order to console myself would be to confess that I had created a reality separate from and with no experience or knowledge of hers.

"Tell me a story," I say, "about your life after the Bronx. Tell me about your mom and dad." I close my eyes, ready to hear the true narrative about Mentayer as a twelve-year-old, a teenager, a young adult.

"Dad says I was a force to be dealt with. Mom says I still am." I hear the laughter in her voice. "They pushed me pretty hard, held me to high standards. As the only black professors in a white university, they knew what the world was like. They wanted to make sure I was prepared. But they doted on me, too. Remember when I thought maybe they'd have a horse? Well, they didn't, but when they saw how disappointed I was, they right away took me horseback riding to welcome me. They understood how much I loved Grandma, so when they adopted me they let me keep her last name instead of taking theirs. They're good people, Sylvia."

She goes silent. I hear her breathing as I drift in and out. "I'm glad they gave you a good life," I murmur, my eyes still closed.

Mentayer takes my hand in hers. "I don't treasure my wounds," she says, "but I do treasure their healing."

My eyes open. Then they close again and I'm back in the fog. *So do I, Mentayer. So do I.*

I wake to the sound of hushed voices in the background. My eyes open to the hint of a small light at the end of a tunnel. I lift my head up from the pillow. Outside the window the sun has gone down: scattered clouds in the sky, a pinkish-gray dusk. The ceiling light has been turned off, the room lit by a bedside lamp. J. B. stands at the foot of my bed, next to Mentayer, his arm around her, both of them tall and lean and looking younger than their actual late forties. Something inside says they're two kindred souls, made wise by life experience and bound together by a shared worldview—one that is diametrically opposed to mine and thus incomprehensible. To me, life's unfairness is an aberration; to them, it's the natural order of things.

"You look tired, J. B.," I say, smiling.

He laughs. "I don't look as bad as you do."

"I didn't say you look bad."

We all laugh. My ribs and my head pound but I can't stop. You'd think one of us had cracked the most hilarious joke in the world.

Mentayer chuckles as she walks back to the cushioned chair. She sits down like she owns it, like it's been her bed for a few days. J. B. brings a small chair from the corner and sits down next to her. His move is circumspect, but I'm awake enough to see him take her hand in his. I'm also with it enough to be discreet about seeing it even as I'm skipping with delight.

"The medical examiner and her mother came to see you while you were sleeping." Mentayer points to a fresh bouquet of yellow roses on the nightstand.

"Bonnie was here? Why didn't you wake me?"

"She wouldn't let me. Talk about a force to be reckoned with." Mentayer laughs. "Dr. Goldmann said in all her years in the medical examiner's office, she's never encountered anyone as persistent as you. Her mother said she wasn't at all surprised. Anyway, you're supposed to call Bonnie when you feel up to it."

"How did they find out what happened?"

"I called Dr. Goldmann to thank her," J. B. says. "She'd already heard about Frascatore's arrest from Detective Crannower."

"Speaking of which," Mentayer says, "Detective Crannower stopped by while you were sleeping and filled me in. As soon as Craine's out of the hospital, he'll have to go to court. He's facing several charges. First-degree murder for Daniel Leacham's death, accomplice to murder for helping Frascatore hide my brother's body, and three attempted murder charges for trying to kill us. They don't have enough to charge him for Dion Brown's death."

"What about Frascatore?" I ask.

"He's still in jail, but he'll be out on bail soon. He's been charged with manslaughter."

I lie back down. "Manslaughter?" My head is fuzzy. *Why not murder? He killed Markus. That's murder, isn't it?*

"Because it wasn't premeditated," Mentayer explains. "I guess he pretty much fell apart when he learned that Craine told us everything. He cried and carried on about how he regretted what happened to Markus, that it was an accident, that he was a stooge for Drake—I mean Craine. That he was desperate for the drugs he provided. Detective Crannower said it was pathetic."

"So he confessed," I say.

"But he's going to plead not guilty. His defense is that he never meant to kill Markus, that he was out of control, hopelessly addicted to drugs. The detective said she almost feels sorry for him."

"Addiction is no excuse," I say. I turn away and stare at the wall, thinking about the look on Frascatore's face that night in the bar, how sure I was that he was putting on an act. *Have some empathy for a fellow addict,* I say to myself. *No,* I tell myself. The answer is no. I can't. *How about praying for the addict who still suffers?* Are you kidding? How can I pray for him when he killed Markus. Who's praying for Markus? *Maybe you could try?* I don't want to. Not until he's held accountable. Not until he pays for what he did. Maybe I can pray for the willingness to pray for him. Maybe I'll talk to Hehewuti about it. I know the subject will be revisited when I'm ready. If I'm ever ready. Maybe. For my own sake. For my own recovery. Good grief, I'm already working at it.

A bubbly nurse rushes into the room to check my temperature and blood pressure, my heart rate. "Congratulations," she says. "All your vitals are normal." As if I had anything to do with it, I think, as a tall, muscular woman with sharp cheekbones but soft eyes comes into the room.

"Hello, I'm Dr. Clark," she says. "We're going to let you out of here tomorrow. Your MRI results show that there's no bleeding on the brain, no internal injuries for us to be concerned about. We kept you here for observation to make sure there wasn't anything more serious going on, and now I'm satisfied that you're going to be okay. You will have to take it easy for a while, though. I'll write up the discharge papers before I leave tonight, and someone will go over them with you in the morning before you're released."

"Is she okay to fly?" J. B. asks.

"She'll be cleared for all normal activities. No lifting or any strenuous activity." The nurse replaces the pitcher of water with a fresh one, tells me dinner will be coming soon, and leaves the room. Then Dr. Clark wishes me good luck, shakes my hand, and leaves.

I turn to J. B. "What about the fraud allegations against CSCH? Is Craine going to be charged with money laundering or something?"

"The fraud investigation is being turned over to the FBI and the Office of the Inspector General in the U.S. Department of Education. It will take a while."

"What about CSCH's plan to take over our Monrow City public schools?"

"At this point in the legal process they can continue to do business as usual, but our mayor is going to cancel the contract. I met with him yesterday to give him a chance to get in front of the story before it hits the news. He jumped at the chance to avoid becoming embroiled in a scandal. He even gets to look like he's saving our public schools. He's planning a press conference the day after tomorrow. He's going to be a big hero."

"Peter Minter is going to be disappointed."

"I had lunch with Peter yesterday and told him the whole story. He's pretty angry about it. People were optimistic that charter schools would be so much better for their kids, and now their hopes are going to be dashed. They're being ripped off once again. By the way, he said to send you his love."

"He did? He said that?"

J. B. grins. "Well, sort of. He said to tell you he understands that CSCH isn't the answer. But he still believes in the charter school movement. He thinks the public schools are so bad for Indian kids that reforming them is no longer a possibility."

"I want to go home. I want to be there for the press conference."

JB takes out his smartphone. "Then let's get ourselves some reservations." He stands up and walks out into the hall.

"Come to Monrow City with us," I say to Mentayer.

"Not right now. Maybe in the summer."

I raise an eyebrow and tip my head toward the door.

"Yes," she says with a conspiratorial grin, "J. B. and I have already talked about it."

"I'm going to miss you, Mentayer."

"Don't worry, I'll write."

"So will I."

"I promise," we say at the same time.

TWENTY-FIVE

Summer 2006

J. B. and I meet for lunch at my favorite spot overlooking Island Lake. It's the third time we've met here since returning from New York. Our bench in the shade of an ancient evergreen provides most welcome protection today from the hot midday sun. We munch on egg salad sandwiches and gaze out at the silver-blue lake, a placid mirror except for the soft ripples left by oars sliding silent and smooth through its surface. Canoes, rowboats, and kayaks are allowed on Island Lake, but no motorboats or swimming. Birds chirp in the deep foliage above our heads and wheel undisturbed in slow, lazy arcs over the lily pads on the lake.

I kick off my sandals. The grass feels warm and soft between my toes. I reach into my purse and pull out a copy of a newspaper clipping. "Mentayer sent me this review. Have you seen it?" I don't wait for him to answer. "Listen to this: 'J. B. Harrell's series on charter schools versus public schools is set apart by its keen precision and sharp analysis, grounded in evidence and absent personal opinion. It will undoubtedly bring yet another award for outstanding investigative reporting.'" I hand the clipping over to him with a smile.

He lays the review on his lap without looking at it or saying anything. But I can tell he's pleased.

"You know how you say I always put everything into whatever I take on," I say with a tease of a smile. "Well, so do you. That's the reason your stories are so outstanding."

J. B. points to a mass of yellow blades of butterflies perched on some red and orange flowers nearby.

I give his arm a playful slap. "Ignore me all you want," I say. "It's the truth."

I reach into the cooler and pull out a bottle of beer for J. B. and a can of Diet Coke for myself. We sip our drinks and eat our sandwiches in companionable silence.

"There was a short article in the *New York Times* today," he says after a while. "The state attorney general has filed fraud charges against CSCH."

"Let's hope that by the time this is all over," I say, "all their charter schools will be shut down."

"Regardless of the outcome in that profit arena for them," he says with a sigh, "the CSCH Corporation will go on. It'll change its name and take its business to another country, maybe somewhere in Latin America."

I groan. "Corporations like CSCH are always going to salivate at the chance to gorge themselves on the public dime, wherever they can," I say. "It gives me a headache thinking about what an easy buck it is for them." Beads of sweat cover my forehead and the bridge of my nose and trickle down my cheeks. I'm wearing the coolest, loosest-fitting lightweight cotton dress I own, and still it's sticking to my back. I grip a wad of the thin fabric at its rounded neckline and wave it in and out. The puff of air cools my skin.

"Frascatore and Craine go on trial next month," J. B. says. He leans back on the bench with his long legs straight out in front of him. The toes of his shoes point to the sky, the heels digging into the ground.

I breathe in the sweet fragrance of fresh-cut grass, the perfume of roses, and the aroma of coconut suntan lotion. My lungs fill with a gratifying sense of triumph. The past has yielded its secrets, and now, at last, Frascatore is going to pay. "Will we be called to testify?" I ask.

"I'll see what I can find out. I'm going to New York next week."

"Oh? Mentayer didn't tell me." A gray-haired couple walks by on the path in front of us, holding hands. I so want that to be J. B. and Mentayer twenty or thirty years from now. I scoot to the edge of the bench and turn to J. B. "Want to know what I'm thinking?" I ask.

"No." There's a shy blush on his light brown cheeks and a hint of a grin on his lips. He turns toward an adjacent garden, pretends to admire the bright yellows and reds of the daylilies and crepe-paper-like poppies.

"Fair enough," I say, proud of myself for having learned when to pry and when not to pry with him. I sit back and listen to the quiet. I watch the sand shimmer on the shore. A stocky white-breasted nuthatch hangs upside down on a nearby tree foraging for insects. Like him, I wait for whatever snippets of personal information J. B. might be willing to offer up.

"Lewis Blair was smart to put Mentayer in charge of his new charter school," he says at last. "He wants to name it after Markus. He says charter schools didn't kill him, a bad school did."

It's a crumb, a snippet, an opening. I snatch it up. "Mentayer's so excited," I say. "It'll take quite a while and a lot of work before the school's up and running, but she says she loves the whole development process."

"They plan to fund it with Daniel Leacham's contributions to the Center for Boys," J. B. says.

"Sweet justice," I say with a laugh.

He smiles, then turns serious. "You don't object?" he says. "I mean, it will be another charter school."

"It's more than a job for Mentayer. It's a calling. You don't mess with someone's calling. And besides, it's going to be a free, non-taxpayer-funded, nonprofit school."

"It's a perfect fit for her," he says. "A school for at-risk boys."

I pause and give him a long, searching look. "You never told me what you think about charter schools."

"It's a complicated issue," he says.

"Cop-out." I slap his arm.

"I'm a journalist, Sylvia, not an activist."

"Come on, J. B. This is me you're talking to. I'm not asking you what you think as a reporter, I'm asking you as a human being. And don't tell me you don't have an opinion, because I know you do."

He stares out at the lake. He rubs his chin. Then he turns and faces me. "Okay, this is what I think, Sylvia. I think that educating our kids is a sacred trust and that it behooves us to do it the best way we can. Nine out of ten American kids attend public schools, so our focus should be on fully funding and improving that system, not siphoning money into private systems, whether for profit or not for profit. That's it. That's what I think. It's simple."

Then he smiles at me, a smile more open than I've ever seen before. I smile back, and something falls away. A lingering distrust perhaps, a sense of caution, some old leftover hint of discomfort.

"We're a good team," I say.

J. B. straightens up and places his feet under the bench. "An amazing feat," he says with a chuckle and that grin of his that always makes me smile.

"You didn't like me when we first met."

"I like you well enough now."

My mouth falls open. Not because he likes me—he's already demonstrated that in too many ways to ignore—but because he said it. Out loud. To my face.

"You and Mentayer are a good team, too." I squirm, worried that I've crossed the line. But J. B.'s amused look emboldens me. "You have a lot in common. You both have haunted pasts."

He looks wistful. "Maybe so. But we're of one mind about it. Our stories are what they are. We let the ravages of life shape us and make our souls stronger."

"And more beautiful," I add.

He blushes. "It made our expectations lower, so life doesn't throw us off so much. You think people have rights, Sylvia. We know they don't."

"I've always struggled to accept life on life's terms," I say. "The religion of my childhood taught that the road to redemption has to pass through suffering. Even as a kid, I rejected that. I have no doubt that's where my acute awareness of unfairness comes from."

J. B. leans down, pulls a weed from the grass and studies it.

"You can't tell me," I say, "that there isn't a fire in both you and Mentayer, a spark that was never extinguished. You see that life isn't fair and want to change that as much as I do."

"Granted," he says, "but we know that if you can't change it, you have to figure out how to live with it."

"I think going back to New York may have helped me with that," I say. "I was able to reconstruct my past and re-create my story."

"Your story is your story, Sylvia. The past can't be reconstructed." His voice is challenging but at the same time filled with compassion and devoid of any judgment. Most people think I'm too passionate. They shy away from me. But J. B. never has.

"In my head it can," I say with a smile. "That's where I constructed it in the first place, after all."

He smiles and shakes his head. I don't know if he's amused or bemused or something else. What I do know is that it's a miracle to be here, right now, with him.

"So, what are you going to drag me into next, Sylvia?" he says with a grin. "First it's a foster kid... "

"Wait a minute, J. B., *you* dragged *me* into that one."

"And then a former student... " His grin turns into a smile.

"And don't forget, a budding romance," I say, laughing.

He rolls his eyes, but they're twinkling. We sit side-by-side, smiling, eyes forward, looking out at the shimmering lake.

"I'm serious, Sylvia," he says. "Ever since I met you, you've been a self-appointed warrior battling for the souls of little boys who no longer exist. So you can see why I wonder what you might do next."

"I don't know what's next," I say with a smile, "but there is always more to do, isn't there?"

Acknowledgments

My deepest gratitude goes to my former students in Chicago and New York City whose struggles to learn in inequitable and entrenched school systems broke my heart in the 1960s and inspired and informed *Death, Unchartered* now. I have been assiduous in protecting their anonymity in the specifics while aiming to capture the essence of their (and my) real-life experiences while attempting to provide as accurate an historical perspective as possible. That said, *Death, Unchartered* is a work of fiction and all persons, geographic locations, agencies, and community organizations are entirely the creation of my imagination.

My early teaching experiences paralleled those of Jonathan Kozol as recounted in his book, *Death at an Early Age: The Destruction of the Hearts and Minds of Negro Children in the Boston Public Schools* (Houghton Mifflin 1967). By giving voice to what it was like for him to teach in a school system deeply entrenched, racially segregated and unequal, and with a crumbling infrastructure, he affirmed my experiences back then and helped me even now to find my own voice in *Death, Unchartered*. A special thank you to the late Miriam Dinerman whose copy of *Bronx: Faces and Voices—Sixteen Stories of Courage and Community* (2014, Texas Tech University Press) by Emita Brady Hill and Janet Butler Munch (editors) helped ground the novel's characters in real places and historical events. Thanks to Jenn Zunt for her stories and insights about charter schools and also to Alan Feldman and Florence Feldman who generously shared their experiences as public school teachers in the Bronx during the long and contentious teachers' strike of 1968.

Writing this book has been a team effort. I continue to be indebted to two outstanding writers, editors, and teachers who have been critical to my development as a novelist. Hal Zina Bennett coached me through those first fledgling steps many years ago, and the wizardry of Max Regan helped transform

Death, Unchartered into the novel you now hold in your hands. Thank you to my writing group members, Mary Kabrich and Roger Roffman, who once again provided wise feedback at every stage of development. A special thank you to readers of different drafts of the manuscript: Stephanie Kimmons, Kristin Ann King, Barbara Leigh, Sue Lerner, Ann Loar Brooks, Rosa O'Reilly, and Mary Swigonski. For the final stages of production I am grateful to Kyra Freestar for her outstanding copyediting and to Kevin Atticks and the Apprentice House publishing team. As always, my deepest appreciation goes to my wife, Susan, whose constant support makes it all possible.

DISCUSSION GUIDE

Questions And Topics Raised In Death,
Unchartered

1. What is the significance of the novel's title, *Death, Unchartered?* Discuss possible meanings and why you think the author selected this title.

2. With which characters did you feel the most sympathy and connections? How did your feelings about them change as the story unfolded?

3. Who or what is the villain of the novel?

4. What does Anthony Frascatore represent? What does Clarke Craine represent?

5. During the 1968 teachers' strike Sylvia Jensen supported the community control movement but it failed. Are there ways to have community control of schools that might have worked? What could have been done differently?

6. Just as issues of race divided people about community control during the 1968 teachers' strike, issues of race continue to divide people now about charter schools. Discuss how the issues played themselves out in the novel.

7. Sylvia Jensen's overarching objection to charter schools is that they drain money from public schools. Do you agree or disagree that that is a major problem? Why? Why not?

8. Discuss Mentayer LeMeur's social justice motivation for supporting charter schools, initially when she worked for a for-profit charter school corporation and later when she devoted herself to developing a nonprofit charter school for at-risk boys. Do you

think charter schools exacerbate or ease inequality?

9. What are your thoughts about the current movement to privatize a variety of public services while continuing to fund them with tax dollars (e.g., prisons, human services, public health, education)?

10. Betsy DeVos, who was appointed by President Trump as U.S. Education Secretary in 2016, promotes the diversion of taxpayer funds to school choice schemes. What are the implications of the policies she promotes for public education in the U.S.?

Further Resources

Movie: *Won't Back Down.* In this 2012 fact-based drama, two women from different classes and races (Viola Davis and Maggie Gyllenhaal) draw on their common bond of motherhood to fight institutional inertia and an antagonistic bureaucracy to improve an inner-city school. The movie stimulates discussion of issues addressed in *Death Unchartered* about failing schools, teachers unions, community control of schools, and public vs. private schools.

Michigan Gambled On Charter Schools And Its Children Lost
New York Times Magazine, **Sept. 5, 2017.** A comprehensive article that provides a balanced overview of a current, real life charter school example in one state. https://www.nytimes.com/2017/09/05/magazine/michigan-gambled-on-charter-schools-its-children-lost.html?hp&action=-click&pgtype=Homepage&clickSource=story-heading&module=second-column-region&region=top-

Two Books That Provide Point/Counterpoint Perspectives:
The Education of Eva Moskowitz: A Memoir, 2017, HarperCollins. **This memoir by the outspoken founder and CEO of the charter school Success Academy** tells one story about education and inequality: that poor children are suffering in bureaucratic and inadequate public schools and need both demanding educators to toughen them up and wealthy philanthropists to fund those efforts.

Class War: **The Privatization of Childhood, 2015, by Megan Erickson, Verso.** This book by a New York City public school teacher tells a different and compelling story about education in which elite corporate education reformers have found new ways to transfer the costs of raising children from the state to individual families. While public schools, tasked with providing education, childcare, job training, meals, and social services to low-income children, struggle with cutbacks, private schools promise to nurture the minds and personalities of future professionals to the tune of $40,000 a year. *Class War* reveals that this situation didn't happen by chance.

About the Author

Dorothy Van Soest is a writer, social worker, political and community activist, and retired professor and university dean. She holds an undergraduate degree in English literature and a master's degree and PhD in social work. She is currently professor emerita at the University of Washington with a research-based publication record of eleven books and over fifty journal articles, essays, and book chapters that tackle complex and controversial issues related to violence, oppression, and injustice. Her debut novel, *Just Mercy*, published in 2014, was informed by her widely acclaimed investigation into the lives of thirty-seven men who were executed by Texas in 1997, and inspired by victim-offender restorative justice dialogue programs. *At the Center* (2015), the first of her Sylvia Jensen mystery series, grew out of her experiences with the child welfare system. *Death, Unchartered,* the second in the series, is based on her experiences with the New York City public school system during the 1968 teachers' strike. She is currently working on the third and final mystery in the series, a story grounded in her experiences in the 1980s with the nuclear disarmament movement. Dorothy Van Soest lives in Seattle, Washington, where she and her wife enjoy spending time with their grandchildren. Her website is http://dorothyvansoest.com/

Apprentice
House Press
Loyola University Maryland

Apprentice House is the country's only campus-based, student-staffed book publishing company. Directed by professors and industry professionals, it is a nonprofit activity of the Communication Department at Loyola University Maryland.

Using state-of-the-art technology and an experiential learning model of education, Apprentice House publishes books in untraditional ways. This dual responsibility as publishers and educators creates an unprecedented collaborative environment among faculty and students, while teaching tomorrow's editors, designers, and marketers.

Outside of class, progress on book projects is carried forth by the AH Book Publishing Club, a co-curricular campus organization supported by Loyola University Maryland's Office of Student Activities.

Eclectic and provocative, Apprentice House titles intend to entertain as well as spark dialogue on a variety of topics. Financial contributions to sustain the press's work are welcomed. Contributions are tax deductible to the fullest extent allowed by the IRS.

To learn more about Apprentice House books or to obtain submission guidelines, please visit www.apprenticehouse.com.

Apprentice House
Communication Department
Loyola University Maryland
4501 N. Charles Street
Baltimore, MD 21210
Ph: 410-617-5265 • Fax: 410-617-2198
info@apprenticehouse.com • www.apprenticehouse.com

CPSIA information can be obtained
at www.ICGtesting.com
Printed in the USA
FSHW02n0358090918
51919FS